Darcy's Tale

Volume II

Into Kent

By

Stanley Michael Hurd

Publisher: Stanley M. Hurd

Second edition, published 2014.

ISBN 13 978-0-9910382-5-1

Cover design: J. E. Hurd

I must again thank my family for their support through this undertaking; it could never have happened, were it not for you.

And I also wish to single out two Jane Austen devotees whose detailed knowledge of the original work, and whose sharp editorial eyes and insightful readings have made this a much better book: J. Rutter and S. Clement—my most sincere thanks.

To my beloved daughters, my excuse for existing, and my brightest hope for the future.

FOREWORD

This second edition has been substantially re-edited for anachronisms and Americanisms; our thanks to those sharp-eyed readers who have helped make this edition possible.

Darcy's Tale is presented in three volumes, as was the original *Pride and Prejudice* 200 years earlier; this has been done both for reasons of historical accuracy and because the story naturally divides itself into three major sections.

For those interested in such matters, this work is set in 1799-1800, rather than the more commonly accepted 1811-1812. The reasons for this lie in a detailed analysis of the times and dates given in the original, particularly around the Easter sojourn into Kent. The argument is convoluted and laborious, so will not be presented here, but it has compelled the author to accept the earlier dates as being the correct ones.

The letters written by Darcy and his sister are included in their entirety in the Correspondence section, as certain letters had no place in the events of the book. They have been included to allow the reader to follow each letter as it was written, without the shifts in time and circumstance which occurred during the intervals between writings. In an age when communications took weeks to complete, letters held their own internal chronology, quite independent of external events; the reader is invited to enjoy this more stately rhythm of life by following the correspondents' individual stories as described in their letters, in the order in which they were exchanged.

Chapter One

*T*he next week was one Darcy would have been well pleased to forego. It had begun with a journey back to London in the company of the Hursts and Miss Bingley, without the alloy of his friend's influence to elevate the tone and vary the content of the conversation. As the Hursts sat together, he was placed next to Miss Bingley, and found that there was no portion of the seat, no matter how small, which left him entirely free from contact with her person. And, throughout that four-hour durance, it weighed very heavily on his mind that he was returning for the express purpose of ruining all his friend's present hopes of happiness.

When the carriage was little more than an hour away from Grosvenor Street, Miss Bingley once again claimed his attention — as she did with some regularity; speaking in accents of warm sincerity, and emphasising her sentiments by placing a hand on his arm, she said, "Mr. Darcy, let me say again how very grateful we are that you are willing to go to such lengths for Charles; you are a true gentleman and friend."

Having already compressed himself close against the side of the carriage, Darcy could not avoid the hand; he wondered whether Miss Bingley were reading too many novels, or not enough: her trite and formulaic terms of approbation, no matter how earnestly articulated, always sounded false in his ears; only when castigating her acquaintance did her words ring with the pure notes of heartfelt sincerity. He merely replied, however, "Thank you, Miss Bingley; I see no other course open to me."

"But it is precisely that which makes your actions so honourable, Sir: only a true gentleman follows the dictates of his conscience in spite of anything!"

1

Decidedly too many novels, Darcy judged. To Miss Bingley, however, he merely bowed his head in acknowledgement.

"Whatever shall you say, when once you have arrived?" Miss Bingley enquired with concern, turning to face him more directly and unwittingly bringing her knee to rest against him.

Hunching in on himself and crossing his legs, Darcy turned his back to the side so he was pressed against the utmost corner of the seat; he answered, "I have no idea; I shall just have to let the moment decide, as the subject does not allow for any clear-cut, logical progression. I shall tell him why I have come, then follow where reason and his responses might lead."

Sitting back and folding her arms in disgust, Miss Bingley cried: "This is just like Charles! He is forever landing himself in trouble of one kind or another." Mrs. Hurst, seated opposite her, added her agreement with a prim, disapproving nod.

Darcy unwound himself from his position with relief, as the cold draught from around the window was icy down the back of his neck. "He is a man of good heart," he said. "He will perceive no fault in his regard for Miss Bennet: that is my chief concern in determining how to dissuade him from his present course."

"Well, it is most inconvenient; he never thinks what trouble these affairs bring to his friends."

"He could have no idea that we should feel the necessity of removing from Netherfield, surely," Darcy said reasonably. "and we cannot compare the slight inconvenience of an early removal to Town, whence we would have gone in any event within days, with the great pain your brother must undergo, on having his cherished hopes with regard to Miss Bennet snatched from him."

"This is hardly the first time Charles has formed such an attraction," observed Miss Bingley unsympathetically. "I have no doubt he will recover without any great difficulty, as he has always done before."

Certainly Darcy hoped that this might be so, although he had never seen his friend show such deep attachment to a young lady before. He nonetheless agreed: "I, too, hope his heart will heal quickly."

At this point, having exhausted his ideas on how to avoid Miss Bingley's conversational sorties, Darcy recalled their trip down to Hertfordshire, during which Bingley had feigned sleep to avoid his sister's discussion with Darcy; he did not think he could very well pretend to sleep, but he saw no reason why he might not sleep in earnest; indeed, it seemed a rather better use of his time. Excusing himself to Miss Bingley, he tucked his hands into his coat sleeves and dosed off, not to rouse until the coach began to clatter over the cobbles of London's streets.

After depositing Miss Bingley and the Hursts at Mr. Hurst's house in Grosvenor Street, Darcy continued across the Thames to Southwark, to recover Bingley from his hotel. As the coach wound through London, Darcy tried to prepare for the coming scene. His first wish would be to have nothing to do with any of this; but he knew his friend's propensity to leap into situations without heed of consequence, and he had not forgotten how ready Bingley had been to help him when he had imagined Darcy to be in difficulties. And, as he often did when considering some action or encounter, he recalled his father saying, "In our position, it is always best to act, Fitzwilliam: to withhold one's hand is an act in itself, and the only one that is doomed to universal failure."

Arriving at the hotel, he was shown up to Bingley's rooms; his friend had naturally been exceedingly surprised to see him in that part of London, and even more surprised to hear what had brought him thither.

"You came all this way to speak to me about Miss Bennet?" Bingley enquired in astonishment, when Darcy had announced his reason for coming. "Whatever for? — Darcy, say she is not ill!"

"No, no, she is well," Darcy said reassuringly; but there he hesitated. There could be no way of softening the blow, so he braced himself and said directly, "In all truth, Bingley, I have come to dissuade you from marrying the lady, which I suspect is your intention."

Bingley looked at him in disbelief, then gave an uncertain laugh. He said doubtingly, "You are not serious."

"I fear I am, although I very much wish I were not," Darcy assured him earnestly. "I find myself compelled to speak on the subject because, even though she is all that is amiable and lovely, I cannot help but think you have failed adequately to consider what having such connections would entail."

"You *are* serious," Bingley said with great bewilderment. "Surely you cannot believe that I would find her silly relations any reason to give Miss Bennet over."

"My dear Bingley, I know very well you would not; but that does not mean that you would not come to regret it."

After a moment's hesitation, his friend said, "You have me at a loss, Darcy. I know you cannot believe that I could be so insensible to my own interests. Is this some elaborate jest—part of our teazing about how easily persuaded I am?"

"No, not at all; on my honour, Charles, I should never take any such liberties with your feelings. I wish I did not have to say these things—it distresses me exceedingly. But I watched the two of you with a most exacting diligence; I was forced to conclude that Miss Bennet, while an indisputably excellent young woman, does not return your affections on an equal footing; that being the case, I feel I cannot stand by and let you enter into an alliance with the Bennets that cannot be justified by the depth of the lady's preference." As he finished, Bingley was holding a measured gaze intently on Darcy's countenance; Darcy could do no more than return his regard with an open, unguarded one of his own.

Bingley remained silent a moment, his brows furrowed in thought. He had great faith in his friend's judgement, more so than in his own, in truth, and Darcy's assurances were sufficient reason for him to distrust his own thoughts on the subject. "How can you be certain?" he asked at length, his face troubled. "Can there be no mistake? I was in no doubt she was beginning to have feelings for me."

Darcy sat down wearily. "I watched the two of you at the ball, almost without interruption from the third dance on, all through the evening—while you were standing out of the dance, during supper—while I could easily perceive *your* warm regard, I never saw the slightest indication from her side that you were more than a pleasant companion; and, you may believe me, I looked for it quite purposefully. Compare in your mind the difference between Miss Bennet's countenance and air, and that of Miss Grantley, for example, when you were in company with each: I am sure you will easily perceive a marked dissimilarity between them. And I hardly need mention, Charles, but you know you could never accept the hand, were the heart not given as well; nor would you, I know, tempt the lady with the choice, where there was any doubt as to her affections."

As he considered these points, Bingley's expression first began to bear witness to a grave misgiving; his eyes drifted aimlessly about the room as he thought back, comparing his relations with the two ladies. At length he turned a pained expression to Darcy. "Fitzwilliam, are you completely sure? I can hardly...I certainly..." shaking his head, he sank down into a chair and sat staring down at his feet.

At length, after a silence of some minutes, he tried to rally, saying, "I believe you to be in earnest, Darcy, but in my heart I know you are in error. I am certain my regard for Miss Bennet is returned—perhaps not equally—but sincerely."

"I believe you do; indeed, that is what makes this so difficult. Without question, if one could open another's heart and peer inside, many of the world's ills would be mitigated. But, given how hard it is to read another's thoughts and emotions, do we have a better measure than their behaviour? And by that gauge, I can swear the lady does not meet your regard with like return. I should never have hazarded this entire undertaking, otherwise."

Again Bingley was silent; after a long moment, as his doubts worked on his natural diffidence, an anguished look passed over his features, and he looked away from his friend. Darcy watched him sympathetically without speaking, knowing that words were insufficient to supply what Bingley needed; only time and care would cure him. The two gentlemen held this tableau for a long minute before Darcy stood and went to his friend. Placing his hand on his shoulder, he said, "Come, Charles; you shall stay with me to-night; I cannot have you staying in an hotel; not now."

Bingley shook his head, but still did not look at his friend. "I shall be well enough, Darcy," he said, though his despondent manner belied his words. "There is no need of that. I was planning to leave in the morning, at any rate, as my business is over."

"I have no doubt of your resources, or your strength, Bingley; I know you will be well. But, truly, I had much rather have you come home with me, rather than stay here amongst strangers, if only because I am in Town, now. Do let me persuade you, Charles—there is nothing to stay here for."

Bingley considered for a moment, but what Darcy said was reasonable; in truth, he seemed relieved to have something to do, and his arrangements were quickly made; the two were off in half an hour. The ride to Grosvenor Square was largely silent. Once there, Darcy poured Bingley a brandy, and one for himself. On taking a seat, Bingley made another attempt to rescue his hopes, although it seemed his protests held less assurance than before, "Darcy, I know Miss Bennet does not much display her feelings, but I was sure that, in her smiles, there was a particular warmth towards myself."

"But Bingley, do but recollect: one of the very first things I noted about her was how she smiles at every one; as I watched at supper, I paid most particular attention to *how* she smiled at you, and contrasted it to her smiles towards her other neighbours. In spite of my most especial attentiveness, I could discern absolutely no difference between her smiles to you and to any one else. Nor was I able to detect any distinguishing traits in her behaviour to you, at any time during the evening: did she ever lay a hand on your arm, to emphasise a point? Or laugh more than she might at some foolish jest? Did she ever slap your shoulder with her fan, if you said anything teazingly? Perhaps brush against you in a crowd, to avoid contact with some one else? These are things I looked for; yet nary a one could I find. I swear to you, Charles, for all I could see she might have been in company with the Bishop of London."

Bingley's eyes left Darcy as he carefully reviewed his time with Miss Bennet at the ball. At length, shaking his head sadly, he allowed: "You are right, Darcy: I cannot think of any such things, myself. My affection would persuade me she has a regard for me, and would have me believe she might come, in time, to match the strength of my esteem." He paused here, then, shaking his head again, he concluded: "But you are right, of course: I could not bear to force such a choice on her, where she might be tempted to do what her heart might learn to regret." His shoulders drooped, and he lapsed into silence again. After some little while, he told his friend, "I shall just go on up, if you would not mind, Darcy."

"Of course, Charles," said Darcy with sympathetic complaisance. "Only let me know if you need anything; I shall see you in the morning." His friend left the room with heavy steps; Darcy sat a while longer, quietly finishing his brandy; trying, if anything, to bias his memories in favour of attachment, he reviewed yet again all his careful scrutiny of the couple: he still could not bring to mind anything which would effectively contradict his arguments.

He thought, too, of his partner for *his* one dance; he retained many lingering and conflicting emotions concerning Miss Elizabeth Bennet, which confounded him: he could not understand why he was unable to bring them to a resolution — a simple, coherent conclusion — and be done with them; he had made up his mind, after all, and it was not his habit to revisit decisions, once made. The situation was clear enough, but each time he thought he had got rid of the matter, around it came again, refusing to sleep in his memory. Eventually he, too, took himself to bed.

Chapter Two

*T*he next morning at breakfast, Bingley was again moved to defend his sentiments and intentions towards Miss Bennet: "Darcy, I have given it full consideration, and I cannot but believe you must be mistaken: I am convinced Miss Bennet has a regard for me." He spoke with certainty, and the look he gave Darcy was almost challenging.

Darcy knew his friend could be stubborn, if pressed, and so replied with all mildness, "All I can say, Bingley, is that no matter how many times I go over it, I come to the same conclusions; I have even put myself in your place, and tried my best to see a mutual regard and esteem between you — but I could not do so, when it came to the lady. It is possible that I might be in error, no matter how certain I may be, but where there can be such equivocation, where the case is so fraught with potential error, is the risk justified? And have you truly reflected on what life in the Bennet clan would compass? Can you imagine that the mother would not be at Netherfield daily? That the younger girls would not make it more their home than that of their father? Or that they would not have every officer in Meryton constantly at your door, and in your drawing-room? Heavens, man, you would never have a moment's peace!"

"Perhaps that is true…But we could always come up to Town."

"Oh, Lord, Bingley — that would be ten times worse! They would never leave! Constantly underfoot — you would have to present them to your entire acquaintance as relations; what then?"

Bingley made no reply.

"Truly, Charles," said Darcy with quiet sincerity, "I have gone through the matter with greatest care, and I cannot but counsel you against the marriage. I think you know I wish only your happiness — your *abiding* happiness — and I hope you would not think I could take up this attitude without being sure of my ground. Nine Seasons in London have surely taught me enough to see a deep regard where it exists, and you have seen it yourself not a few times, or something very like, from the ladies whom you have honoured with your favour."

Bingley remained quiet, his eyes thoughtful and doubting. Darcy went on, "Assuming it were only the lady concerned — amiable, reasonable, and lovely as she unquestionably is — if she returned your feelings from her heart, I should say you could do no better; but, when one takes into account her family, and, to say no less, the uncertainty regarding her esteem for you, the conclusion must be contrary."

During this speech Bingley listened attentively to his friend, clearly weighing Darcy's words; at its conclusion he said dispiritedly, "I cannot argue with you, Darcy, I never could; nor could I swear that you were in the wrong, given the study you made of us together; and when I compare it with my own memories of her company, I can find nothing to contradict you. And, while I know how far you are willing to go in pursuit of a debate, I am also certain that you do not persist in this solely to win your point: you are not a man to toy with others' hearts for your own amusement. But…still, I had thought Miss Bennet…" he did not finish, and Darcy did not belabour the subject further; it would be best to let Bingley's own good sense guide him, and let him make of it what he could. Darcy knew his friend's honour and principles would never allow him to persist in his attentions to a lady of whose esteem there could be any question, and, moreover, who had so much to tempt her into the union. And, convinced as he was of Miss Bennet's own delicate sense of honour, it were an ungentlemanly thing to place before such a lady a choice so easily misled by interest; Bingley, he knew, was incapable of acting with such disregard for what was upright and fitting.

Shortly after breakfast, however, Bingley's sisters arrived and the topic was again canvassed at length; Bingley showed a much greater inclination to argue with his sisters than with his friend. Having to stand by, unable to say anything that might help his friend while he listened to the sisters' more interested views and protestations, was very distressing to Darcy. Listening to them urging their own embarrassment, their sense of the match being a degradation, and how *they* must suffer from having such relations, while their brother was clearly suffering to a much greater degree from the pangs of loss and love unrequited, made Darcy wish from his heart that he could take sides with Bingley against them; but he could bring no arguments to bear that might aid his friend. In Bingley's disappointment he saw a magnified reflection of his own, and he could therefore easily imagine how Bingley, who obviously cherished much deeper intentions towards Miss Bennet than any he had let himself feel towards her sister, must be the more affected in having to let them go. And that it should be by Darcy's own hand that his friend's hopes were dashed, made him all the more sensible of Bingley's distress. And, certainly, having the two sisters adding their voices to his, did nothing to relieve his mind of those qualms he could not help but entertain from time to time in the face of his friend's heartsick protests; he continually challenged his observations against the arguments going forward, to ensure that nothing which might contradict his reasoning escaped his notice; however, no such benevolent contradiction came to light.

But Darcy was not one to shirk a duty: why it always fell to him to act, he did not know — others of his acquaintance did not seem to carry that burden in life — but he persevered nonetheless, lending his support to Bingley's sisters' when necessary. Reminding himself frequently of

the careful observations he had made of Miss Bennet's demeanour towards his friend, and, just as importantly, of the
many instances of improper behaviour in the Bennet family—and, most particularly, the kind of home-life his friend
could expect with the Bennets as near relations—he was
able to continue in good faith, if not without regrets. At
length, therefore, Bingley's confidence in his friend's
judgement, his doubts as to his own acuity and, in truth, his
own worth, finally convinced him that Miss Bennet was not,
after all, to be his.

When his sisters were gone, carrying all their acrimony
and contention with them, there was a long period of quiet;
at length Bingley asked: "What should I do about Netherfield, Darcy? I do not know that I could face going back,
now."

"My advice would be to do nothing, for the time being," Darcy gave as his opinion. "Netherfield is not a
problem that needs solving right away, so I suggest you
leave it till a better season for thought. You have made no
plans, I think, for the holidays?"

"No; none at all," Bingley replied.

"Then leave it at that. Dismiss all but a caretaker or
two, and wait to see what lies in the future."

There being a marked lack of gaiety amongst the
Bingley family at this time—Bingley's sisters having been
exceedingly generous and unreserved in their condemnation of the Bennets, and their brother's intention of forming
a union with them—Darcy was prompted to invite his
friend to stay with him for a time. While this arrangement
spared his friend the trouble of opening the house in Manchester Square for the holidays, of greater import was
Darcy's very real concern on his friend's behalf; Bingley's
spirits were exceedingly low the days following these
events, and Darcy knew he would receive little enough
sympathy from his sisters. He had observed that, when secure of themselves in the house in which they had been

raised, the sisters were wont to exercise their opinions even more vocally than usual, and he wished to shield his friend from their gentle urgings on the subject of his disappointment.

For his part, Darcy had persuaded himself with reasonable certainty that a few weeks' diversion over the holidays, away from Miss Bennet's charms, would be sufficient cure to relieve Bingley of his current infatuation, as had happened in the past. Bingley had known Miss Grantley much longer than Miss Bennet, Darcy assured himself, and he had got over her well enough; there ought to be no great delay in Bingley's return to his own, lively self. Darcy's confidence might have been less if he had stopped to consider his own sentiments towards one of the Bennet sisters: he was daily experiencing surprising difficulty in overcoming that regard for Elizabeth which he knew must end, for both their sakes—yet he had, in fact, known her for less time, and pursued their acquaintance with less interest, than his friend had Miss Bennet.

Indeed, with each passing day, Darcy was becoming more aware of how much he felt Elizabeth's absence—how much he missed seeing her, missed indulging himself in her conversation, and watching her serenity in repose and grace in activity. He wished from his heart that he had done more at the ball to have countered Wickham's lies, to have convinced her of Wickham's want of character and honour; that she should think ill of him now was a persistent and acute source of regret, and added yet another injury to the list of those received at Wickham's hands. He could only hope that her regard for him and estimation of his character, based on the six weeks of acquaintance and four days of close association they had shared together, would eventually restore him to her good graces.

Yet each time he entertained these thoughts, in the next moment he would be asking himself, how could it matter? They were never to see each other again, so her opinion of him could have no effect for either good or ill, nor was there anything he could do that might make it right.

These and other thoughts regarding Elizabeth plagued him more and more in the days succeeding his return to London; while it irritated him to find such conflicting and ill-regulated feelings in himself, it was also beginning rather to anger him to feel Society interfering with his wishes. The thought that a man like that parson might court her, but he could not, made him want to strike something. Indeed, the thought of that repellent man paying his addresses to her, and the appalling apprehension that—for the sake of her family at any rate—it was conceivable she might be compelled to accept him, made him want to lash out. If the purpose of society was to promote order, harmony, and justice amongst the populace, he thought angrily, he failed to see how the proscription of any possible union between himself and a lady like Elizabeth served any of the three; and surely there could be no justice or harmony in her union with the parson, or with Wickham—Dear God, the very idea! —or any one else she was ever likely to meet with in Hertfordshire.

Chapter Three

*T*he first week of December was gone, and the holidays were fast approaching; it was time to be bringing Georgiana up from Derbyshire. Darcy had requested the favour of his friend's company on the trip to escort Georgiana back to Town, he had often thought that, should they happen to suit one another, Bingley and his sister would make a fine match. She would benefit greatly from his general amiability and social ease, and he, especially now, might find happiness in her soothing sweetness and quiet accomplishment; in addition, the thought of being related to Bingley was highly gratifying to Darcy. Until now, indeed, there had not seemed to be any attraction between them, but they had both of them undergone some trials of the heart of late, and given the vagaries of spirit humankind is prey to—in short, who knew but what they might suit now? This seemed to Darcy a perfect opportunity to bring them together and let their mutual goodness have a chance to exert its influence.

The second week in December, therefore, the two friends set out for Derbyshire on a cold Monday morning under heavy skies and a light snow. Bingley, who for the past week had lived entirely with Darcy, had little to say as they passed through Buckinghamshire, and sat gazing out the window eastward towards Hertfordshire. He spoke but little, and when he did, it was without his accustomed good spirits. As they were leaving the outskirts of London he had observed in an abstracted manner, "When last we came through here, it was to go down to Netherfield."

Darcy nodded, but did not reply.

"Do you recall how eager I was to go to the Meryton assembly? I told you we might meet some one special."

"Yes, I do recall," Darcy said. "But, Charles, to allow such license in your thoughts cannot increase your happiness."

"No, of course, you are right; I shall get the better," Bingley assured his friend. Then, almost as if to himself, he said, "But I was right about that evening: I did meet some one special, even if..." he trailed off into silence. Darcy's thoughts naturally turned to the singular young lady whom *he* had met — well, not met, precisely — but had been in company with, that night. After this, neither gentleman spoke for some time.

Bingley did not fully revive until they reached Dunstable for their evening meal, and throughout the afternoon Darcy would often find *his* gaze drawn eastward towards Hertfordshire in their periods of silence; his too-brief acquaintance with Elizabeth certainly had not left his heart unaffected, for all his rational side sought to deny the fact. Unlike Bingley, however, he was able to console himself, to a degree, with the assurance that the pangs he suffered were borne on Elizabeth's behalf, which at least allowed him to feel that his trials of the heart served some worthy purpose.

Their journey the day following proceeded much as had done the one before: colder perhaps, but no more conversible; they reached Pemberley late in the morning of the third day. Georgiana, who had been wandering about the ground floor all morning awaiting their arrival, ran to greet Darcy as soon as he entered. She stopped short of him, however, and looked up uncertainly; Darcy reached out and gathered her into a glad embrace, which she returned with great relief; notwithstanding the reassurances he had given her in his letters, she still needed to see the proof of his continued love and esteem in his eyes. He held her thus briefly, until Bingley approached to offer his greetings. Georgiana extricated herself hastily from her brother's arms, embarrassed by her show of feeling, and welcomed

Mr. Bingley with warm, yet quiet, propriety; then, tucking her arm demurely but happily into her brother's, she led the gentlemen directly to the south dining-room, where the servants were just finishing laying out an early dinner. "I was certain you would be hungry on your arrival," said Georgiana.

"You remembered rabbit," Darcy observed to his sister fondly. She coloured and nodded without speaking; Darcy could see she was pleased that he had noticed, but anything resembling a compliment always sent her into an embarrassed silence.

"You must not bother to wash and change," she then said. "I have had this prepared to be ready the moment you arrived." As was often the case, there was a delicate mix of pride and reticence in her tone, as she was pleased with her scheme, yet remained unsure as to how it would be received.

"Unfortunately, Miss Darcy," Bingley told her lightly, "your brother will find it absolutely necessary to change before sitting down to eat; he is very nice about such matters. Are not you, Darcy?" Without waiting for Darcy's reply, he added to Miss Darcy: "But not to worry—I shall be sure to leave him a scrap or two from my ravening."

Miss Darcy looked at Mr. Bingley with mild alarm, but her brother told her: "Bingley is only trying to teaze me—he is taking his revenge for some foolishness at Netherfield, Dearest. Be assured: I am perfectly ready to eat just as I am in my own dining-room." Bingley laughed—the first open laughter Darcy had heard from him in many days, and he hoped that this might be due to his sister's influence. The three of them sat down together to the laden table.

The meal was sumptuous, savoury, and warming: besides braised rabbit there was chicken *en casserole*, hearty soups, and fresh warm breads, and there was easily enough to feed twice their number. The two men were exceedingly glad to relax and take their ease after the long, cold, rattle-

and-bounce of the chaise, and Darcy felt the weight of many months' absence fall from his shoulders.

Indeed, in the affection and thoughtfulness of his sister's greeting and preparations, Darcy found much to be grateful for; altogether his home-coming brought him a sense almost of deliverance. Whenever he left the estate he felt like a man setting out to sea: bracing himself for long days and short nights, storms and hardships. Returning to Pemberley afforded him an almost physical sense of relief; no longer holding himself constantly ready, set to meet whatever might come at him—he fancied at times that even his breathing came easier at home. While he could, and did, remind himself that there were few in England who lived in easier circumstances, nevertheless his journeys drained him, and being at home soothed his spirits like rain after a drought.

Although their conversation at table remained on inconsequential matters of travel and weather, Miss Darcy was in a torment to hear the details of the Netherfield ball, which her brother's brief letter from London had not done nearly enough to satisfy. She knew but little of her brother's dance with Miss Elizabeth Bennet, and wanted him to particularise very fully; she knew the reason for his removal to London, but not the outcome. These points were most insistently on her mind, yet, uncertain where things stood on so much that touched Mr. Bingley, his presence placed an embargo on all such topics. The gentlemen, paying rapt attention to the meal in front of them, spoke but little, and Georgiana could do no more than wait with as much patience as possible for the opportunity to speak with her brother in private.

Towards the end of a quiet, but very contented, meal, at which Miss Darcy was pleased to see her efforts well-rewarded, by the quantity of food consumed and the silent attention it commanded, her brother enquired: "Is all in readiness, Georgiana? Are we still to leave to-morrow?" On receiving her affirmation he said, "Then if you will ask Reynolds to show Mr. Bingley to his rooms, I have some necessary business with Stevenson, after which I wish to speak with Mr. and Mrs. Reynolds; I shall finish with Mrs. Annesley: if you might let her know, I should be obliged. I shall have done in the library in perhaps two hours—shall I come find you then?"

"Yes, Fitzwilliam, that would be nice. I spend much of my time in the front parlour up stairs; I shall wait for you there." Miss Darcy, however disappointed she might be by this delay, knew her brother well enough not to attempt to deflect his accustomed activities on his arrival home. He always met with his steward, Stevenson, to hear how things stood on the estate, after which he would turn his attentions to the household servants; finally, his business finished, he might relax and be himself.

Mr. Bingley, amiable as always, suggested that, after he had managed to remove the dust of travel, he, Miss Darcy and her companion might play at cards together until her brother should be ready for them. To this Georgiana agreed with pleasure, but not before looking to her brother to be sure of his approval, which he of course gave willingly; the three of them set off to tend to their separate concerns.

Darcy strode purposefully to his library and his business with Stevenson; on reaching it and closing the door behind him, however, he became suddenly irresolute. A discontented sigh escaped him as he looked about the familiar surroundings where he spent so much of his time at Pemberley. He drifted vaguely about the room, lost in thought. He could tell from certain looks during dinner that Georgiana had a good many questions on her mind—and some regarding Elizabeth most certainly among them. His ideas revolving around the discussion of Elizabeth he knew was to come, combined with the nearly palpable relief of being home, which enabled him at last to relax his guard, brought forward many of the emotions he had striven to hold in check during his journey homeward. On the way north he had been troubled to find his heart much heavier than he could have imagined it might be; he had been nearly continuously preoccupied by thoughts of Elizabeth. Indeed, over the last several days, even in London, he had found himself deeply engrossed by such thoughts, and perplexed by the persistence of his attraction to her. Her face had been before him constantly, and throughout their journey he had had to resist introducing her into conversation with his friend almost hourly. Her relationship to the object of his friend's attentions naturally placed a bar on the subject that could not be breached—yet he longed to speak of his own difficulties, and perhaps, to let his friend know he was not alone in having found something to regret in leaving Hertfordshire.

As he wandered about the room, he saw her about him in imagination; her smile shone at him from every chair and corner, by every window and doorway; at this moment, the dearest wish of his heart was that she might truly be there, and not merely a phantom of his imagining. While musing thus, his mind pictured her standing at the door, dressed for the evening, come to find him at his work before dinner; he realised with an ache of longing that he would have no difficulty whatever envisioning Elizabeth as mistress of Pemberley House: her bright laughter, her quiet purpose and grace, her wit…she would win the servants over in a day's time, and Georgiana would be so *very* pleased with her as a sister. The thought that followed hard on this one— that it could never be—gave him an almost physical pain. When they had been together in Hertfordshire, while knowing that they could have no future together, still—being with her and knowing he was protecting her by his silence, he had been able to support the idea that it was all for the best, even to the degree of experiencing a sort of pride in his sacrifice; but now, with no prospect of ever seeing her again, all he could feel was the bleak emptiness of her absence.

When he had met Elizabeth, Darcy had all but given up on the other sex, insofar as any romantic attachment might be considered. Then, to find some one whose nature seemed so completely to complement his own, had struck him with more force than he could have had any idea of — so unforeseen that it seemed nearly miraculous — and, unanticipated as were his emotions, he was wholly under their influence before he could realise their existence. Now that his feelings for her were become clear to him, as well as their utter hopelessness, he was the harder struck by his loss because his feelings for her *had* been unexpected and miraculous. And now, his emotions having broken free, he found himself unable to force them back down, although he tried daily to do so; his awareness, however, of Elizabeth's superior claims, in almost every aspect of her character and person, made this a daily, in fact, an almost hourly exercise in futility.

Determinedly pulling his gaze away from the door, where her image still stood before him, he forced his thoughts away from the tempting illusion of felicity she represented. Why should she dominate his mind in this way? he demanded of himself. His judgement and his resolution concerning her were unaltered, so whence came this unrelenting and self-imposed affliction? He prided himself on his discipline over his thoughts and emotions: this want of regulation was almost as troubling to him as the sensations that caused it. Their acquaintance was over, it was done: the decision made, he must move on. Before the thought was even fully formed, though, he knew he was lost, for he had had the same thought before, and a hundred like it: whether he would or no, he could not keep his mind from straying to her: not in London, nor in the chaise coming northward, nor here in his own familiar library.

The arrival of his steward finally brought his thoughts to order. What little news he had to offer was good, and as the winter months were quiet on the estate, there was little to be put in motion. Towards the end of the interview, Mr. Stevenson said to him, "There is, Sir, a difficulty in the town that I should like to place before you." When Darcy was at the estate he was often asked to intercede in local affairs, as his father had always done before him. He had not exercised his right to the post of magistrate for the county, as he felt himself too often absent; if he should ever have a settled life in Derbyshire, though, he would probably find himself assigned that duty whether he would or no, since his tenants and dependents always seemed to prefer to come to him with their troubles.

"Go on, Stevenson," Darcy invited.

"It is James Sayers, Mr. Darcy."

"William Sayers' son?" Darcy asked. Sayers had been a builder in the village, who had often worked on the Pemberley estates. He had died about the same time as had Darcy's father, and, Darcy recalled hazily, had left a widow and a son, James, then in his teens.

"Yes. The boy…well, to be perfectly blunt, the boy is a drunkard. A good-hearted lad, even in his cups, but he cannot sustain any sort of employment in his condition. His poor mother is at her wit's end, and his custom at the alehouses is costing her what little savings her husband left her. She has desired me to ask you, Sir, if there might be anything he could do about the manor."

"Well, Stevenson," Darcy said in mild surprise, "you would know better than I what might suit."

"Yes, but, between the family's history with the manor and the facts of the present case, I was uncertain as to what your wishes would be."

'I see," said Darcy. He thought for a moment or two before pronouncing: "We cannot leave William Sayers' widow in distress. I noticed last summer that the walls in the south fields were getting rather tumble-down: surely a builder's son will know how to stack rocks together, no matter how besotted he might be. And when the snow is too deep for stonework in the fields, have him work the walks and walls about the manor."

"Very good, Sir," replied Stevenson. "And his pay?"

"Twelve pence a day." Stevenson frowned and began to question the amount, as it was half a normal day's wages: surely not enough to keep body and soul together for two people. Darcy held up a finger, and went on: "And each week, enough food for the two of them will be sent his mother." As an afterthought, he added, "Make that six pence; send the other six to his mother. He should not be able to do too much damage to himself on six pence a day."

Stevenson smiled. "Yes, Sir. Very good, Mr. Darcy." And with that, he took his leave.

Next were come the Reynoldses. A pleasant older couple, staid, solid, and respectable; Darcy had known them both since earliest childhood. With them, Darcy had but one issue on his mind: the newest member of their staff. "How does Mrs. Annesley get on?" he enquired.

"Very well, Sir," replied Reynolds.

"A very good woman," agreed his wife. "Nice in her ways, and not at all above herself: always willing to lend a hand, even before asked."

Darcy was glad to have such a good account of her; companions were difficult: neither family nor quite servants, they could cause a good deal of friction within the household.

"Excellent; I am delighted to hear it. Is there anything I need be aware of, otherwise?"

The couple looked at each other. "Well, Mr. Darcy," began Reynolds, "do you mind Hadyn, the footman?"

"Young lad, sandy hair?" asked Darcy.

"That's him," confirmed Reynolds. "Well, Sir, he...that is, there is a young woman in the village..." Reynolds seemed to be having trouble coming to the point.

"Your pardon, Mr. Darcy," broke in his wife, "but Mr. Reynolds will be all day about it—Cyril, you know it's true; men never can talk of such things. The fact is, Mr. Darcy, that Hadyn has got a village girl with child, and is now loath to marry her."

"I see," said Darcy. "What sort of girl is she? Mrs. Reynolds?"

The good woman pursed her lips and said with deliberate judgement, "She's a good girl, for all she's saucy in her ways. I don't doubt but what she believed he meant to do right by her before she ever...well, having spoken with them both, I'd give my oath he sang her a pretty tune: but when the time came to pay the piper, well..."

Darcy, considering, said, "I see. Well, he has two choices: marry the girl, or leave my employ. If she cannot trust him, neither can I." He looked to the husband. "Reynolds, I shall want you to look into the matter, too. Make sure the girl is not pulling the wool over our eyes; but mark you, if the case be such as is stated, I want no misunderstanding on how to proceed."

To this Mrs. Reynolds nodded in complete agreement; Reynolds nodded, too, but with less enthusiasm. "I'd hate to lose him," he said. "He's a powerful good worker."

"Then let us hope he will make the right choice," Darcy said firmly. "Was there anything else?" Neither one had aught to add, and he dismissed them to their duties with a request that Reynolds send Mrs. Annesley to him.

Darcy was very keen to hear from Mrs. Annesley: his sister's concerns had the strongest of claims on him, and he very much wanted to know what that lady had to say about her. She arrived very shortly after, a pleasant-faced woman of middle years. She seemed at first rather anxious to make the right impression; as their discussion proceeded, however, she became more comfortable, and her expressions more candid. For the next quarter-hour Darcy listened attentively to what she had to relate: her arrival in Derbyshire, her first thoughts concerning Miss Darcy, and her opinion as to her current state of mind. When he had interviewed her for the post of Georgiana's companion in London, he had found Mrs. Annesley to be thoughtful, amiable, and perfectly gentle in her manners; she now justified his judgement by the sensibility of her observations of his sister's condition over the last several months. He was greatly aggrieved by her description of Georgiana's dejected spirits in October, but even more greatly surprised to learn when they had lifted, and what had seemed to be the cause.

"You are an exceedingly generous correspondent, Mr. Darcy," Mrs. Annesley had observed, "and it has done your sister more good than you may know."

"How is that, Mrs. Annesley?"

"Why, Sir, your letters from Hertfordshire were her constant study," she replied. "And if I am not mistaken, they raised her spirits quite considerably. I know nothing of their contents, of course; but she was always excited to receive them, and always appeared happier for having read them."

This startled Darcy a good deal, for, while he had certainly hoped that he might in some way have bolstered Georgiana's spirits and offered her solace, he hardly thought what he had written could have worked so great a change as this. "I confess," he said after a moment's reflection, "she seemed to have read into them things I had no idea I was writing, and her replies have often left me wondering if I had not told her much more than I remembered. I now begin to think that whatever she discovered in them could only have come from her attentiveness and insight — not my abilities as correspondent."

"Whatever the cause, what you wrote her has certainly lifted her spirits. Even her playing on the pianoforte is livelier."

"I am very glad to hear it, though I cannot think how my letters might have had such effect. If she found anything to value in them, I assure you it was rather due to her generous interpretation, than my writing." He added affectionately, "Her goodness colours every thing she touches."

Mrs. Annesley, smiling, said "If you will allow me, Sir, I have to say that Miss Darcy is one of the most thoughtful, and sweetest, young ladies I have ever met with. Are all the ladies of Derbyshire as delightful? If they are, be sure to keep word of it away from the fashionable young men in Town: no doubt there would be a sudden exodus to Derbyshire if it were widely known—and the peace of the country would suffer for it, I fear."

Darcy smiled back. "I would not make that claim, Mrs. Annesley; but, as I have told my sister, England's heart is in the country, and I can tell *you* that she was principally in my thoughts when I said it." He stood to signal the end of the interview. "Thank you for your time; I am well pleased with your efforts on Miss Darcy's behalf."

"My efforts have been slight, Mr. Darcy," said she. "It has done me good, I am sure, to be with her, and to see one so young and so good-hearted regain the lightness of spirit due her."

Darcy replied, "Again, thank you; I am very satisfied with how things stand. And as to Miss Darcy's good heart—I am prejudiced, of course, but I truly believe her to be the most genuinely good person I have ever known, save possibly my father."

The good woman had also risen in preparation for leaving, but she turned back at the door to say, "Based on my own knowledge of brothers, and what their sisters may expect of them, Mr. Darcy, I would venture to guess that it must be a family trait." She smiled gently and closed the door behind her.

Her implication rather startled Darcy and made him pause to assess himself: on serious reflection he found he could not entirely agree. Responsible, certainly. Charitable? Yes, he could allow himself that; he certainly tried to be liberal with those dependent on Pemberley. But good? Georgiana was good, Elizabeth was good, Bingley was good, but he could not accuse himself of deserving the term; his flaws were too numerous, and too grave. These reflections brought to mind an evening during which Elizabeth had teazed him with: "I am perfectly convinced by it that Mr. Darcy has no defect..." A moment's warmth spread through him at the memory, until he remembered, too, that it had been that very evening when he had realised the necessity of distancing himself from her. Reining in his wandering thoughts yet again, with resolute purpose he picked up the papers Stevenson had left. The figures were good; the next year should proceed well...But how would Elizabeth fare in the coming year, and beyond? He saw still a drudging, dreary future for her, even if there were no parson—Heaven forbid—in the offing. She could be such a...with a gesture of frustration and disgust at his want of self-discipline, he firmly pushed the papers from him and left the room in search of his sister and Bingley.

He found them in the front salon up stairs, as Georgiana had said he might; on entering it he remembered that Georgiana and his mother had often used it together when Georgiana was quite a girl. He also saw that it was largely unchanged since that time, and was in want of new furnishings. Not that the room was shabby, but the colours were dark and muted, and the style was from a generation past; he would see to it that it was lightened and brought up to date before Georgiana returned to Pemberley. Dismissing Reynolds, who had stayed to attend Miss Darcy in Mrs.

Annesley's place, Darcy went over to join his sister and friend.

Bingley and his sister were seated together on the sofa by the window playing vingt-un between them, and as Darcy went to join them he was highly gratified to see that Bingley seemed in better spirits than he had been this last week and more. As he reached the window, Darcy was pleased to refresh his memory on the fine prospects the windows afforded of the river and fields in front of the house; he had not taken in this view for some years.

"Well, then; all serene?" he asked, leaning against the corner of the window.

"I have been telling Mr. Bingley about our plans for Christmas," Georgiana informed him with a degree of pride and pleasure in her voice.

"Your sister has a magnificent scheme laid out for the holidays, Darcy," said Bingley admiringly.

"Hardly magnificent," Georgiana demurred quietly. "Mostly it will be only family and friends."

"Precisely as it should be," Bingley stated firmly.

In jest, Darcy fixed his sister with a stern look and said, "So, you have let my friend in on the secret before telling me? I see now in what regard you hold me!"

Instantly, Georgiana was all over confusion: "No, Fitzwilliam…truly," she stammered, "we were only just talking…I was waiting until you should have done…"

"Dearest," Darcy interrupted her gently, "I was only teazing; it meant nothing." He smiled at her and kissed her hand reassuringly. To his friend he said, "She kept her plans from me, even pledging my own butler to secrecy."

"Aunt Eleanor wanted it to be such a surprise!" cried Georgiana, still upset that she might have offended him. "You were not to know until we were sure the plans were complete," she explained hastily. She looked as though she would say more, but had not the courage.

"Well, your holidays promise very well, I assure you," said Bingley, taking pity on Miss Darcy's confusion and shifting the burden of conversation to himself: "She has planned every evening: games, entertainments, all the best dishes of the season: the perfect Christmas."

"Merely what one expects, nothing extraordinary," Georgiana protested again, softer still.

"That is exactly what makes it extraordinary," Bingley insisted. "This modern idea that English food and English customs are out-dated offends me; why should the French and German holidays be held in higher regard than our own?" he protested. "The vogue to-day for pretending that the old-fashioned holidays are beneath us is stuff and nonsense. Do not you agree, Darcy?"

"I am entirely of your opinion, Bingley," he answered pleasantly.

"Not that I do not enjoy variety in cuisine, or feel it right that other countries should have their own way of doing things; I am not so illiberal as that," Bingley said. "But why our own should be any less agreeable or proper is beyond me."

"Well, then," said Darcy, "we must venture to bring a touch of the old ways back to England's capital city, must we not?" To his sister he said, "So tell me, then, what have you planned?"

Georgiana, searching her brother's face anxiously for any sign of disapproval, said hesitantly, "Well, we have plans with our friends for most evenings, but the Saturday before Christmas we are giving...a rather large dinner party." At this last Georgiana looked at her brother with a fearful and apologetic face.

"A dinner party? How large is 'rather large'?" Darcy asked curiously.

"We are not sure yet."

"And who might *we* be?"

"Aunt Eleanor has been doing most of the work; it was her idea to begin with."

"I see; and do *we* know how many invitations have been sent?" Darcy smiled at Georgiana.

Georgiana hunched in on herself and answered in nearly a whisper, "Almost fifty."

"My *dear* Miss Darcy," her brother said in amazement, "you are planning an evening entertainment in our home with nearly a hundred guests?"

"I am sorry, Fitzwilliam!" she cried. "It was all Aunt Eleanor's idea — to begin introducing me."

Bingley laughed delightedly at his friend. "Forced into Society with a vengeance! The leopard had best change its spots, make no mistake — and right away: you have only ten days to prepare yourself. Oh, Miss Darcy, please — pray do tell me that there will be a ball after!"

Georgiana, her eyes still on her brother, shook her head at this: "No, even my aunt agreed this was too much to expect of my brother," said she.

Bingley made a disappointed face. "What a shame! I should so love to see your brother opening his own dance."

Darcy, knowing Georgiana's eyes to be upon him, slowly spoke, "Do you know, the notion is not altogether bad; Georgiana *will* be mistress of the house soon, and ought to begin being known as such."

Bingley directly threw a pillow from the sofa at Darcy, startling Georgiana considerably. "What!" cried he. "You misbegotten lout! You fraud! After how you go on about being in company, how much you despise it — and here you are, happy as you please, to be having your own Society dinner!"

"An English gentleman is always happier in his own home, no matter what might be passing," Darcy told his friend loftily; he found Bingley's good humour very encouraging. "Here, allow me to rearrange your pillow." Taking the pillow he had caught, he stuffed it down behind

Bingley's back with such force that Bingley was nearly thrown from the sofa.

"Fitzwilliam!" cried his sister, alarmed at such violence, even in play.

Bingley took advantage of the moment Darcy looked towards his sister to strike him a blow across the chin with the pillow. "Ah, that is better!" he exclaimed. "Your cravat was crooked." The two friends regarded each other warily for a moment, waiting to see what the other's next move might be, but then Darcy's shoulders relaxed, and he laughed. "Always happier at home, no matter what might be passing," said he, picking up the pillow and setting it with precision back in the corner of the sofa. Still laughing, he poured Bingley and himself a glass of wine; offering to pour a small glass for his sister, which she declined, the three sat down in excellent spirits.

Darcy was exceedingly glad to see his friend's spirits lifted. He hoped it might presage a faster recovery than he had had any reason to suppose up until then. The rest of the evening passed quietly away with cards and conversation. After a lengthy but guarded observation of his friend, however, Darcy decided that the improvement in Bingley's mood had less to do with his sister's influence in her own right, than it was simply the effect of being with others. Bingley's nature was such that he was always in better spirits when he was in company, especially mixed company, and with only Darcy at Grosvenor Square, his mood was unlikely to have improved; but in the schemes Georgiana had in motion, and the entertainments and diversions that must attend them, Darcy had reason to hope for better. His misgivings where his friend was concerned were materially lightened as a result, and he flattered himself that he had done right by him.

Their plan was to start their return shortly after breakfast on the morrow, and so the card game broke up early. Up in his rooms, while Darcy was laying out some things he wished to take back with him, a light rapping came at the door.

"Fitzwilliam?" his sister's voice came softly.

"Come in, Dearest," he answered.

The door opened quietly. "I am not disturbing you?"

"Not at all," he assured her. "I was rather expecting you; I am sorry we have had no time before now to talk. How are you? You seem well."

"I am well, I think. Better, at least. Well, except for dreading Aunt Eleanor's dinner; this is not at all what I came to speak with you about, but I do not wish it, Fitzwilliam, truly I do not—how could I wish to be in company? Can *you* not stop her? It is *so* wrong! She wants me to meet people! If she knew…"

"Now, Georgiana," Darcy interrupted her, "calm yourself, do; there is no need for alarm; come, sit by the fire." He wrapt her shawl more carefully about her shoulders, then sat down across from her. "I believe I understand some part of how you are feeling, you know; I imagine I find these social affairs no more rewarding than yourself. But, I assure you, Dearest, you will have little enough to do. From what you have said, I gather Aunt Eleanor means for you merely to sit with her at dinner, and not much more."

"But, Fitzwilliam, I have no business being amongst such people—with any one, in fact; if they knew what I have done…"

Darcy looked at her troubled face sympathetically. "First, your one great error was to trust some one: I hardly think that breaks any of the Commandments; but, second, I am sure *you* would not want to be with some of them either, if you knew what *they* have done, I promise you," he assured her gently. "You cannot put ten people in a room, but one of them, at least, has secrets they would die before revealing."

Georgiana said nothing for a moment, then asked wretchedly, "Must I do this?"

"No—well, yes; not this time, perhaps," he replied reasonably, "if you are positively set against it; but at some time, you must, indeed. Your aunt has been pointing you in this direction for the last two years, after all; but it is in my power to forbid that the dinner should go forward—is that your wish? If it is, I shall comply." Darcy did not, in all honesty, think he could dissuade his aunt that easily, but Georgiana fancied his authority absolute, and in this way she would come to her own decision on the matter.

"Yes!" she replied hastily, followed immediately thereafter by: "No...I should not wish to disappoint Aunt Eleanor, after all her hard work and preparation." She looked earnestly at her brother. "You will be there to help me, will you not, Fitzwilliam? I do not think I shall be able to go through with it on my own."

"Of course, Dearest; if it were for my sake alone, I should never let you face anything by yourself: seeing you in difficulty is something I should never choose. But for your own sake you must learn to take on such tasks: you must learn to know your own strength. And allow me to point out that a great many ladies before you, and I dare say not a few who were far less gifted with resources than yourself, have managed to assume similar rôles. Aunt Eleanor is so insistent that you be brought forward because she knows—not imagines out of love, mind you, but she *knows*—that you are a very capable young lady. And you know what my mother would have wished for you: she believed strength in a woman benefited both herself and her husband; and I must say I agree. Her strength was something Father relied on, and when he was bereft of that reliance, I believe he suffered for it."

"Yes, I know she was strong: every one says so. But Fitzwilliam, that is why she...she always rode alone, and joked that she had no wish to wait for a man to catch up; but if she had not been riding by herself that day, she would still be alive," Georgiana said sadly.

Darcy was shocked: he had never before heard this idea from Georgiana — nor from any one, for that matter. He said, "No, that is not so, Dearest: why would you say that?"

"I do not know," said Georgiana uncertainly. "But I thought…I always just assumed that if she had not been alone, she should not have…"

Darcy gave his sister a sympathetic look. "Ah, I see," he nodded. "Well, that would make sense, at the age of seven," he allowed. "But Georgiana, that had nothing to do with it. A buckle on her cinch gave way during a jump; there was nothing any one could have done: she would have fallen the next time she took a jump, no matter how many others had been with her."

"Then it was not what Father said? That she was headstrong?"

"Did he say that? In your hearing?" Darcy felt for what his sister's youthful feelings must have been on hearing this. "On my honour, Georgiana, that was not the case at all. And, to the best of my memory, her being 'headstrong' was never a thing he complained of when she was with us; quite the contrary, in fact: he was proud of her abilities, and counted on them a good deal, I believe."

Georgiana was quiet for a moment; her own recollections of her mother were not extensive, and were largely coloured by what she had heard said of her by their relations after her death. Georgiana's character, being naturally sympathetic, had been influenced to a degree by the thought that her mother's boldness had contributed to her death, and this new intelligence brought an entirely new view of the matter to her. "Are you certain, Fitzwilliam?" she asked.

"Completely," said he with confidence. He looked at her enquiringly. "I hope that will ease your mind; does it help?"

"It does," she acknowledged tentatively. "But I shall have to think on it some time, I believe." She sighed and said, "I am learning a great deal this year, it seems. But, Fitzwilliam, I came to speak of *you*: I have been very worried about you — will you not tell me about Hertfordshire? And London?" Her voice was calm, but her eyes were troubled.

"Well, Dearest, I shall tell you what I can," he said. "Your letters caught up to me in London, so I think I know pretty well what you wish to hear. I am sorry you have been so racked for want of information, but the whole affair has been such a jumble..." he broke off and stared into the flames on the hearth.

"You said he..." Georgiana began hesitatingly, "he was not at the ball."

"No, he did not attend," Darcy said briefly.

She nodded without looking up at him. "You danced with Miss Elizabeth Bennet...?"

He drew a deep breath, and said, "I did." His reply was short, as he had no wish to relive the affair.

Georgiana looked up at him. "And did you...did she...it was pleasant?"

"It was at first, very," he allowed.

"In your letter you said it ended differently."

Darcy sighed. "Yes, it ended differently. I fear she has no very high opinion of your brother at present."

"But how can that *be*?" Georgiana demanded in a distressed tone. "Whatever can have happened? Please, Fitzwilliam — tell me every thing."

Here Darcy paused; the truth, he knew, would give Georgiana pain, and he was disinclined to exhibit more of Wickham's misdeeds to her. "Dearest, what is done, is done. It would be best, perhaps, to leave it at that."

But Georgiana was determined; convinced as she was that her brother was merely hiding his emotions from her, and himself, she could not let his reluctance prevent him from seeing where his heart might lead him; taking her courage in both hands, she asked the question that had worried her since first reading his letters: "Did you say anything, Brother? Forgive me, but you know you can sometimes speak in a manner not best suited to please your listeners."

Darcy smiled gently at her. "You think then that *I* might have offended Miss Elizabeth Bennet in some way?"

Georgiana's diffidence again made her hesitate, but concern for her brother's best interests drove her on. "I confess that when I first heard that Miss Elizabeth Bennet had declined to dance with you, I wondered if she might not have heard you speak your mind in an unguarded manner."

Darcy, amused, said, "I own that I am at times too...forthright...in my comments when in company, but such was not the case here, I assure you. I can remember every word I ever spoke to her."

"But then, what can have happened at the ball?" she cried. "Why should she dislike you now?"

In the face of such sincere distress, Darcy felt obliged to tell her a little of what happened at the ball. As he spoke, however, he found himself becoming more diffuse, and by the time he had done, he had told her every thing that happened that night at Netherfield, and also later in London with Bingley. It had been some years since he had established the custom of speaking openly with his sister—it had been directly after their father's death, in fact, when the practice had been of service to them both—and the habit was difficult to break.

Tears came to Georgiana's eyes more than once during his narrative as he exposed Wickham's rôle in setting Elizabeth against him, but she kept her silence until the end. "I am so sorry, Fitzwilliam," she said, bowing her head and clasping her hands tightly in her lap. "This is my fault."

"No!" cried her brother in alarm and surprise. "Why should you say so? You must not think that: nothing you have done has any bearing on this, surely!"

"He is striking back at you, because of me."

"No, Georgiana, *truly*," he replied, taking her hands in his own. "He may be striking out at me, that is true, but not because of you; he has always sought to injure me, in ways both large and small."

Georgiana's tears began again. "And I chose *him*!" she denounced herself bitterly.

She would not meet Darcy's eye, and he knelt down next to her to look up into her face. "Dearest," said he in the gentlest of accents. "Georgiana—no. It was not you who sought him out; he needed money, and picked you as his quarry—that is all; I know this is so because he had come at me for assistance not long before. I do not deny that his dislike of me might have been a factor in his choice, but that makes it rather more my fault than yours."

Georgiana slowly recovered herself, and Darcy brought her a glass of water. After some little time spent speaking quiet words of reassurance, Darcy sat down next to her. Taking her hands again in his and looking down at them, he said regretfully, "Regardless, I do not know what I could have hoped for: no matter how things had gone at the ball, Miss Elizabeth Bennet and I could have no future." He had never spoken these thoughts aloud before, and as he did he felt a wrench; saying the words had driven it home to him as never before. His spirit cried out against this truth, but, try as he might, he could see no other way through the matter.

"Dearest Fitzwilliam, I have never seen you upset so; *why* should not you and Miss Elizabeth Bennet have a future together?" Georgiana asked, her eyes again becoming unhappy. "This is the one point that has puzzled me so in your letters."

Darcy looked at his sister gravely. "Can you not see how impossible it is? Her family, her sisters—her mother! Connections the likes of which have never been remotely considered by our family; notwithstanding her qualities and abilities, it is impossible."

"But what family does not have its weaknesses and follies?" she protested. "Aunt Catherine, you must agree…"

Darcy broke in with a shake of his head: "Dearest, there can be no comparison between Lady Catherine de Bourgh of Rosings and Mrs. Bennet of Longbourn. Truly, you must believe me when I tell you that her mother stands alone in her genius for folly and impropriety. Nor, I have to say, are her three younger sisters without their share in full measure."

"I do believe you, Fitzwilliam. It is only my heart that wishes it were otherwise."

Darcy released her hands, and, kissing her forehead, said, "As does mine—more than I can say. Come, now, it is very late: you need your rest." He escorted her to the door, wrapt her shawl once more around her shoulders, and bade her goodnight. Unfortunately, he was unable to take his own advice, and sleep evaded him until late in the night.

Chapter Four

*D*arcy, Georgiana, and Bingley made the return to London without incident. Darcy still kept watch for any signs of regard that might pass between his companions, but, aside from the fact that Georgiana was more at ease around Bingley than she was with most others outside her family, he could discern no evidence of any particular attraction developing between them. Darcy's own mood being sombre, he was glad that the two of them got on together; they kept each other occupied while he brooded. Again and again he found his thoughts straying to Elizabeth; in his mind he could see their life together with perfect clarity, stretching before him in every detail—at Pemberley in the breakfast parlour, and in London with him at the theatre, always the kindest and brightest part of his life. Periodically he would try to lift himself out of his mood and attempt conversation, but he would invariably lapse back into melancholy. On the heels of that melancholy often followed a sharp frustration; nearly three hundred years of privilege and position imperiously demanded within him that his desires be met; and, removed from rational thought, removed from the rules of propriety, his irritation and impatience at being thus thwarted continued to churn inside him.

London, when they arrived late on Saturday afternoon, was busier even than when they had left it six days earlier, as the holiday season expanded its influence. Festive ornaments and bright colours were every where seen, and Darcy was gladdened by the sight of his sister's eyes lighting up with pleasure as they arrived at Grosvenor Square. Mrs. Annesley, who had travelled slightly ahead of them that day, was already at work with the servants to begin preparations for meals and entertainments; Georgiana dutifully went off to join them on her arrival, leaving the two gentlemen to settle in on their own.

"Something to drink, Bingley, to warm the bones?" Darcy asked after they had shed their coats.

"A good cup of tea would not go amiss," answered his friend. "But if you wish something stronger, do not let me influence you."

"Tea sounds perfect," Darcy concurred amicably. Glancing out the window, he saw the street in front of the house transform itself into a charming holiday picture, as a thick snow began to fall among the cheerful lights shining from around the Square. The two gentlemen settled themselves in the lower drawing-room by a fine blaze, and enjoyed that feeling of good fortune which any one must have when within doors in front of a comfortable fire, just at the beginning of a heavy snowfall.

The friends sat before the fire for half an hour, warming themselves and talking of the journey. At length Darcy said to his friend, "I want to thank you, Bingley, for coming with me to fetch my sister. It is a long ride, I know, and I make it all too often by myself. I was glad of the company, I assure you."

"Not at all, Darcy," his friend replied. "It is I who should thank you, for having preserved me from *my* sisters' company these past weeks."

"Will you be needed at home? Selfishly, I should like you here with us, at least until after the New Year."

"Just as selfishly, I should like to remain, and I thank you. I shall, however, have to go back to the Hursts' for a bit, if only to keep Caroline from bankrupting me in my absence."

Darcy gave a laugh. "My father used to say: no matter how large a man's income, his family could always outspend it."

"How true; I only wish that she might marry, so she might impoverish some one else for a change," said Bingley with one of his grins. To this Darcy made no reply; his silence did not go unnoticed, and after a pause Bingley spoke uncertainly, "Darcy, I have been meaning to say…there can be no question about Caroline's interest in a certain quarter—but I should just like to say that, however all that might turn out, I do not intend that it should have the slightest effect on our friendship."

"I am very glad to hear it," said Darcy, "but why say so now?"

Bingley was quiet for a moment. "I am not sure, to say the truth: to do some good where it is wanting? Perhaps it is only that my own recent…difficulties…make me want to keep anything else from going wrong—at least for a while. We neither of us have had much of a year, and, while I am endeavouring to get the better of things, I should hate to have anything more to contend with, for either of us."

Darcy shook his head at his friend. "Indeed; I have never known a year such as this." A moment of silence stretched between them. Darcy firmly put down his cup. "I find that tea no longer satisfies me. Something with more authority? And perhaps backgammon?"

"Billiards," Bingley said with decision. "And claret; too early for spirits."

"Done, and done. But I warn you—I am in a mood to crush you utterly."

"Then you must still be smarting from the way I trounced you last time. Bring on your worst—you will find it insufficient to your needs, though, I fear." So saying, the two lovelorn companions went off to soothe their savaged spirits in the linked arms of Mars and Bacchus.

Chapter Five

*F*or the next day Darcy had invited the Hursts and Miss Bingley to dine with them; Georgiana, he knew, had already invited them for various entertainments during the holiday season, but he felt the need to have them on his own behalf, in return for the hospitality he had received at Netherfield. In support of his aunt's efforts to bring Georgiana more to the fore, and to encourage her to accept her rôle as mistress of the house, he had asked her approval for the dinner, and received her rather bewildered blessing. It was to be a small affair, one that asked little of her beyond setting the menu. But it had been agreed that she might be allowed to retire early: she did not like to think of herself as being out, running the household, and feared her aunt's soirée marked the beginning of the end of her peace; she wished to enjoy her tranquillity for as long as she could.

"I am required to be in company this Thursday, Fitzwilliam," she had argued, "Please — might I have one more evening of quiet and ease?"

"Very well," he acquiesced. But, turning a penetrating eye on her, he added: "But mind you, I feel it wrong in me to be so lenient; as you are to run things eventually, you must begin sometime, and it were easier, I should think, to start out among a small group well-known to you, than to wait until the dinner."

His sister had thanked him with a quick peck on the cheek, and then hurried away before he could think better of it and change his mind. Darcy smiled at her back: he knew he was letting himself be manœuvred, but making Georgiana happy was one of the things he took most pleasure in; and, so long as he did not allow her to become lax in her duties, or ill-equipped to take her place in life, it pleased him to indulge her.

Therefore, when the loo table was placed after tea, Georgiana bade every one a gentle good evening and went upstairs to enjoy one of her dwindling nights of freedom.

Their play was sociable and easy, much to Mr. Hurst's annoyance; but the ladies were, neither one, adepts at the science of chance, and Bingley and Darcy were inclined to let the cards play themselves that evening, so Mr. Hurst spent much of the evening fuming over the lack of sound play.

"Miss Darcy is even lovelier than last year," Miss Bingley had complimented Darcy at one point in the evening, not long after Georgiana had retired. "Louisa and I are thrilled that she is to be hostess for the dinner next week."

"You must not let her hear you call her that," Darcy advised, "unless you wish to see her discomposed beyond all measure: in her mind it is her aunt's dinner, and no other."

"Oh! —Poor dear!" cried Miss Bingley. "Is she much worried, then?"

"I believe she would give a great deal never to have heard the word 'dinner'," Darcy replied. "But her aunt is in the right on this matter, I believe: it is time my sister took on more duties and began moving into society."

"You, recommending your sister move into society?" Bingley demanded. "How would you know anything of that? *You* never have!"

Darcy cocked an eyebrow at him, but made no reply.

"Charles," cried Miss Bingley, "how can you speak so to our host? Is he not in Society now, or do you not count your own family among the people of fashion hereabouts?"

"Caroline, this is hardly 'Society'; surely it is more like a family gathering: we are all well acquainted with each other, and perfectly easy. Much different from being at a grand social event where the strangers far outnumber the friends."

His sister sniffed disdainfully. "Well, it is still abominably rude to accuse your host of being ill-bred." She turned a relieving smile at Darcy; he recognised the truth in her brother's accusation, however, and therefore had taken no offense at his jibe.

At this point, Hurst, who had often been chafing under such conversations at Netherfield, apparently felt that such goings-on simply were not to be tolerated in Town; he threw in his hand without speaking and went to pour himself a glass of wine; drinking half of it straight down, he lay down on a sofa some distance from the group. Those at the card table looked at each other in surprise, although no one seemed to feel any great contrition, nor to mourn the loss of his company. Indeed, his wife directly went to the instrument, and, looking first at Darcy for his permission, began a lively piece within a few paces of her husband's back.

Mr. Hurst having broken up the card game, and his wife having taken upon herself their entertainment, the three remaining got up from the table as well. Darcy went over to a chair well away from the instrument, as Mrs. Hurst was holding forth with commendable energy; Miss Bingley followed him, while her brother stationed himself by the fire, gazing into the flames.

"Well, Mr. Darcy, it must be pleasing to see your sister moving into her rightful place as mistress of Pemberley," Miss Bingley said; to Darcy, however, her comment appeared to have a faintly downcast air about it.

"Indeed," said he, "although I could wish it were easier for her. Her diffidence has always held her back; I only wish my mother…" he trailed off, and did not finish his thought.

Miss Bingley looked at him not unsympathetically, but then her gaze sharpened, and she said with interest, "Have you considered, Mr. Darcy, that having a more experienced lady to guide Miss Darcy would be of invaluable assistance to her, in finding her way in Society?"

Darcy thought it best to deflect her from the true object of her question—how *she* might become that helpful lady. "I agree with you," he replied, "and my aunt has taken that task largely upon herself." An association of ideas led him to add: "She is to take my sister to Bath later in January; I am glad of it, in a way, as it will give me a chance to send certain things from here to Pemberley; I am doing over my sister's favourite room there, and, in addition to new furnishings, I have a mind to send some of the small *objets* from the drawing-room here that will suit it, and there is bound to be a certain commotion about the business."

"Goodness, Mr. Darcy; would that Charles were half the brother you are! Have you chosen a theme for the room? That is critical, you know, to the proper selection of new furnishings; I should be very glad to be of assistance," she said, looking at him speculatively. As her ideas developed, so did Miss Bingley's enthusiasm for the project increase. "Truly, it would be my greatest

delight. Perhaps we might go shopping together, when I return." Darcy appeared dubious at this. "Please, I insist," she appealed with a sincere and winsome manner, "—do promise me!"

"In truth, Miss Bingley, it had been my plan to attend to it sooner rather than later," the gentleman prevaricated. When she looked so very down at this, though, he could not but relent to some extent: "Very well; I have no doubt that there will be any number of things I shall have forgotten: we shall go out and finish the list together one day."

Miss Bingley was overjoyed at his acquiescence; she smiled very broadly, thoroughly delighted at the prospect of being able to buy even the least thing for Pemberley, with its master's full permission; then, her face becoming more serious, she began ticking points off on her fingers: "Only be sure to tell me what you have purchased," said she, "and remember the colours exactly; get a swatch if you can; the merchant is sure to have some to hand. And best quality, of course: perhaps I should write down some of the better warehouses for you…"

Darcy thought it best to head off this torrent, lest, in her enthusiasm, she re-furnished all of Pemberley, and Grosvenor Square into the bargain. "I assure you, Miss Bingley," he interrupted, "this is not the first occasion on which I have made purchases for the estate. And I always buy at Wilson's; we have traded there since my mother's time."

"Wilson's, of course; unquestionably first quality; but perhaps I should just jot down some of the main pieces; German, do you think, or French? And tapestried fabrics are all the rage just now…"

But Darcy had no intention of letting Miss Bingley use Pemberley as her dollhouse, and put an end to her delighted imaginings by saying, "Thank you Miss Bingley, but I have some things already in mind; but I shall make sure Mr. Wilson delays the shipment until you have seen the pieces I select, and then you will have all the information you require."

Miss Bingley began a pout, but, seeing Darcy's cool gaze in response, she instantly turned it into a smile, thanking him with an abundance of delighted sincerity, while leaning closely in on his arm, almost as though she were going to rest her head on his shoulder. Darcy defended his claims to the unfettered use of his person by stepping away and gesturing to the pianoforte, diverting her with the request: "Perhaps you and Mrs. Hurst might favour us with a duet?" He knew the sisters enjoyed displaying their abilities, and his application was rewarded with her immediate and gratified compliance. Darcy removed himself to the fire, taking up the position opposite his friend; securing themselves by the hearth, with the safety of numbers and occasional lauds and smiles, the two gentlemen managed to keep each other out of the line of fire from the ladies' attentions and machinations for the rest of the evening.

Early the following Thursday brought the arrival of Darcy's nearest, and dearest, relations: the Fitzwilliam family. His cousin Edmund, of course, had been an intimate friend and confidant since childhood, and Edmund's parents — Darcy's Uncle Jonathan, Earl of Andover, and his aunt Eleanor, Lady Andover — were great favourites with both Darcy and Georgiana. The elder brother, however, George, Viscount St. Stephens, was not. Cursed with a deadly combination of arrogance and ignorance, his affected manners and superciliousness, even towards his own parents, often grated on Darcy; fortunately, Viscount St. Stephens preferred a public life, in consequence of which he and Darcy rarely found themselves in company together, even in Town.

Lord Andover had, in some respects, come to stand in place of Darcy's father. Darcy had the highest opinion of his uncle's abilities and wisdom; he was one of the very few men Darcy would turn to for advice on thorny matters. On his side, Lord Andover looked upon Darcy as a younger version of himself, and had been a close friend to Darcy's father for many years; on the death of Darcy's father, it had been Lord Andover who had stepped in to support Darcy and his sister during that very difficult change of life. Whenever the two men met, they were sure to give themselves the pleasure of a lengthy, comfortable, private conversation.

This time was no different. No sooner had the family settled in — that is, when Darcy's Aunt Eleanor had bustled off with Georgiana to review, thoroughly approve, and completely rearrange all that Georgiana had already begun; Cousin George had hastened away into Town on "matters of import"; and the Colonel had ensconced himself in his apartments to write letters—than Darcy and his uncle took possession of the library

"Well, then. —My dear Mr. Darcy," began the Earl with a rather florid bow and a cheerful grin.

"My dear Lord Andover," Darcy returned with his own bow and grin to match. This was their formula on re-union, a kind of mutual acknowledgement, and it meant a good deal to Darcy. His uncle had begun the mock formali-ty of their greeting as a way of making light of the new responsibilities Darcy had assumed on his father's death: a reminder of sorts, that the mantle of duty, while heavy, need not be a crushing and inhuman burden. To Darcy it was even more: a symbol of their connection and of his un-cle's faith in him. They were Andover of Clereford and Darcy of Pemberley—men of good will and repute, who stood high in each other's estimation.

"Well, then, Uncle, how stands the nation?" Darcy en-quired, drawing a chair over by the fire for his uncle and taking another for himself. Andover was active in Parlia-ment, and was always abreast of what was moving in England and abroad.

"Ah…My boy, the nation, as it always has and, to my belief, always will, does not stand at all; it stumbles and ·blunders along somehow or other, lurching this way and that like a drunken hod-carrier under a heavy load. We can only pray it continues to remain miraculously upright."

Darcy laughed. "And Clereford?" he asked.

"There, I flatter myself, we see at least *some* coherence, and a sense of direction," Andover acknowledged. "Per-haps that is merely the reflection of my own arrogance, however."

"It was a good year at Pemberley," observed Darcy.

"Yes…for us it was, too." replied his uncle hesitatingly. "But I get a sense of unease, somehow. People are not hap-py."

"The war with the French?" surmised Darcy. "It has taken away a number of our tenants, and those who come back often are not fit to work the land."

"Perhaps, but I think not..." Lord Andover scowled at his hands for a moment, then shook his head to chase away the thought. "Time will sift through that problem," he said confidently. "But I want to ask you about this dinner your aunt has forced on you: are you being too much put out? Can I do anything about the expenses?"

"No, I thank you, Uncle Jonathan: that will not be necessary; it is for Georgiana's sake, after all. And my aunt is taking most of the burden off Georgiana's shoulders, and all of it off mine: it is no trouble, I promise you."

"Good," said His Lordship. "But now, Darcy; what about you? Truthfully, this last twelvemonth you have been looking rather down; your aunt is worried about you. Anything troubling you?"

Darcy hesitated. This was twice now that one of his intimates had addressed him on this subject in as many months. He decided to open his mind to his uncle. "Well, frankly, the Season last year left me rather in despair at the hope of ever finding a wife. I am very sorry, though, that I should have been so transparent as to have distressed my aunt."

His uncle waved away the latter part of this speech. He looked Darcy in the eye for a moment, then said, "Your aunt and I were discussing that very subject on the ride up from Hampshire; a man needs a wife, and your station both increases the need and complicates the choice." He hesitated again. "Darcy, may I ask — do you seriously contemplate a union with your cousin Anne?"

"No" Darcy said decisively. His uncle looked at him expectantly, so he expanded: "If it comes to that, there is a lady here in Town, a Miss Hartsbury, with more capital, more personality, and a far more complaisant mother — Heaven help me."

"Ah. 'If it comes to that…' — the lady does not entirely please, then." His uncle looked at him closely. "Is there, indeed, no one amongst your entire acquaintance you would wish to see as mistress of Pemberley?" Elizabeth's face rose instantly in Darcy's mind, but he could not speak of her. He slowly shook his head.

His uncle saw more in Darcy's face than he realised he had revealed. "I see," Andover said gently. "*The* lady does not suit, is that it?" Darcy looked up, startled at his uncle's penetration, but still did not speak. "Difficult; very difficult," murmured his uncle thoughtfully. "Is she…the lady is not already spoken for, is she?"

Darcy shook his head. "No, Uncle, nothing like that…it is a matter of her connections." He did not elaborate.

"I see. I am very sorry, my boy. What will you do?"

Darcy shook his head again. He attempted to put the proper face on it: "What can one do? It cannot be, and there is an end to it." His disappointed hopes, however, which had wounded him ever since he had first spoken aloud his conclusion regarding Elizabeth at Pemberley, caused a constriction in his chest that could scarcely be concealed. After a moment he asked, "Uncle Jonathan, did you never feel an attraction for some one who was not…a potential match?"

"No, Fitzwilliam, I never did; I am afraid I can offer nothing on the subject worth the hearing. I was fortunate enough to fall rather deeply in love with a girl unexceptional both as to connections and fortune. I honestly do not know what I might have done if things had gone otherwise. It does happen, of course; sometimes it works, others it does not. So far, it has not happened in our family — although it was a near thing when my sister married Sir Lewis."

"What do you mean?" asked Darcy; he had only dim memories of Sir Lewis de Bourgh, who had died abroad at an early age.

"Did you never hear the story?" his uncle enquired. Darcy shook his head. "Well, Sir Lewis' antecedents were a trifle murky; the family was an old one, but no one seemed to know them; and he had gone abroad as quite a young man, after certain rumours surfaced...regardless, he had made quite a bit, one way and another, from holdings in the colonies. But the ink on his letters patent was barely dry when he married your Aunt Catherine. At the time, my own father hinted that his "services to the Crown" were purely financial in nature."

"I never heard anything of that," said Darcy in surprise.

"No, I should not imagine you would. Your mother would not speak of it, naturally, and your good father had too kind a heart to say anything to any one's disadvantage."

Darcy mulled this new intelligence for a moment. "Wait a moment," he said, "are you suggesting that Aunt Catherine married beneath her?" Darcy was stunned at the idea.

"And for money," his uncle acknowledged blandly. "But Sir Lewis was anxious to secure his own standing — Catherine, of course, being of noble blood, would give him an indisputable legitimacy — and he was rich and ambitious, and not an ill-looking fellow, so the match was made. The marriage, I understand, was not to take place until he had got his baronetcy."

"But...but Aunt Catherine is the most unbearably proper person I know!" Darcy protested.

"*Now* she is, of course; but she was not always so. I rather imagine that is her way of making up for her one great lapse — and, I suspect, is also the reason she is so anxious to have Anne marry back into the Darcy family. But at the time — well, you *have* met my sister, have you not? How many suitors do you suppose could withstand that tongue? She was not overburdened by admirers, you may believe me. And Sir Lewis had the advantage of being out of the country much of the time, so the marriage worked — after a fashion."

Darcy was amazed, and not a little amused, at this new view of his aunt.

"Does this do anything to allay your reservations about this young lady of yours, by the way?" his uncle brought the discussion back to Darcy's concerns.

Darcy shook his head. "I fear, Uncle, that the two cases bear no real comparison. Her father's estate is an old one, although small, but he married beneath him. She has an uncle in trade, an aunt who married a law clerk, and her own mother is a veritable paragon of impropriety."

"I see," said he. "Shame. You are quite certain? If her father is a private gentleman…"

"You can have no idea, Uncle; there can be no question."

His uncle nodded thoughtfully, then placed a reassuring hand on Darcy's shoulder. "Well, do not give up hope; we cannot see the future, and if this lady is not the right one, we must be patient yet a while longer. I came here determined not to see you become my sister's son-in-law, if such had been your bent, and we must not allow the somewhat less troubling Miss…Hartsbury? …to have you out of sheer despair, must we?" Darcy tried his best to smile, but his heart refused to relent: within him frustration and anger vied with pain and sadness for precedence. "Come, my boy, the heart will heal," his uncle assured him. "There is still time; nothing need be done just now: it is hard to see from your position, but these things do seem to work themselves out, you know." He clapped Darcy again on the shoulder, saying, "But, come—I must not monopolise my host; let us go see what the ladies are about."

Chapter Six

*I*n truth, Darcy saw very little of either his sister or his aunt for the rest of that day, as they were very busily making final preparations for the dinner two days hence; there was still a great deal to do, making certain every least detail was complete. Periodically through the morning Georgiana would stop in to see him for a brief respite, and for reassurance; notwithstanding Darcy's assertions in Derbyshire, she felt it deeply wrong that she should be the centre of attention for an entire evening, as thoroughly discredited as she held herself to be, and was still more than a little frightened at the prospect of being noticed by so many people; this, combined with the effort required to ensure that all would go well, was beginning to wear on her. But each time she came to see him, five minute's support and encouragement would send her back out into the fray.

If Darcy's Uncle Jonathan had been somewhat a father to him, his Aunt Eleanor, having no daughter of her own to cherish and guide, had served as Georgiana's mother after the death of her own. Each year since Georgiana was ten, Aunt Eleanor had taken her to Town with her in the autumn, and they had also been together in Bath not unseldomly; Lady Andover's connections were from Somersetshire, and most of the family spent some or all of the winter season there, allowing her aunt to take Georgiana to visit in style and comfort. Lady Andover had also overseen Georgiana's education in London, entering her in one of the better seminaries for several terms, as well as teaching her at home. Lord Andover chose not to maintain a fixed abode in Town, so this arrangement had given Georgiana the chance to stay in many of London's more fashionable neighbourhoods, while the Darcy home in Grosvenor

Square had provided her a permanent address and a sense of stability.

Georgiana's aunt had the highest opinion of her abilities and sense, and it had been her idea the year before that Georgiana was ready to have an establishment of her own; she was determined that Georgiana should take that place in their circle she believed was her due, and so had begun to bring Georgiana forward at the early age of fifteen. She and Darcy did not always concur on how best Georgiana's education might be forwarded, but she had discovered that Darcy could not argue with the statement: "As a woman of some standing myself, I believe it to be in Georgiana's best interests…"; after that discovery, she had pretty well had the upper hand in their disagreements where Georgiana was concerned. Darcy knew he could, if need be, bring out his own status as Georgiana's guardian and brother to overrule his aunt, but he rarely chose to exert his authority in such an arbitrary manner.

Darcy had been especially careful to protect his aunt from all knowledge of Georgiana's intended elopement; Georgiana, he knew, would die of shame to have her aunt discover her secret, and, as Darcy considered it his own fault that the affair had occurred at all—he being the one who had engaged Mrs. Younge, the lady who had been Georgiana's chaperone and Wickham's conspirator—he was all the more assiduous in keeping the affair secret from those Georgiana respected most.

Early in the afternoon, at about the time he thought he might receive another visit from his sister, his Cousin Edmund appeared at the door of the library instead, come to see if Darcy wished to accompany him to amuse himself for a quarter-hour by watching the preparations under way. Darcy agreed readily, and they found the ladies of the house in command of the entire assemblage below stairs. As the two of them approached, Lady Andover cast a brief glance at them over her shoulder, then turned immediately back to her work. "Yes, gentlemen?" she enquired coolly, "Are you in need of something?"

"No, Mother," answered the Colonel, "we were just curious about the goings-on."

She gave them another glance, then said complacently, "I am the more pleased by your leisure and curiosity in that I am most particularly in need of two strong men to run to the fishmonger's; I had thought to send some footmen, but as you are here…" Edmund snatched Darcy by the lapels and pulled him away at a run. As they scrambled up the stairs, Darcy demanded, "But Edmund, does she not need our help?"

As they gained the landing, Colonel Fitzwilliam slowed down and assured him, "Not at all, Darcy; you may believe me: that was just the warning shot across the bow. What she wanted was for us to be elsewhere — we are safe enough, now, I think, but having brought ourselves to her attention, rather than trust to luck I shall go ahead and *be* elsewhere, entirely; I shall wander over to Knightsbridge, to see if there is any news." Colonel Fitzwilliam was attached to the First Dragoons, and their barracks was no more than a five-minute ride. He went up stairs to change, and Darcy returned to his library, cautiously and securely closing the door behind him.

Later that afternoon, perhaps two hours before dinner, Darcy finished his work in the library and wandered out past the front drawing-room; he saw that the Colonel had returned from the barracks and was staring out the window onto the Square with a preoccupied air and a cup of tea in his hand. "You are back!" Darcy cried. "Anything left in the teapot?"

Colonel Fitzwilliam turned to face him: "Of course, Darcy," he replied. "Shall I ring?"

"No; I had rather not bring myself to my aunt's attention by taking away one of her minions," Darcy said with a grin. "Besides," said he, "I believe I can manage to pour a cup of tea in my own home without injury, or loss of dignity." He proceeded to demonstrate, and the two men sat down by the fire.

"Do not let my mother catch you performing servant's duties," the Colonel warned.

Darcy smiled at him and took a sip. "I have not seen her above stairs all day; I believe we are safe enough. Well, Edmund, I really have not had a chance to catch up with you since last summer; how are you?"

Colonel Fitzwilliam blew out a breath. "Well enough, Darcy," he replied. "I am very glad to be here; Georgiana is looking better, I believe."

"Yes; I, too, see some improvement—I have hopes the worst is past. I do wish we could find the means of overcoming her reticence, though; she has no concept of her own worth and accomplishment."

Colonel Fitzwilliam nodded. "So true. Why is it that those of least ability so often enjoy the greatest assurance?" he mused. Looking at his cousin, he went on: "But Darcy, you were not much different from your sister at that age; when we were at Eton, I swear you some times went a week without speaking to any one."

"I was not being shy, Fitzwilliam—only uninspired. If I said nothing it was because I could think of nothing worth saying."

"That hardly matters to most people; they are perfectly happy to prattle away about nothing to each other."

Darcy shrugged his indifference to such.

"There!" his cousin laughed. "Bingley would have used two dozen words to say that others' ways were not his own."

"Making me more efficient in my speech than my friend," Darcy scoffed. "Need I point out that this is not a profound revelation? But, if you are right, and there is a similarity of mind between Georgiana and myself, then I have failed to see it in that light; to me it has always seemed she was merely timid, and too hard upon herself."

"That, she certainly is," the Colonel agreed. "But as she is easy with us, I do not see it as an essential aspect of her character; only that she has too little appreciation of her strengths, relative to others her age."

"We must hope so," Darcy said. "I keep trying. But what of you, Fitzwilliam? You look well; how do things fare in His Majesty's service? What news from Knightsbridge?"

His cousin made a face. "No news at all. Lord, Darcy, it is a dog's life, I can tell you. They have me stuck here in London trying to turn men who barely know one end of a horse from the other into cavalrymen. It is heart-breaking work; and meanwhile, Bonaparte is back in Paris, Batavia has turned into a rout, and I wish nothing better than to be over there, doing something worthwhile."

"So this is why we hardly see you! All your letter-writing — you are fishing for an assignment in Europe."

Colonel Fitzwilliam looked cautiously over his shoulder towards the door and nodded. "Yes; but only Father knows, so I trust you will keep it in confidence."

"Of course; is there anything I might do to help, Fitzwilliam?"

"I do not think so, but I thank you; Father is doing what he can." The Colonel here paused a moment; he then cried with some heat, "The Devil of it is, the Russian army is making such a mess of it that we need all our best on the continent, not here on a parade ground! You heard about that fool, von Fersen, being taken at Bergen? I swear to you Darcy — without conceit, I am five times the horseman he is. If I had been there with a battalion of our Dragoons, we should have taken Bergen!"

"Calm yourself, Edmund!" Darcy said in a placating tone. "Heavens, man, it was not I who held you here."

"I am sorry, Darcy," his cousin apologised. "The truth is, I am fit to be tied. There's more than one title to be had by the men who bring Bonaparte down, and here I am, twiddling my thumbs in Knightsbridge."

"I can think of no one who deserves success, or the dignity that goes with it, more than yourself," Darcy assured him. "What kept you out of Batavia? I know your superiors think well of you, and I should have thought my uncle would have had sufficient influence to get you any posting you wanted."

"Father and York do not get on," Colonel Fitzwilliam grumbled.

"The Duke of York?" Darcy asked.

"Yes, he led the campaign in Batavia. Well, his reputation is a little blown upon these days, and the French are not slowing down in the least in their annexation of all Europe, so I may get a look in soon enough. At least, that is what I keep telling myself: if only some other rascal does not take Bonaparte down before I can get assigned…"

Here Darcy had to laugh: "My dear Fitzwilliam, you do realise that you are very near to treason by wishing Bonaparte continued success?"

"Only until I can get to him!" the Colonel cried. "I have been studying him, Darcy," said he with fervour, "and he is a very logical thinker. I tell you, I believe I could reason out his battle plans almost before he made them."

Darcy shook his head over his cousin's martial enthusiasms, but he respected his cousin's intellect: very possibly he could do just what he said. "Well, I certainly hope you get your chance. Only let me know if I may be of any use to you."

After dinner that evening, Darcy invited Bingley to a rematch at the billiards table; he had not seen his friend's grin for some time, and it seemed to him that Bingley's manner was becoming withdrawn. Bingley's play was strong, but his conversation remained muted, and Darcy thought perhaps he drank a half-glass more wine than usual, though this could have been merely his imagination.

Darcy kept the conversation studiously light; he attempted one subject after another, though, with little success. At one point he had mentioned hunting, and Bingley had said in an abstracted fashion, "I shall have to find another manor, I suppose; but Netherfield was so well suited to my needs, and so conveniently located…"

He did not continue, and Darcy looked at him closely; he suspected that his friend's thoughts had travelled beyond Netherfield to Longbourn. But here it appeared that Bingley had reached his low point, and realised how cheerless his manner must seem; quickly rousing himself, he changed the topic determinedly: "May I say, Miss Darcy is a delightfully accomplished young lady, Darcy: I congratulate you."

"Yes, she surprises even me; my aunt has done very well by her education."

"But I think I remember you saying that you had had her taught at Pemberley?" Bingley said.

"I did; we had the masters for her from the time she was seven — after my mother's death, that is — and of course, she has always had the Pemberley library at her disposal; indeed, while my father lived she was very fond of lingering there, while he worked. But when my father died as well, Aunt Eleanor decided she ought to be enrolled in one of the seminaries here in Town; I was against it at first: Georgiana did not wish to leave the estate, and my experience with ladies who have gone to these places leads me to conclude that they are an utter waste of time."

"What? My sisters both attended seminaries in Town," said Bingley with a sardonic air, "and who could *possibly* object to how they were turned out?"

Darcy laughed. "To speak the truth, your sisters are not as bad as many to whom I have been introduced. But my aunt took pains to inform me that for most young ladies, rather like Eton and Oxford for most men, seminaries are less about the education, than about forming the appropriate acquaintance. And I believe she did form some acquaintance there; she still corresponds with some of them, at least."

"Well, your sister has done marvellously well, regardless of who, where, or why. There is only one question in my mind, however: has she attained that one true measure of the accomplished woman?"

"Yes?" Darcy enquired.

"Can she net a decent purse?" Bingley joked, at last showing Darcy the grin he had hoped for.

Chapter Seven

*T*he next day in the mid-morning, Georgiana came again to find her brother in his library.

"Am I disturbing your work, Fitzwilliam?"

"Not at all. There is a notable dearth of work to be done, just at present; most every one is putting aside their affairs now, until after Christmas"

Georgiana wandered over to the large globe in the corner. Turning it slowly, she said, "Father liked this globe."

"Did he?" Darcy replied.

Georgiana nodded, "When he took time from his work or his reading, he would show me places on it, and tell me their stories." Darcy smiled, but had no such memories to share; his own time with his father in the libraries of Grosvenor Square and Pemberley were less personal, but no less important, as it was largely in them that he had learnt to be Darcy of Pemberley.

Georgiana asked, "Might I ask a question?"

"Of course," answered Darcy with a smile. "Something to do with your dinner?"

"*Please* do not call it that! It is not *my* dinner; say rather it is Aunt Eleanor's dinner." She sat down in a deep chair and curled her feet in under her; leaning back against the cushions, her face was sad: "No Fitzwilliam, it is...something else. I was listening just now, as Aunt Eleanor and Mrs. Annesley were talking about the entertainments they had gone to as girls: they went with their sisters. And afterward, they told each other about the men they had talked to, and whispered and giggled together the whole night long." She laid her head down on her arms. "Will I ever have a true sister, Fitzwilliam? I had so hoped that Miss Elizabeth Bennet..." her voice trailed off without finishing.

Darcy had never before been aware that his sister was in any way affected by his parting with Elizabeth, other than how she might regret the loss for his sake. The sadness in her voice was almost more than he could bear; realising she was in pain on this point released his own in some way, as though the injury he saw reflected in her eyes were more real, more tangible, than his own.

He rose from his desk and came to stand by her chair. In softest tones of compassion and remorse he told her, "I am so *very* sorry, Georgiana: I should never have written to you about her. It never occurred to me that there might be disappointment for you in all this. In truth, I had no idea that it might come to this at all—that either of us might be…disappointed."

In this Darcy was less foresighted than he would wish to be. While he knew himself to be distanced from most of his circle, he did not grasp how this isolation rendered his feelings susceptible of being wounded—especially when, as in the present case, the injuries came at him through one of those few to whom he was close. His sympathetic affection for Georgiana, who was closer to his heart than any other, provided a ready conduit through which his wayward emotions might run; his sense of *her* pain and distress caused his own to well up in a shocking rush, unexpected both in strength and kind.

Darcy stroked his sister's temples—as his mother had done for him as a boy, and as he had done to comfort Georgiana when she was ill as a child—saying with an attempt at humour, "Quite the pair, are we not? 'Lucky at play, unlucky in love'—is not that the saying? We must surely have earned some luck at cards this past twelvemonth, then." Georgiana tried to smile, but shook her head, her eyes rimmed in tears. His sensibility of his sister's trials at Wickham's hands, her lonely childhood as a near-orphan, and most particularly, how much she must rely on him to fill those voids the events of her young life had created, could only increase his pain. Seeing the mild and the delicate come to grief will ever touch the heart of the strong, and to see Georgiana so, quite nearly rent Darcy's in two.

Coming to himself, though, Darcy tried to force down his regrets, and to say the right thing as her guardian and older brother. "Come, Dearest, we must resist. We cannot know what may yet betide, but we must look to what we *do* have: you have friends, I know, and we can always look to our family." It did not seem that Georgiana felt his words any more than he did himself.

"Acquaintances I am friendly with," Georgiana said disconsolately, "those I have; but no true...no one to confide in. I should *so* like to meet Miss Elizabeth Bennet. Tell me more about her — please?"

Darcy was uncertain how he might do so without discovering to her just how much the loss of Elizabeth had cost *him*, but Georgiana looked altogether so forlorn, so young and vulnerable, indeed, that he could not but give in to her request. Pulling a chair next to her, he sat down and began the narrative of a tale he had gone over in his mind, many and many a time: "I first saw her at an assembly..."

"The one where Miss Bingley wanted to tell you how to dress?"

"Yes, that was the one," Darcy smiled to recall that evening. "I remember her dancing; she has a natural grace, and such a fine tempo she hardly seems to *dance* at all: it is hard to say whether she follows the music, or the music follows her; she almost flows *with* the music — inside it, if you follow my meaning."

"Did you ask her to dance that night?"

"I did not; we had not been introduced, and I was, I fear, rather out of sorts to be there at the dance at all. We met again, at Netherfield, and were introduced; I thought her very lovely, and found the sound of her voice very pleasing, but we had no conversation that day. On another occasion we dined together at a small dinner party, and I first heard her wit. Next, at an evening party where we were in company together, our host attempted to give me her hand for a dance; she resisted, mostly out of pique at being thus accosted, I think: that was the first time she declined my hand; but her manner in doing so was charming. Then at Netherfield, one evening when Miss Bingley was playing, I asked her to dance—but she thought I was only teazing, and turned me down again."

"Then at Mr. Bingley's ball?"

"At the ball she accepted me. We danced a minuet; I was..." Darcy looked away with a slight shake of his head, unable to speak his memories of how it had affected him to take Elizabeth's hand. He said simply, "I was very happy to stand up next to her."

"What is she like, Fitzwilliam?"

Darcy sighed deeply. He said, "Well, she is very caring: she came to Netherfield to tend to her sister, and walked three miles through the fields on the morning after a soaking rain to get there; then she barely left her sister's side for three solid days. Her sister had not asked her to come, Miss Bingley told me—she did it on her own, to be of comfort to her sister. She is forthright, and strong where she knows herself to be in the right, but her manners are always gentle and considerate, even under the provocation Miss Bingley at times would offer her. And she loves to teaze in fun, and to play with words and ideas: her conversation is a treat like no other I have known."

"Hers is a happy temper, then? She smiles often?"

This question affected Darcy deeply—so often had he seen her in imagination, smiling at him in the life they might have had together. He set his jaw and looked away, that his sister might not see how much he felt. "Yes," he said softly, "she smiles very often." Turning back and kissing her hand, he stood up. "I have things I must do now, Dearest," said he in a stronger voice, "and you ought to be helping to prepare for to-morrow; the dinner, whosever it may be, is nearly upon us, you know."

Georgiana obligingly stood up and gave him a quick hug before going. Darcy sat back down at his desk; he remained there without moving for a very long while, staring unseeing at the walls of the library.

Chapter Eight

*B*y Friday evening, preparations for the party were well in hand: the kitchen and larder were stuffed to capacity, as deliveries had been nearly incessant through the previous two days. The ball-room had been transformed into a grand drawing-room, and richly decorated, while the drawing-room itself was to be used for cards. Lady Andover and Miss Darcy were both showing signs of fatigue, but seemed pleased with their progress.

Their party that evening was confined to the family and Darcy's friend; dinner was a simple affair, as far as the menu went, for an overworked kitchen staff had not the resources to meet the usual standards of the house; but though the bill of fare might be simple, it was all done superbly well. When every one was seated, Lord Andover, with a sympathetic eye to his wife's fatigue, asked her to join him in a glass of wine, for which she smiled her gratitude. As the soup came out, almost every one, it seemed, breathed a sigh, and let go their various struggles from the day.

At table, Cousin George contrived to remind Darcy most amusingly of why he had looked forward to seeing him again, as he was in rare conversational form, drawing upon himself the notice and ire of both his parents, and offering incredulous diversion to the rest, save possibly Georgiana. During dinner, the concerted efforts of Lord and Lady Andover—most notably the latter—were in play to constrain his near complete want of tact; he sat next to his mother, who, whenever she was displeased with anything her eldest might say, showed a highly developed skill in striking exposed parts of his person with a spoon. The first occasion of its happening, St. Stephens cried out, rubbing the back of his hand, and the whole table looked at him; his mother, ignoring his outburst, asked him in the most decorous manner to pass her the salt. Her husband looked at her thoughtfully, then poured them both more wine. Georgiana had rarely been in company with her eldest cousin, and, not having perceived the blow, knew not what to make of his exclamation, no more than she had his impertinences and extravagant airs: she caught sight of her aunt's second strike, however, and her shriek of surprise fairly drowned out St. Stephens' own; she quickly lowered her eyes to her plate and pretended hard she had been mute since birth. Bingley laughed outright, but, turning immediately to Darcy, covered his lapse by saying, "Darcy, did I tell you what Stroudmeyer said the other day? It was so droll…" and led off in a low voice to an anecdote that, in truth, had but little humour in it; this was of use to Darcy, however, as his gravity too had begun to fail him.

St. Stephens, who had always been a slow student, spoke again: "Speaking of amusing stories, t'other night Fox was saying about that strumpet of his…Yeogh! —Mother, by the fiends of…Gad! —Mother, will you stop that!"

"Finish your soup, George, dear," the lady said calmly, taking a sip of her wine, "the others have finished, and the fish will be getting cold." Bingley was forced to excuse himself from the table at that moment, and Darcy was very near joining him. He caught Georgiana's eye and gave her a private wink, at which she giggled openly before cutting off abruptly.

"Georgiana, dear," said her aunt, still unruffled, "something seems to have slipped. Goodwin?" The butler came to Georgiana's chair and, with preternatural gravity, bent down and feigned retrieving her napkin from the floor, his bulk effectively covering her face from her cousin's view while she recovered her composure. Colonel Fitzwilliam, seated next to his father, turned a burst of laughter into a coughing fit, for which his father very obligingly struck him on the back.

"Edmund," enquired his mother, "are you quite well?"

This, of course, only made matters worse for the Colonel. "One, moment, Mother," said he with difficulty, "I shall be well in just one moment."

"All is well, then," Lady Andover said with a complacent smile. "Goodwin, the fish?"

After this, all signs of the stress of the days prior fell from the party — save for Lord St. Stephens, admittedly, although his pouting face served rather to increase the high spirits of the table. Darcy was pleased that both his sister and his friend had been able to enjoy even a momentary lightness of spirit, even though it came at the expense of his cousin's lack of manners, and through the rest of the meal he would periodically share a private look of amusement with each. Every one enjoyed a most congenial air during the remainder of dinner, and even St. Stephens came out of his ill-humour to laugh at one of Bingley's jests; the occasion reminded Darcy that no man is wholly without some benefit, of use to his fellow beings — even if it is only to ease their cares by his heedless folly.

The following evening was, of course, The Dinner. With what exertions Georgiana, her aunt, and Mrs. Annesley had brought the menu, decorations, and in sum, the whole scheme, to fruition, only the three of them might know. But it all proved highly successful, and even Georgiana had to confess that she had gained a great deal by working alongside her aunt. As the ladies had descended before the guests were to arrive, Darcy was startled to see his sister, looking very grown up indeed, come down on her Cousin Edmund's arm, in a new gown of very fashionable cut.

"Does not your sister look well?" asked his Aunt Eleanor, beaming with pride and pleasure.

"Very well, indeed," Darcy replied. He took Georgiana's hand and bowed over it gallantly, just to see her blush, which she did, and very prettily, too. He tucked her arm under his and escorted her to the front entranceway, where they were to receive their guests.

To attend the dinner, Lady Andover had selected a large number of old friends and family, to make Georgiana feel at ease, mixed in with enough new acquaintances to lend novelty to the conversation; her intentions, at least where Georgiana was concerned, were not entirely successful, however. As Darcy walked his sister and their aunt and uncle towards the entrance hall to greet the arriving guests, she whispered to him earnestly, "Fitzwilliam, I shall faint—I know I shall! I do not know even half these people!"

Darcy looked at her with concern; she did, in truth, look pale. "Stand next to me, Dearest, and do not let go of my arm. Remember: you need only smile and curtsey; you are only to be seen, so you will not be speaking to them, unless they address you directly—which none of them unknown to you will do." Georgiana looked him in the eye a long moment: she nodded and gathered her determination, but said nothing.

Darcy began to understand her misgivings as the reception line grew and grew; he asked his sister in an astonished whisper, "Good Heavens, Miss Darcy—are you sure my aunt did not send out more invitations without telling you?"

She whispered back, terrified, "Would she do that, Fitzwilliam?"

"No, no, Dearest; I am sure she would not—I was only joking; but there are quite a number, are there not?

"Aunt Eleanor said she meant to see me get a proper start in Society."

"Well, I must say, this ought to do it."

Aside from having to move Georgiana into a more forward position once or twice, Darcy thought she bore up well. He saw his aunt lean in and whisper to her with smiles and encouragement more than once, and between them they managed to keep Georgiana from being too overwhelmed during the three-quarters of an hour they stood there together.

For Darcy, these affairs were rather more work than pleasure; even just greeting the new guests was laborious — more an exertion of the mind than of the body, however. Not having Bingley's great enjoyment of people in general, just holding himself in an attitude of expectant pleasure as each couple came up to convey their compliments, was a wearisome and unrewarding task. It helped that Georgiana was at his side, as he felt he must set an example of fortitude for her sake.

Afterwards, on the way back up the stairs, Darcy quietly told his sister, "In all honesty, Dearest, I do not like performing that office, any more than you; by the end, I thought my jaw would crack."

Georgiana looked at him in surprise, but then giggled behind her hand when he winked. "By the way," Darcy asked, "did you mark Lady Swyndham?"

"Which was she?" Georgiana asked, furrowing her brows as she cast back in her mind over the many people she had seen pass.

"Just recall the largest lady to arrive — or gentleman, either, for that matter — with a very high coiffure, and a rather prominent string of pearls," Darcy prompted. Georgiana nodded, her eyes wide. "You should see her on the dance floor: she moves as if she weighed no more than a feather; it is truly remarkable. And do you recall Sir Reginald Crevis? Tall, serious-looking man, black coat, and a very full beard? He is an enormously successful banker, and well-bred in his manners; but, upon my honour, the man is an absolute witling. I have heard it said that, had he no valet, he would go about Town all day in his nightshirt." Georgiana giggled again, and with such little stories and anecdotes about their guests, Darcy contrived to entertain her and revive her spirits as they returned to the dining-room.

For Darcy, however, dinner itself was something of a trial. Seated at one end of the table, he had his uncle on his right, and his cousin George had seated himself to Darcy's left, thereby putting Lady Andover's table out of order; Darcy's aunt was unfortunately at the far end with his sister: he felt the want of Her Ladyship's restraining influence on St. Stephens throughout the meal. The conversation at his end of the table — a monologue, really, dominated by the viscount — Darcy found to be a challenge to both his equanimity and his manners; he had to remind himself frequently of his realization the night before, that no man was without some benefit to his fellow beings.

Towards the end of the meal, shortly before the ladies were to retire, Darcy's cousin addressed his father thus, in a voice that carried half-way down the hall: "Father, some of us are going 'round to a chase on St. Stephens's Day — I ought to be in luck, eh? — and I have been meaning to ask if you should care to join us; my good friend, Mr. Fox, will be there; he would, I'm sure, be delighted to see you."

"Thank you, George," his father answered in much more regulated tones, "but as you know, my plans are already fixed; and our dear Georgiana has gone to such trouble…"

"Trouble?" St. Stephens sniffed disdainfully, making application to his snuff box. "This? It may do for Derbyshire, but it don't answer for London! You should have seen Carlton House last month, at the Prince's masquerade." Darcy, who was not only insulted by his cousin's comments, but also despised the use of snuff at table, drew himself up and turned a thundering brow on his cousin. His uncle placed a restraining hand on his arm.

"George," said His Lordship dryly, "do please *attempt* to think before you speak; you are seated at your cousin's table, and speaking to her brother." To Darcy he said, "Georgiana is doing marvellously well: I doubt London will have seen such a Christmas these twenty years."

"Come, come, Father," said St. Stephens disparagingly, "that is precisely the point. No one of fashion follows these worn-out old customs. Beef pudding? —Lord, who could believe it! At this rate I shouldn't be surprised if we were actually to have mince pies and plum pudding at Christmas dinner. And you know I always speak my thoughts, Father: if one does not speak out, how is one to correct the behaviour of others?"

"I am well aware of your readiness to speak—it is the thinking part of which I remain uncertain," replied his father dryly. More sharply he added: "And in order to instruct others in correct behaviour, one must be at least passing familiar with it oneself—I fear, boy, you are under-qualified for the rôle."

St. Stephens only laughed merrily, as though his father had made a fine jest. Lord Andover's features became momentarily blank. "Crosses to bear," he muttered under his breath.

Darcy let down his shoulders and smiled at his uncle, as though to show appreciation at a jest, though he knew there was little enough humour meant. He was well aware Lord Andover recognised his eldest son was lacking in certain aspects of his character, nor did he disagree; Edmund was beyond all comparison the better man, but there it was—the inheritance was George's, and, as he was unfortunately of robust health, there was nothing to be done— except to hope for a providential hunting accident.

St. Stephens rose to his feet, announcing to the whole room with some ostentation: "Well, I regret that I must ask you all to excuse me; I have an important appointment with certain gentlemen who stand very high in the first circles of our nation." With a bow to Georgiana he said, "I pray you will forgive me, dear Cousin. Would you be so good as to have a footman stay up? I shall not return until late."

To this, poor Georgiana could only return a confused nod of the head; even she, who seldom felt the wrongdoings of others, could not but feel the thoughtless affront being offered by her cousin. At her side, her aunt was ominously fingering her flatware and frowning at her firstborn, as though wondering if she might hazard throwing something, without putting others at risk.

"You were speaking just now of behaviour?" Lord Andover asked his heir softly. "But no doubt this is an important matter of state, and demands the sacrifice of your better feelings — dog race?"

"Lord, Father, no one goes to dog races now," chided St. Stephens. In an enthusiastic undertone he added: "No, two of the finest pugilists in England are to toe the mark down by the river, beyond Cheapside. Fox said he might attend, and there's even a rumour that the Prince himself might be there. If I don't hurry I shall miss it." Straightening up he asked, "Should you care to join me?" and, evidently not wishing to snub his host, he added: "And you too, Darcy, of course; you would be very welcome to come along."

Darcy hardly knew how to reply. He only shook his head wonderingly. His cousin's brilliant unconcern for those not in his set had often confounded Darcy's civility in the past.

"No? Well then, I must be off," said St. Stephens with a decided air of relief. Bowing with a flourish to the company he walked, with a certain amount of parade, out of the dining-room. Many stared, but few had the assurance to speak in the presence of the family. To Darcy, however, his cousin's behaviour was too familiar for surprise, and too often discussed to merit further comment. But St. Stephen's leaving effected a notably lighter spirit in the room, at least amongst the family; Darcy turned back to his uncle to continue their discussion of matters on their respective estates, and the general conversation drifted on to more amusing matters.

After dinner, when the gentlemen were to join the ladies, the company gathered in the ball-room. There was a quartet of musicians playing, and the room was delightfully arranged. There were, here and there amongst the company, various young courting couples, and as Darcy went in with Bingley, he saw his friend watching the young people reuniting with smiles and glad cries; a sigh escaped him, although his countenance gave away nothing of his sentiments. After a time drifting about, chatting with his guests, Darcy approached his friend and asked, "Is all well, Bingley? You seem unusually quiet for such a gathering."

Bingley looked at him with a ghost of a smile and said, "A little tired, I find; I think I shall retire in an hour or so: you will not mind?"

Darcy placed a hand on his friend's shoulder and assured him, "Of course not; were I not the host, I should join you."

Turning away, he very nearly tumbled over Miss Bingley, who, it seemed, was coming to speak to him. "Miss Bingley," he bowed.

"Well, Sir, I congratulate you; your dinner is a grand success."

"I had nothing to do with it, I assure you," he replied. "It was my aunt and my sister who managed the whole affair."

"I have just been speaking with Lady Andover and Georgiana," she began, but on seeing Darcy's eyebrow rise, she hastily amended: "Miss Darcy, I mean, of course—dear girl that she is. What a charming woman your aunt is, Mr. Darcy!"

"Yes, she is indeed; a delightful lady."

"Is she often with you at Pemberley?"

"Not as frequently now as in prior years, mostly because my sister and I have been in Town more of late."

"What is Her Ladyship's home like?"

"Clereford? A very lovely estate; much the same size as Pemberley, but far older, and, to my thinking, more dignified in appearance."

"More dignified than Pemberley?" cried Miss Bingley in disbelief. "My goodness, Sir; if that can be true, I should very much like to see it some day."

Darcy, who realised instantly that she was expecting to hear him say that he would take her there, hardly knew what to say; in her mind, he knew well enough, any such offer would be taken as very nearly a betrothal; yet it was an innocent enough expectation, and, on the face of it, one which he might, in all propriety, easily accommodate. Doing his best to safely traverse this treacherous ground, he answered carefully, "I am sure you should; it is a sight any one in the nation might enjoy and feel a certain pride in; and the distance is little more than that to Netherfield."

Miss Bingley looked at him for a moment from the corner of her eye, obviously waiting for something more.

He hurriedly bore on, changing the topic determinedly: "And speaking of travel, Miss Bingley, I understand from your brother that you and the Hursts are off to Bath for Christmas."

"Indeed," Miss Bingley replied coolly, still studying his face. Then, with more warmth she said, "We shall miss your company, Mr. Darcy."

"Which do you prefer for the holidays: London, or Bath?"

"Why, Mr. Darcy—wherever the company offers best: as you once said, it is the company, not the location, which determines the pleasure taken. This year, I fancy, it will be better in London. Fortunately, we will be returning before New Year's Eve."

"You had rather not go, then?"

"Oh, I am sure it will serve," she answered with an indifferent air. "Only, I shall be missing certain company."

Darcy, feeling the ground shift again beneath his feet, offered this in return: "Perhaps we might find time for our shopping expedition on your return."

He succeeded beyond his intentions, for the lady had by no means forgotten about their planned excursion. "Oh, Mr. Darcy! That would be so delightful! Now, please, do let me arrange things; it would give me such pleasure! We shall begin at Wilson's, of course, then I know ever so many quaint little shops in that part of town! We shall have no trouble whatever finding every thing we shall require; I would stake my honour on it."

Darcy did, in all honesty, believe Miss Bingley to be well acquainted with the places where one might divest oneself of any amount of money on trifling purchases, and could foresee a reasonably successful hunt for the objects he would need, when led by such a guide; his only concern was how to avoid making far more purchases than he intended, or could ever find useful.

While listening to Miss Bingley go on to enumerate all the places one simply must go for the most *recherché* and very highest-quality trinkets, he led her slowly back to the neighbourhood of her brother; Bingley stood at the edge of room, still watching the courting couples with what, to Darcy's eye, seemed a wistful demeanour. He brightened as they approached, however, and the three of them talked amicably until Mr. Bingley excused himself for the evening. Darcy excused himself to Miss Bingley too, pleading the necessity of seeing to his other guests.

As host, Darcy was well pleased with the evening's success, and on Georgiana's behalf, even more so. Through the dinner she held up quite well in her rôle as hostess's assistant; Darcy even had the pleasure of seeing several young men afterwards approach to speak with her, or beg an introduction—but her aunt was there to manage the demurrals. Georgiana staid with her aunt, limiting her conversation to ladies of Lady Andover's close acquaintance, and one or two of the younger ladies who had but recently come out. Towards the end of the evening, however, Darcy could see how fatigued she was become; he returned to her and assisted her in her conversation with their guests, that she might husband her strength to last out the evening.

Finally, however, the evening ended and the last of the guests were gone; Georgiana blushed and smiled as she received congratulations from her aunt and uncle. Her aunt hugged her delightedly, saying, "It was perfect, my dear; and you were a wonder!" and her Uncle Jonathan bowed and kissed her hand. "There is no denying it, my dear; you are nearly grown up; much as I shall miss my little moppet, I expect I shall take equal pleasure in the grown-up Miss Darcy." He then kissed her cheek, causing her to colour again, and took his wife on his arm to go up to their chambers.

"Was it good, Fitzwilliam?" she asked him when they had gone.

"It was excellently done," he assured her. They left the room and Darcy escorted her to the stairs going up to the family quarters. "Your family, you see, had every right to be confident of your success; I only wish you could be as well assured of your abilities as we are."

"I do try, Fitzwilliam, truly; but you are not upset with me, after all? You do not blame me for taking part in an entertainment? Aunt Eleanor said we were not going to give you a chance to say no; nor me, to say the truth."

Darcy laughed. "Are we sure she is not the one related to Aunt Catherine? Never mind, I shall find a way to avenge myself on her." Georgiana looked at him in alarm, but he patted her arm with a chuckle, telling her, "And, no, I do not blame you in the slightest: I am delighted. Now, I have a detail or two to attend to before going up; sleep well. And, Dearest—it was very well done."

The young lady covered quite a considerable yawn before saying, "Thank you—oh, dear! —I did not know it was possible to be as tired as this. Sleeping well will not be hard, but rising may be more difficult." So saying, she trudged slowly up the stairs.

Before going up stairs, Darcy remembered to relieve Georgiana of the task of speaking to Goodwin regarding a footman for St. Stephens, further suggesting that the footman be allowed to sleep until Lord St. Stephens himself should awaken. He also reminded himself to make certain that Georgiana had included mince pies and plum pudding on the menu for Christmas dinner.

As he was retiring and his thoughts were wandering back over the evening, they lit at length on one who had barely attended: Viscount St. Stephens. He was struck, not for the first time, by how odd it seemed that Cousin George should have manners so very different from the rest of his family; Uncle Jonathan and Aunt Eleanor, Edmund—they were some of the most agreeable, reasonable people Darcy knew. How then did St. Stephens manage to make himself into such an unpleasant fellow? Darcy had always known his cousin's was not one of the leading minds of the age, but his manners seemed unrelated to that; Darcy had known several men who were stupid as owls, but had impeccable manners. He suspected it came from St. Stephens's decision to enter public life; men who strove for advancement in those circles Darcy had always found to be unpleasant: like all others who sought fame, he thought—actors, singers, entertainers of any stripe—no matter their rank, they were best kept at a distance. They were all, to some extent, dissemblers, he believed: playing a rôle, disguising their true natures—and those who sought to rise in political life were the worst: since they never stepped out of their rôles, one could never know their true characters. To Darcy, this disguise was different from an outright lie in method only; he could not imagine how one could allow oneself such disgusting license in dealing with others—such continual dishonesty violated all principles of honour, and Darcy hardly knew how such people could support the shame of their existence.

Chapter Nine

*T*wo days later, on Monday morning, Darcy sat once more in his library; the household was largely returned to normal, and Darcy needed no longer anticipate the disruption of his work, what little there was of it. Not for the first time since returning to London, his thoughts turned to Meryton, and, of course, Elizabeth; he could not forget that Wickham was installed in the neighbourhood at least for the winter, and he was well aware that he had failed to adequately warn Elizabeth against him at the Netherfield ball. The image of Wickham standing next to her in Meryton Square, not a care in the world, as if he had any right to be there, came often to his mind. The longer Darcy was from her, the more he became convinced that Elizabeth was just the lady Wickham would choose to prey upon: her father was certainly among the wealthiest men in the country, she was lovely, lively, and charming, and, while Darcy himself detested the sight of him, he could not be insensible of the fact that women seemed to enjoy his company. He was undeniably a better dancer than Darcy, which Darcy had noted at several evening entertainments given at Pemberley during his father's life, and which had contributed in no small amount to Darcy's disgust for the pastime.

There were, of course, difficulties in his way in connection with Elizabeth's protection: supposing Wickham was in fact determined to pursue her; what could he, Darcy, do to stop it? With an exacting observance of propriety, he had no right to involve himself at all; Elizabeth would not thank him for his officious interest in her affairs, certainly. But against that, she could have no idea of the danger Wickham represented, any more than had Georgiana; he could not stand by and let Wickham do what he would with another young lady. No, he would not let Wickham have free rein in Meryton, no matter what it might cost him in Elizabeth's eyes.

Darcy had been exercising his mind on this problem off and on ever since leaving Hertfordshire, his disquiet growing daily as he imagined Elizabeth's smiles being directed at Wickham; knowing nothing of what might be going forward in Meryton was now become intolerable: it was imperative that he find a way to get news of Wickham. Of course, the receipt of any intelligence regarding Mr. Wickham must also put him in the way of receiving news of Elizabeth, but this, he assured himself, was not a motive; it was merely that, in apprising himself of Wickham's activities, which was no more than his duty, he must unavoidably discover more about Elizabeth, too. In any case, to-day he was finally moved to act: he rang the bell for Perkins.

When that worthy appeared, Darcy said, "Perkins, I want you to do something for me."

"Of course, Sir."

"You recall, I expect, that the individual we dislike is to be in Meryton for the rest of the winter?"

"Yes, Sir."

"I wish to keep an eye on him—to know what he is up to: have you any acquaintance about the place that might be of service to us?"

Perkins cleared his throat. "There was a...young person...who worked at the Boar, Sir. I dare say she might be as like as any to know any gossip about the town."

Darcy looked at his man in surprise. "Perkins—is there an aspect of your character hidden from me?" His man looked straight ahead without speaking. "Yes, by Heaven," said Darcy with some amusement, "I can see there is; in spite of your self-effacing behaviour in your duties, it strikes me that privately you are like to have a bold and roving eye; nor are you an ill-favoured individual—yes, I can see it now—all in all, I am persuaded you have a way about you."

Perkins coughed and studied the carpet modestly. "Would you be willing to put your no doubt considerable personal claims to use, for the good of a young lady?" Darcy asked more seriously.

"That young lady would be...Miss Elizabeth Bennet, Sir?"

"Yes, Perkins. I am concerned lest that individual should begin to have undue influence over the lady."

Perkins nodded. "Very understandable, Sir,"

"I should like you to go down to Meryton after Christmas," Darcy told him, "and see what your 'young person' has to say. Stay at the Boar, if you like. But Perkins," here Darcy hesitated, but could not forebear to teaze his man again: "I should hate to have to extricate you from the clutches of an irate father, so I trust you will exercise restraint in the execution of your commission."

Perkins's ears reddened, but his training held good and he made no reply; bowing, he left the room. Darcy chuckled at having piqued Perkins's dignity, but then, more soberly, he reminded himself that it was far from amusing: Wickham could do immeasurable harm to Elizabeth and her family. He reassured himself that Perkins would discover whether there was any likelihood of that occurring; until then, he could think of nothing more to do at present.

Satisfied at having taken what steps he could for the moment, to preserve Elizabeth from any interest Wickham might take in her, his mind travelled back to his own interests where that lady was concerned. His thoughts, as always, could rest on no one conclusion: in one moment he was arguing that to bring the Bennet family into his would violate generations of dignity, standing, and accomplishment. In the next he was arguing the opposite: he cared little enough for Society, certainly, so why should he allow his wishes to be dictated to by a collection of faceless fops,

whom he would as soon affront as not? Elizabeth's worth
was far greater than theirs, even without his esteem for her,
so why should he not follow his inclinations, and ignore
them? But then he would hear his father's exhortations to
remember his birth and position, and think how all propriety would be violated by their union. These and other such
musings, while they did little to move Darcy forward in his
thinking, were sure to consume a considerable amount of
his time each day.

That evening was to take Darcy and Bingley to a ball at
the home of Mrs. Delacroix, wife of that same Delacroix
who had sent Bingley down to view Netherfield the summer before. All of the men at Grosvenor Square had
received invitations, as the affair promised to be one of the
most complete of its kind; Delacroix had been heard to
boast that he meant to give the Season a proper start. The
Colonel was required at the Knightsbridge Officer's Mess
that evening, nor was Darcy's uncle to attend, but Lord St.
Stephens had accepted on hearing a rumour that the Prince
of Wales might consider making an appearance; notwithstanding, Darcy had accepted, largely at the urging of Lord
Andover: "You might find it diverting, and your friend
seems very fond of company. Besides, you might be of service to me in case your cousin decides to get himself into
trouble, which you cannot but allow is a distinct possibility
whenever he steps out of the house."

Darcy smiled at this, saying, "Perhaps you are right,
Uncle. And I am sure Bingley would enjoy it; very well — we
shall go."

"Just be sure to take your own coach," advised his uncle wryly, "else, Lord knows when you might be home."

Darcy actually entertained some hopes for the evening,
at least for Bingley's sake, as Delacroix was renowned for
festivities at which a substantial representation of London's
most eligible young women would be in attendance. In
point of fact, during his University days Delacroix had had

a reputation as being something of a rake, and his appreciation of a fine countenance seemed to have outlived his
bachelor days—at least to the extent of filling his home with
beauty on social occasions. Curiously, although he and his
wife seemed as close as any couple among Darcy's acquaintance, Mrs. Delacroix was quite a plain woman.

Darcy and Bingley went to the Delacroix's without the
company of St. Stephens; indeed, Darcy, not having seen his
cousin St. Stephens at the house all day, could not even say
with certainty whether his house-guest had slept at
Grosvenor Square; that Cousin George treated his home as
if it were an hotel was a fresh source of irritation to Darcy.
None of that had any bearing on the entertainment before
them, he reminded himself, and he put it out of his mind so
he might enjoy the evening. Arriving at the Delacroix's and
having greeted their hosts, the two friends entered the hall,
where Bingley was immediately hailed by five or six of his
dearest friends, who dragged him gaily off into the depths
of the house. While pleased on Bingley's account, Darcy
was therefore left, as often before, to his own devices. Looking about him at the congregation, he saw no one of his
immediate circle; he drifted over to the side of the room,
where he might be out of the way and observe the proceed-
ings, as was his wont at such gatherings. He had just taken
a glass from a passing footman when he heard his name
called and a hand was placed familiarly on his shoulder.
Turning, he found he was being greeted by St. Stephens.
"Darcy! Good Lord—is it you? Finally decided to live like a
gentleman and make an appearance in Society, eh? Never
thought I'd live to see the day."

Darcy nodded a greeting to his cousin. "Where have
you been all day, St. Stephens? I do not think I have seen
you amongst us at all."

His cousin, as usual, missed the implicit dig at his failure to do what was right by his hosts. He laughed and said,
"Had myself quite the evening last night; Fox and I with

some of the others were at a private showing at Drury Lane—a *very* private showing," he added with a leer, nudging Darcy in the ribs with his thumb. "Ha! Didn't get in till dawn. Then I had to be at the club for cards; Fenton and I took on Fox and Lord Haraldson. Had to be damn' careful not to play too well, I can tell you: Fox is a wretched man at cards. I say, Darcy, give my compliments to Georgiana, would you? I meant to find her to-day and, you know, pay my respects to the lady of the house and all that, but Pater has been hectoring me lately about the company I keep, and 'comportment becoming a gentleman', and whatnot, so I thought it best to avoid his august presence."

Darcy stared at his cousin, once again momentarily speechless, but gave it up as useless to pursue. He said at length, "I shall let Georgiana know you thought of her." He then turned to go.

George laughed at this and held him by the arm, saying, "Lord, what a conversationalist you are! Here, no— wait, Darcy!—don't pull away like that; let me introduce you to some people. If left on your own, you'll never meet a soul." Darcy was mustering the composure to decline this kind invitation without recourse to violence when the two men were approached by Miss Caroline Bingley; never had Darcy been so happy to see her.

"Miss Bingley," he said with considerable relief. "What an unexpected pleasure!" A delighted smile spread across Miss Bingley's features at this unlooked-for enthusiasm, and after her curtsey she linked her arm through Darcy's. Even this familiarity was acceptable to Darcy in his desire to deflect his cousin's good offices. "Cousin, allow me to introduce Miss Caroline Bingley; Miss Bingley, my cousin, Viscount St. Stephens."

George looked Miss Bingley broadly up and down, and bowed so low and so long over her hand that Darcy feared he might devour it; Miss Bingley gazed at him with a mixture of pleasure and astonishment: pleasure at his title, and astonishment at his manner. She recovered directly, however, and said with a curtsey, "My Lord St. Stephens — you must be Colonel Fitzwilliam's elder brother, I take it."

"Your servant, dear lady," said St. Stephens, smiling up into her face from where he still held his bow. Looking down again to where a simple chain locket rested above the rather daringly cut neckline on Miss Bingley's gown, he said, "That's a capital necklace, I must say!" He then straightened, saying, "But don't let's talk about my brother; what do you say to a turn on the dance floor?" Leaving her barely enough time for a response, he led her by the hand, which he had yet to relinquish, out into a set that had already formed. At least, Darcy reflected, Cousin George was consistent in his courtesy; those in his family were not the exclusive victims of his etiquette. Miss Bingley looked enquiringly back over her shoulder at Darcy as St. Stephens carried her off, but he smiled at her and nodded encouragingly; then, as they disappeared into the swirling couples, he let out a deep breath. A warm feminine chuckle came from nearby, and he turned in time to see a rather beautiful and very fashionable young woman watching him; she immediately hid her smile behind her fan, but a pair of grey, remarkably intelligent eyes continued to hold his over the top of it. Then, turning away with a demur drop of her head that might have been taken for a curtsey, she made her way off through the crowd. Darcy, his interest piqued, was turning to follow her with his eyes, but was at that moment approached by Bingley, who had come in search of him.

"Darcy! What — all alone still?"

"No, not at all; your sister just left me to dance with St. Stephens."

"Caroline? Here already? I had thought she would be later, to make an entrance. And with your cousin — what a pairing *they* must make!"

Darcy chuckled in his turn. "Quite. What have you been up to?"

"I was in the game-room—Delacroix was there with some of the fellows from University. Pender is there."

"Vincent? I have not had a line from him in months."

"Well then, if I were you I should not waste any more time," his friend suggested. "You go along; I have some others to meet out here."

Mr. Vincent Pender had been tutor at Christ Church to both Darcy and Bingley, although they had not then known each other, Darcy being six years ahead of Bingley; Pender was one of the few who knew them both well and was not surprised at their friendship. Indeed, it had been his presence that had brought the two of them to the same soirée on the evening they first met.

Darcy left his friend directly and went in search of his old mentor. He found him ensconced in a corner of the game-room with a small circle of Darcy's contemporaries gathered around him. As always, it gave Darcy a mild surprise to see Pender out of academical dress; he looked so ordinary in this setting, with his simple attire and spectacles, yet he was anything but simple and ordinary—his was one of the finest minds at Oxford. He had tutored Darcy to a First in Philosophy, but Darcy always had the sense that in all their convoluted debates and discussions, the older man had been merely strolling along, while he, Darcy, had been sprinting for all he was worth and panting to keep up. Darcy also appreciated his wry humour and sardonic view of the world. Darcy's uncle, having met Pender once at a reception, summed him up thus: "If that man had no sense of humour, he would be the youngest Vice Chancellor in Oxford's history; but I fear the post wants him more than he wants the post."

The two men exchanged warm greetings, and the circle expanded to admit Darcy in a place of prominence. They were discussing, of all things imaginable, the rôle of the Hessians in the loss of the American colonies. Pender was defending the position that the augmentation of the British forces had been necessary, given the situation in Europe; then, when the consensus began to turn in his direction, he laughed and began arguing the other side, that the involvement of foreigners in what was an essentially British dispute had so outraged the colonists that it had tipped the balance in their favour. Darcy, as often before, shook his head over Pender's intellectual antics. "Great Heavens, Pender: is nothing either true or false to you?"

That gentleman laughed again, replying "Not in history, my boy—especially not in recent history. The real truths in history are very simple, very old, and very well concealed. What historians argue over are the little issues, and their arguments are driven entirely by whether theirs was the winning side, or the losing."

"And are not all of us here on the losing side in this case, Sir?" Darcy placed the gambit casually before his mentor.

"Mind your treasonous tongue, you young upstart! The Crown has not lost—it is cleverly biding its time until the moment is right to strike." He fixed Darcy with a hard, but comical stare. "Ha! Try to catch *me* out, would you? Allow me to remind you, Sir, that scholars have no side; and if you have forgotten that, then best you come back to Oxford and stay out of London until you are old enough to keep your mind on what matters!"

Darcy grinned at him: his attempt to force the other into an untenable position, an old debater's trick, had not worked. But, graceful in defeat, he supplied the question he knew was expected: "And what is that, Sir?"

"Women—and beer!" Pender declared, taking a long quaff from his glass. Then he lowered his eyes and scratched the back of his head. "Or was it beer, and women? I think my age is beginning to tell on me—they do say the mind goes second."

Darcy knew this one and forbore to respond, but it was not long before one of the younger men supplied the wanted question: "What goes first, Sir?"

"I…well, I cannot seem to recall." The older man's bright eye appeared above the rim of his glass, and he drained it with a laugh.

Darcy staid with Pender for three-quarters of an hour, then, with mutual assurances of early correspondence, went back to the ball-room in search of Bingley. His friend was dancing, which gratified Darcy; his sister Caroline appeared at Darcy's side only moments after he entered the room.

"And may I ask where you have been, Sir?" she began with an arch expression. "It was most unkind in you to abandon me."

"I beg your pardon, Miss Bingley," Darcy replied, pointing vaguely back towards the game-room. "I was called away to see a good friend whom I had not heard from in some time."

"I forgive you," said she, resting her hand on his sleeve. "In any event," with a glance over her shoulder to an exceedingly animated crowd at the other end of the ball-room, "your cousin has only just now released me."

"Really? As you once asked me, when am I to wish you joy?" Miss Bingley laughed and daintily slapped his arm with her fan. Darcy, remembering his sister's advice from her letter, recovered himself and said more distantly, "And have you seen any one else of our acquaintance?"

"Oh yes; Mr. Hurst's older brother, Sir Walter, is here, and the Edgertons, and the Armsteads, and oh! —Miss Lavinia Hartsbury was asking after you." At just that moment Darcy heard a familiar feminine chuckle from behind them; turning, he saw the young woman from earlier standing quite near, with her back to them, talking to a small gathering of men. There was nothing in her demeanour to indicate it, but he had the distinct impression that she had laughed on hearing Miss Bingley mention Miss Hartsbury's name.

"Miss Bingley," said Darcy in a low voice, turning back to his companion, "Do you know that young woman?"

Miss Bingley looked over his shoulder and sniffed disdainfully when she saw to whom Darcy was referring. "That," she replied in a whisper, "is Miss Susan Chesterton; as unaccomplished a woman as any you will find in all of London. She has nothing but looks to recommend her, and, in my opinion, they are fading fast: in five years she will be nothing but a haggard shell." Darcy saw Miss Chesterton turn her head to stare through Miss Bingley for a single, brief moment, then turn back to her own companions. Shortly thereafter the gentlemen surrounding her gave forth gales of laughter, looking pointedly away from Miss Bingley and Darcy; Miss Bingley took Darcy's arm and moved determinedly away to another part of the room.

Chapter Ten

S ome while later Darcy was again by himself in a relatively quiet room off the main ball-room, Miss Bingley having been taken for a dance by a gentleman unknown to him. St. Stephens appeared just then at the door and looked about until he spied Darcy; turning, he briefly beckoned to some one out of sight, then entered with Miss Susan Chesterton on his arm.

"Darcy!" George cried boisterously, although not without a slight muddling of his speech. "There you are! Been searching the whole house for you. I ought to have known you'd be hiding in some corner or other. Come, I promised you I'd introduce you to some one — come make the acquaintance of Miss Susan Chesterton; as charming and delicious a woman as any man could ever care to meet!" Darcy, galled and embarrassed as always by his cousin's manners, was somewhat relieved to see the young lady turn her smile from him to look at his cousin in shock, then cast her eyes down modestly. Here, at least, Darcy thought, was an acquaintance of St. Stephens' with a sense of propriety. St. Stephens whispered tipsily, and perfectly audibly, in his ear, "Never say I've done you no favours."

Drawing apart from his cousin, Darcy bowed to Miss Chesterton, saying, "Rather than challenge my cousin's courtesy any farther by waiting for him actually to make the introduction, Miss Chesterton, allow me to express my pleasure at making your acquaintance."

With just a hint of an amused smile playing around her lips, the lady made him a deep curtsey and favoured him with a flash of her intelligent eyes.

"You are most kind, Sir," said she. St. Stephens let out a guffaw, and, clapping Darcy on the back, said, "Such a proper lady! Well, there you are, Darcy; I'll leave you to it."

So saying he left the room, with only a slight encounter with a disobliging door-frame to impede his progress.

"How is it you know my cousin?" Darcy enquired, staring thoughtfully at the door through which he had quit the room.

The lady replied: "Actually, we met here, it must be—two years ago. I have known the Delacroix family some time."

"I see. I wonder at my cousin's never having mentioned you before."

"If I may say, Sir, I have never heard Lord St. Stephens mention any one who was not of superior rank or position—which certainly is not true in my case."

Darcy inclined his head with a smile. "I see you do know His Lordship well."

After a moment's pause, during which Darcy rather expected her to bring up Miss Bingley's name, the lady instead commented: "I do not believe I have noticed you dancing this evening, Mr. Darcy; do you not care for it?"

"Ah; there Miss Chesterton, you have me at a loss. If I say I do not, you will think me churlish and unschooled—but if I say I do, it would be an untruth."

She looked into his eyes with an amused smile, then said, "And if I were to say to you, Sir, what very great pleasure it would give me to be on the dance floor this moment, with a rather tall, handsome gentleman, of unexceptional fashion and bearing, what should you say?"

This question, clever in being so very forward yet strictly proper at the same time, and an arch, acute glance which was softened by a sweet smile, rather reminded Darcy of Miss Elizabeth Bennet, and prompted him to offer an unwonted response: "I would have to say that no man could be so churlish as to deny such a lovely lady such a simple pleasure."

"Prettily said, Mr. Darcy," said she with a pleased smile, stepping to his side and looking expectantly at him until he offered her his arm. As they made their way to the dance floor she asked, "But do you really find dancing to be 'simple'?"

Darcy paused, considering. "Yes, rather; I dare say some steps are more complex than others, but on the whole...in what way do you see it otherwise?"

"Why, to me it is a metaphor for life."

"'Metaphor for life'? — Truly? How so?"

They took their place in the set just forming, and Miss Chesterton gestured to indicate their two selves. "Two people meet; formalities and compliments are exchanged," here the couple bowed to each other to start the dance, "and their acquaintance begins. During the time they know each other, they spend time together, then apart." They moved down the dance, their actions framing her words. "They meet others, change partners; the dance of time twirls on..." here they separated, then, on coming together again, she continued: "...bringing them together again and again, and each time their steps get a little closer, a little surer, until..." here they separated and joined again, "...at a particular moment, it is decided — neither one knowing who decided, or exactly why — but it is decided, and forever, that either it is over between them, or that they will dance on and on, ever closer, ever surer." She finished speaking as the two of them, moving in perfect harmony, reached the end of a pass. Darcy looked down at his partner; her eyes shone happily and a delicate flush suffused her features, giving her the countenance of a young girl in her very first Season, rather than the two-and-twenty Darcy took her for.

Darcy, who had never once given a serious thought to the subject, was struck by her exposition, but more so by her insight and intelligence as she expressed herself: no mean feat to match one's words to the cadence of a dance so exactly. Remembering Miss Bingley's slight on her accomplishments, he realised that this was nothing more than her jealousy at work again, just as it had been with Elizabeth.

Indeed, Miss Chesterton struck him as being altogether so much like Elizabeth that Darcy felt that they had known each other rather longer than was the case.

"An elegant argument, Miss Chesterton," said he with some admiration. "I confess it had never occurred to me to think of it that way; and, may I say, it is a very romantic way of looking at it."

Miss Chesterton demurred: "Nay, Sir, I assure you: I am no romantic. But I own I do adore a dance with a worthy partner." Here she looked at him fully and smiled warmly, bringing an uncharacteristically open smile to Darcy's face.

The two of them finished the set, but sat out the next. Darcy found her company engaging and her conversation stimulating; in her opinions he found an intriguingly refreshing view of the world. In comparing her with another lady whose wit he recently had had occasion to admire, Miss Chesterton had not Elizabeth's informed mind, perhaps, on learned matters, but her understanding of London, particularly its most notable citizens and their characters, foibles, and motivations, was far more complete even than his own. She had an intimate knowledge of every one in the first circles, and could relate anecdotes illustrative of their characters with amusing insight. At one point Darcy had asked her, with some perplexity, about her willing acceptance of St. Stephens' society: "Might I ask, Miss Chesterton, why a woman of such sensibility as yourself would vex herself with my cousin's acquaintance?"

Miss Chesterton laughed at the question. "But he is only a duckling! One cannot be offended."

"'A duckling'?" asked Darcy in surprise. "Whatever do you mean?"

"Oh—I *do* apologise! I ought not to say such things, and to his own family!" she covered her face with her fan and turned away from him.

"No, no—please, I insist: in what way is Viscount St. Stephens a duckling?"

"Why, the way he follows along behind Mr. Fox: is not he just like a little duckling, all puffed up and waddling along, chasing with all his fellows after their leader?"

Darcy laughed heartily at this image of his cousin.

"You see?" said Miss Chesterton with a smile. "It is rather endearing, actually—as long as one never takes him too seriously."

Darcy laughed again and wondered if he might share this with his uncle; he must share it with Edmund, certainly. But George, a duckling—that was he, to the very life: an exact image. Suddenly his cousin did not seem so offensive; just a bumbling, fuzzy little creature, pursuing its own obscure goals with little or no intention of either good or ill.

Darcy said with appreciation, "Miss Chesterton, you are a wonder; in seven-and-twenty years I have never been able to see my cousin so clearly as I do right now."

Miss Chesterton smiled her pleasure at him. "And now, Mr. Darcy, it is your turn: how is it you are acquainted with Miss Bingley?"

"Ah...her brother is my close friend; my closest friend, in fact."

"I see. I thought perhaps...there seemed...forgive my mentioning it...but it did seem as though there might be a slight degree of interest...on her side at least—when she was speaking with you."

"I can, of course, have no knowledge of Miss Bingley's motives or intentions."

"No, of course not—I see," said Miss Chesterton, giving him a sidelong glance. "And yet, so eligible a gentleman as yourself, surely you cannot be entirely unattached."

"I am, most assuredly, Miss Chesterton," he confessed. While nine years' of Seasons had left Darcy somewhat inured to the fact that a woman might exhibit an interest in him, Darcy could not but be gratified by *this* lady's notice:

her ease, her elevated conversation, and her fine person, placed her personal claims high among the women of Darcy's acquaintance, and her presence at the Delacroix's spoke for her character.

"What a surprise, Mr. Darcy," the lady replied, "and a shame. How sad that such a charming gentleman should have to pass through life alone." The lady patted his arm sympathetically and sat back deeper into her chair. She did not press Darcy further on the subject, but instead led their conversation off into an anecdote on some entertaining exchanges between St. Stephens's friend, Mr. Fox, and one of his adversaries on the floor of Parliament.

Throughout their time together he found Miss Chesterton's conversation, views, and information all to his liking: she seemed to know instinctively the right thing to say on every occasion. In addition, his turn on the dance-floor with Elizabeth at Netherfield had awakened in him an appreciation of the benefits of the exercise, when paired with the right woman. On the whole, he was enjoying himself this evening far more than he had had any idea of before the event.

A little while later in the evening he was at a refreshment table securing glasses for Miss Chesterton and himself; they had danced again, at Darcy's instigation, and the room was warm. When dancing with Miss Chesterton he could only compare it with one other dance; this time, however, there were no unwanted references to other persons, no accusations, no interruptions. And while Miss Chesterton did not have Elizabeth's playful intellect, she had about her a more composed charm; altogether Darcy was well pleased by her company.

As he turned from the table with glasses in hand he encountered Miss Lavinia Hartsbury, whom he had not seen since the prior spring. She met him with her usual open enthusiasm, saying with all her accustomed rapidity of speech, "Mr. Darcy! What a pleasure! I had no idea of your being back in Town! You are well, I trust—and your sister? Where have you been? You have passed the autumn pleasantly, I hope? I was with Mamma in Bath, but this year I found it rather dull."

Darcy smiled into her blinking face; he had found during the last Season that her manner of speech and constant blinking did not disgust; instead, it engendered a sympathy which quite surprised him: in his estimation, though, her obvious sincerity and good will mitigated strongly against her personal shortcomings. After giving her his compliments he told her, "Yes, Miss Darcy and I are both well, I thank you. I was with my friend, Mr. Bingley, at his new manor in Hertfordshire after Michaelmas, and this is the first time I have ventured into company outside my own house since returning to Town; we have had friends staying with us this last fortnight."

"Well then, Sir, we must count ourselves fortunate to have you among us this evening," Miss Hartsbury enthused, her whole person seeming to radiate pleasure. Then, noting that he held two glasses, she said, "Oh—are you here with some one?"

"No, not really. I have been dancing, and I just came to get us something cooling to drink."

"You, Mr. Darcy? Dancing?"

At that moment they were joined by Miss Chesterton. "Mr. Darcy," said she, "I was beginning to wonder if you might were in need of help carrying." Turning to face Miss Hartsbury, she said, "But I see that it is our dear Lavinia who has detained you. How are you, dear?"

Darcy was looking at Miss Hartsbury when she turned to see Miss Chesterton; to his surprise, she coloured deeply—and her blinking stopped entirely. Said she in confusion, "Miss Ches...I...Mr. Darcy, I...I must go. Forgive me, please." She turned and hurried away. Darcy stared after her in mild shock until he felt a glass being taken from his hand. Miss Chesterton, he found, was frowning after the retreating back of Miss Hartsbury. "Dear, strange, little creature," she murmured. "What can have come over her?" Darcy could only shake his head in wonder.

Shortly thereafter Miss Chesterton had been forced to excuse herself; pleading a prior commitment, she had left the ball; Darcy finished the evening drifting from room to room, stopping occasionally to exchange comments with some one of his acquaintance. Miss Bingley found him again and spent some time spelling for information about his time with Miss Chesterton; failing in that, she began alluding to the dance-floor, but Darcy refused to take the hint. She had eventually been approached by a gentleman Darcy knew by name only, asking her to dance, which released Darcy to his own devices once more.

Perhaps half an hour later, Bingley sought him out to say he had had enough for the evening; even though it was still relatively early, the two repaired to their carriage.

"How was your evening?" Darcy enquired.

"The evening went well, Darcy; quite well. I am glad to have come; it was marvellous to see every one again, and Pender — what a mind the man has! I could listen to him for hours."

"Indeed. No matter the subject, I have never caught him out — regardless of how hard I tried — and Heaven knows I tried often enough. I think I saw you dance?"

"Oh yes…once or twice," Bingley replied, his manner becoming constrained.

Darcy asked casually, "Did you meet any one?"

"No, no one like…that is, every one was very pleasant. I had an excellent time."

"All is well, then," Darcy offered.

Bingley's reply was a muted: "Yes, all is well…" This, of course, was very unlike his friend's normal high spirits after an evening's entertainment, and he compared this carriage ride to another he had recently shared with Bingley on the way back from a dance: he could not but be affected by the difference in his friend—Bingley obviously still pined for Miss Bennet. Well, he thought, one must not expect immediate success: this will be a campaign, not a sally.

Chapter Eleven

*T*he following Thursday, after a delightful Christmas during which Darcy had enjoyed quite a sufficiency of mince pie and plum pudding, he had gone out into town to see to purchasing the furnishings for Georgiana's drawing-room at Pemberley, as he had intended. Mindful of Miss Bingley's advice, he had spoken with Mrs. Annesley before starting out, wishing to have her thoughts on a suitable décor. She made several suggestions, and had mentioned the window seat: "Your sister seems very drawn to that window; does it hold any special significance?"

Darcy cast back his memory. "Not especially, I think. She did sit there with my mother fairly often when she was but a girl, but that was years ago, now."

Mrs. Annesley looked at him momentarily, as if expecting him to continue. At length she said, "Perhaps I might best deal with the window seat, Sir? I am sure you will have your hands full with the rest."

As his chaise pulled up in front of the warehouse, Darcy heard the sound of another carriage pulling up behind him. Descending, he glanced around and was surprised to see Miss Susan Chesterton was at that same moment alighting from a hackney coach, evidently with the intent of visiting the same shop as he.

'Miss Chesterton!" he spoke in greeting. "This is an unexpected pleasure."

"Why, Mr. Darcy! Indeed it is. *What* a surprise! How odd that we should both choose to-day to come here, of all places."

"You are in need of furnishings, too, then?" Darcy asked.

Miss Chesterton glanced casually into the window he was indicating. "Indeed; I am in desperate need of a new carpet for my chambers; the housemaid spilled some coals on my old one—it is quite ruined, I fear."

"What a shame."

"Oh, well, I was planning on replacing it anyway, so I was not too upset with her. And now she has given me the chance to meet you again, I have forgiven her entirely." She smiled at Darcy and gestured. "Shall we?" Darcy opened the door for them and they went in.

The proprietor came bustling towards them, recognising Darcy as a regular and valued customer: "Mr. Darcy— what a pleasure, Sir!" When he saw Miss Chesterton, however, his face became suddenly blank: "Ah…Miss Chesterton," he said with a restrained bow to her; Darcy understood: it had always appeared to him that one of the great difficulties of being a tradesman was the necessity of maintaining the strictest propriety with all persons, which, when dealing with a woman as lovely as Miss Chesterton, must call for a high degree of discipline.

"How might I be of service, Sir?" the man asked.

"I am looking for a new suite of furniture for a moderately sized parlour," Darcy informed him.

Miss Chesterton looked up at him in surprise. "Are you in the habit of buying such things, Mr. Darcy? Surely this is a woman's duty."

"In the normal course of events, I should leave it to my sister and her staff to attend to these matters," he agreed, "but this is to be a surprise for her; the room is one she favours, and I should like to have it brought up to date for her."

"What a marvellous brother you are, Mr. Darcy," Miss Chesterton said warmly, smiling up at him. She held his gaze a moment, then said. "Well, I shall leave you to your task. Mr.…?" she hesitated, looking at the proprietor.

"Wilson, Madam," he supplied with a slight bow. "Perhaps you may recall the purchase of a German clock you made here some months ago," he supplied. "It came back to us, I believe."

"Of course—Mr. Wilson. If you would show me to your carpetries, then?"

Darcy thought the man hesitated briefly before saying, "Certainly, Madam. Just this way."

Darcy wandered off to explore the warehouse. Before long he had selected a sofa and matching chairs in a soft lemon colour that would set the tone for the room. He walked deeper into a quiet, recessed area where pianofortes of various styles were kept; Georgiana so enjoyed playing, and he was contemplating including one in his purchase, when some one reached past him, brushing up against his arm. Surprised, he looked down to find Miss Chesterton at his side: she lightly played a chord or two. "Is your sister's parlour in need of an instrument, then?" she asked, still leaning against his arm while her fingers passed over the keys.

"No, no; but my sister plays exceptionally well, and I was thinking of giving her a new one: the one in the music-room is rather old."

"Such an extraordinary brother! Your house is a large one, I take it?"

"The manor is," he said. "The house here in London is, of course, smaller."

"And where do you reside here in Town?"

"Grosvenor Square."

"How lovely! You are not far from my dear friend, Mrs. Johnson. Do you know Mr. Rupert Johnson? His house is near Bedford Square."

"No, I have not had that pleasure."

"Well, perhaps I should remedy that; Mrs. Johnson, I am sure, would be delighted to know you. I am staying with them, now, in fact." Looking about, she said, "Heavens, but this is a dark, lonely corner, is not it? One might think we were the only ones in the place."

Darcy agreed and, sensible that their present isolated situation might be mischievously interpreted by any one coming upon them, he detached himself gently from contact with Miss Chesterton, that no hint of impropriety might be ascribed to her, should any one happen by. Moving to the side of the instrument he suggested: "Perhaps you might like to play a piece?"

Miss Chesterton looked at him curiously, then smiled. "I fear, Mr. Darcy, that even though I studied as a girl, my abilities have declined. I cannot boast, with your sister, of my performance."

Darcy shook his head. "My sister would never boast: I almost wish she would; but her abilities are eclipsed only by her modesty."

"What could be more attractive in a woman?" said Miss Chesterton admiringly. "Surely a delicate sense of propriety must make any woman — nay, any man, as well — modest in behaviour." As she concluded, she favoured him with a very open and approving look, smiling warmly. Darcy, his thoughts going instantly to Miss Bingley and her frequent attempts to put herself before Miss Elizabeth Bennet, as well as her numerous challenges to her brother's authority, not to mention the occasional brazen manœuvre towards himself, could not but concur. "I agree entirely," said he, returning her smile. "There can be no surer sign of proper thinking than modest behaviour."

After some time further looking about the place, and giving Mr. Wilson his shipping instructions, Darcy and Miss Chesterton prepared to leave. As they stepped out onto the street, Miss Chesterton turned and said, "Mr. Darcy…" but here the lady hesitated, her eyes downcast. She appeared to gather her courage, and said, "My hosts are giving a small party this Saturday evening; would you be willing to accept an invitation to attend? I am myself without escort—I...I should very much like to have you be part of the company for the evening."

Darcy might have been surprised at such an invitation, as lately as the lady had been introduced to him, but he knew that, in Town, people of fashion were wont to form—and in some cases, dissolve—acquaintances much faster than in the country. He smiled, and said, "Of course, Miss Chesterton; it would be a pleasure."

"You will? Oh, how lovely! Really, I am so delighted...that is, I am very obliged to you, Sir. You will hear from Mrs. Johnson within the day." With this they parted; Darcy returned home in fine spirits to enjoy an afternoon with his relatives.

He found his Aunt Eleanor and Uncle Jonathan having tea in the drawing-room when he returned. Helping himself to a cup, for which his aunt reproached him, first with a frowning look at him, then with a pointed glance at Goodwin standing in the corner by the door. Darcy bowed to her with a smile, then took a satisfied, and rather noisy, sip; he arched a brow, with an impish grin, at his uncle, who chuckled. "You men behave yourselves," his aunt reproved them both, but a faint smile played on her lips.

"Fitzwilliam," said she, as she continued her needlework, "your uncle tells me you met some one in Hertfordshire. Is it so?"

"Well...yes, Aunt," said he with a pained expression, "but it is nothing."

His aunt sniffed. "It did not sound like 'nothing.' What is her name?"

"Indeed, you need not concern yourself, Aunt Eleanor."

"Darcy," his aunt chided him, "you always assume that every woman you meet is well intentioned; if you will not look to your own best interests, then your family must."

Darcy shook his head. "Believe me, Ma'am, the lady can have no idea of having aroused my interest, and I have no thought of pursuing her acquaintance. It is not to be, and the only effect my feelings can have is to plague their owner."

Lady Andover looked at him closely and said, not unkindly, "Well enough, Fitzwilliam; if that be the case, I am sorry it should be so. We *do* worry about you, you know: it is time and past time for you to settle."

"While we are on the subject, Darcy," his uncle said, "George tells me he introduced you to some one at the Delacroix's last week; who is *she*, now?"

"Her name is Miss Susan Chesterton. As a matter of fact, I have just left her: she was at the same furnishings warehouse as I this morning."

Lady Andover said, "And who are *her* people?" Turning to her husband she said, "My dear, do we know any Chestertons?"

That gentleman shook his head slowly, "I do not believe so. Who is she, my boy?"

"Honestly, I know very little about her, aside from having met her at Delacroix's, and that she is a very charming lady."

"'Charming', you say? I shall make enquiries," said his aunt primly.

"That is hardly necessary, Aunt Eleanor," Darcy protested. "I hardly know the lady!"

"Did you spend any time with her at the Delacroix's ball?"

"We danced…"

"*You* danced?" demanded his aunt.

Darcy nodded. "Twice. And we had a cup of punch. That is all, I assure you."

"I see. And this morning: you met in passing?"

"No, she was arriving just as I did, and we left together; she has invited me to an evening party this Saturday."

Lady Andover gave him a look compounded of mild reproof and disbelief. "I shall enquire," she said dryly.

Into Kent

"And when next you allow yourself to be seen buying furniture in the company of a young lady, do let me know
beforehand, that I might make sure the proper notices of
your betrothal are sent, before you appear in public together."

Darcy, not having given any prior consideration to this
aspect of the business, now thought back and realised, not
only what might be thought of his outing that morning, but
what might *not* be thought of the excursion he had let himself in for with Miss Bingley. His aunt noticed his look of
concern. "Is there something else, Darcy?"

Darcy, with a slight grimace, said uncertainly, "I told
Miss Bingley I would let her buy some things for a drawing-room I am refurnishing for Georgiana, at Pemberley."

His aunt stared at him, dumbfounded, and even his
uncle winced. His aunt finally said, "I had thought you possessed of some sense, Darcy. What on Earth were you
thinking! This *is* the young lady at whose brother's house
you spent the entire autumn, is not it? Well, you might just
as well stop by the jewellers while you are out, and buy her
a ring—and give the jeweller the hint to spread word to the
newspapers, into the bargain."

Georgiana's letter, in which she had warned him of
Miss Bingley' use of stratagems, came instantly to Darcy's
mind; but he made what attempt he could to defend himself: "Aunt Eleanor," he said plaintively, "you know I had
no such intention! I had no thought of anything beyond being civil to the sister of my friend, with both of whom I am
nearly constantly in company; I mentioned my plans in
passing, and she asked if she might help: it was no more
than that, at least on my side. I do not see why I should
need to watch my tongue every moment of every day! Men
do not ascribe consequence to acts where no such significance is intended."

His aunt Eleanor gestured to her husband as though to
say, "You reason with him!" That gentleman said, "Perhaps

that is true, Darcy, but you had better learn to interpret these actions in light of how they will be taken, or you will wake up one morning to find you are married to a woman you barely know."

Lady Andover sighed deeply, shaking her head, and told him, "I shall attend to it, Darcy. A formal invitation from me, to grant me the favour of her company while pursuing the thankless task of guiding my poor, naïve, insensible nephew in the purchase of some household goods, will be sufficient I should think. But *do* be more careful, for Heaven's sake."

Darcy nodded. "I shall, Aunt Eleanor," said he unenthusiastically. "But why must women always seek meanings within meanings, and import deep significance into the simplest civilities?"

"And why must men be always blind to what is plainly in front of their noses?" she asked pointedly, holding Darcy's eye. His uncle made a gesture of decided warning from behind her shoulder, and Darcy wisely let the challenge go unanswered. She looked quickly around at her husband, however, whose return look of angelic innocence might have explained his successes in Parliament, but, unhappily, in the present case served only to convince his lady of his duplicity. She crossly struck him a blow to the shoulder with her fist, and, rising with dignity, left the room.

"Well done, Darcy," his uncle said in an aggravated manner. "Now we'll both be sleeping in the stables. I claim the hayloft." To which Darcy could reply only with a very sheepish shrug of the shoulders; his uncle lifted himself and went off in search of his wife, to begin the process of making amends. Privately, Darcy was not wholly displeased on his own behalf; his aunt's scheme would do for Miss Bingley, and it occurred to him that an afternoon in company with Miss Bingley, whilst not precisely the revenge he had thought of for his aunt, in exchange for her having given an unauthorised Society dinner in his home, would still serve well enough.

Darcy went to in his rooms shortly thereafter, where he was surprised to come upon Perkins busily employed in rearranging all his closets; he had not known his man had returned from Meryton. As he entered, nearly every door and drawer was open, and his man was buried to his shoulders in the interior of a capacious wardrobe; various other articles of furniture were liberally bedecked with drapings of clothes, as was his man, himself. With a mixture of pleasure and puzzlement Darcy said, "Perkins! You are back—at least, I trust that is you under all that."

"Mr. Darcy, Sir," his man's muffled voice came from within the wardrobe. Perkins emerged and greeted him with a rather stiff bow, the formality of which was marred by the loose flapping of various sleeves and collars that were festooned about his person. "I returned nearly an hour ago. As you were occupied in the drawing-room, I came up stairs, where," he finished with some heat, "I found that James had completely rearranged your closets!"

Darcy realised from his tone that this was a catastrophe of the first water; it certainly boded ill for poor James, the footman who had stood in Perkins's stead while he was away. With some sympathy, he said to his man, "Yes, I see; most unfortunate: well, when you have things back in order, I shall be glad to hear how things went in Meryton."

Perkins, having been brought to himself by this comment, turned away from his work, and, bowing, said, "I beg your pardon, Sir; I meant no disrespect, but I fear my feelings had got the better of me. I shall report immediately."

So saying, he divested himself of the several layers of clothing bestowed about him, and, coming almost to stand at attention in the centre of the room with his hands behind his back, began as though reciting at school: "I arrived by coach at two in the afternoon, and, per your instructions, Sir, I took a room at the Boar. Finding Lara…the young lady of my acquaintance…was off for the afternoon, I took advantage of the time allowed me to reacquaint myself with the barman at the Boar. From that individual I learnt that the person we are interested in was a frequent patron, and often spent a fair amount of money standing rounds of drinks for the other officers. I was already aware that in a certain back room of the establishment, there was a nearly constant assembly of those interested in games of chance, and I discovered that the man in question was also to be found amongst them most evenings.

"Later, when my acquaintance came back to work, I had the opportunity to enquire into further aspects of his behaviour. My acquaintance confirmed that the individual was known to show some interest in Miss Elizabeth Bennet; but my informant believes that his real interest is directed towards a young woman in the town: a friend of my acquaintance, to whom, I am told, the individual has apparently made sincere overtures of a permanent nature.

"I did not feel comfortable accepting this report without more information, so I staid on to attempt to confirm what I had been told. I fear I was unable to do so; I did, however, become sensible during my enquiries that the individual was even more widespread in his interests than at first it appeared: at least one other girl in the town seemed to think *she* was his choice. I also found some of the tradesmen were less than enthusiastic in their opinions of the man, but whether from financial concerns, or concerns where the women of their families were involved, they were reluctant to say. Leaving Meryton on Monday, per our discussion I used the remainder of the time you so generously gave me, Sir, to visit my mother in Bakewell. Her rheumatics are improved, I am happy to report, and she was very touched by the gift she received from you at Christmas. That, Sir, is my report."

As Perkins spoke, Darcy considered the intelligence he presented. None of it was surprising, but the one thing that concerned him, Wickham's interest in Elizabeth, did not, at this juncture, seem too worrisome. He certainly was not pursuing her exclusively. Indeed, if he kept on at his present rate, the little town of Meryton would soon be too small to hold all his schemes and indiscretions, and Elizabeth would surely hear of his carryings-on; that was Wickham's greatest weakness: he never could restrain his misdeeds. The entire town of Lambton near Pemberley had eventually been awakened to his character, simply because he could not keep from committing the same sins over and over. Darcy reflected on this, and was reassured.

"Very good, Perkins," he said. "I think we may rest easy, for a time. I might, perhaps, ask you to go back again, but for now I feel reasonably certain of the lady's safety. Oh, and I am very happy to hear your mother is doing well." And, his own world secure, he took himself off to allow Perkins to finish re-establishing a sense of order and correctness in his.

It was on the following morning that, on the pretext of speaking to her brother, Miss Bingley came to see Darcy with the important news that Miss Bennet was arrived in London. "I shall not be able to avoid seeing her, but we cannot allow Charles to know; I am sure he is not yet sufficiently recovered from his regard for her to do so without ill-effect." Darcy was loath to agree, but neither could he disagree; such a low artifice, knowingly withholding information that would be of great consequence to *her* brother and *his* friend, was very wrong. But he knew in his heart that Bingley was not yet ready to meet Miss Bennet again without relapse, and so, reluctantly, he agreed; so now, he told himself, you are become a deceiver, as well: look down on the *ton*, would you? —if this is how you treat your friends, you have little enough to say for yourself. But Bingley was his *best* friend, and for that reason he was willing to accept the lesser evil of artifice, rather than see the unhappiness and degradation of his friend; he only hoped that Elizabeth would never hear of any of it.

Chapter Twelve

*T*he invitation from Miss Chesterton's friend, Mrs. Johnson, had arrived the very evening of their meeting at the furnishings warehouse, and two days later, as Darcy prepared himself to go the neighbourhood of Bedford Square, he was looking forward to a pleasant evening: he was, at least, well assured of agreeable discourse; Miss Chesterton he knew to be a very accomplished conversationalist: her comments and questions were always astute, and, within the sphere of her own knowledge, she was as sharp and insightful as any one could wish. As Perkins put the finishing touches on his attire, Darcy felt an unwonted keenness; an evening with Miss Chesterton promised edification and diversion, at the very least. He was even beginning to be sensible of a cautious optimism that this Season, perhaps, would prove less desolate than the last. As he looked back over the year, his thoughts naturally turning to Miss Elizabeth Bennet, he wondered whether it were possible that she might be at an entertainment this evening, too. One felt a little guilty to be going off to enjoy oneself, perhaps, but, he reminded himself firmly, it was necessary to move on, and to spurn the company of Miss Chesterton would be an unwarranted contravention of his decision regarding Elizabeth.

And, in fact, the evening proceeded so as to fulfil his hopes entirely. The party was small, only twelve or fifteen couples, but, as the rest were unknown to Darcy, Miss Chesterton devoted herself to him almost entirely; the two of them spent most of the evening together chatting. His host, Mr. Johnson—an older gentleman, whose solid, rather stiff figure was mirrored by his outlook and his manner— was complemented well in his wife; a little older than Miss Chesterton, she was a lively, entertaining lady, whose manners formed a pleasant counterpoint to her husband's. Surrounded by laughter and small talk, Miss Chesterton and Darcy kept quietly to themselves on a sofa to one side of a comfortable fire.

Late in the party, when some of the others began taking their leave, Miss Chesterton's conversation—and, it cannot be denied, her more strictly personal charms—kept Darcy's attentions so firmly fixed in their corner of the room that he barely noticed when some of the others were bidding their hosts good night. Their dialogue flowed with great spirit, and the lady's eyes shone with enthusiasm and humour.

"And so, Sir, you are quite devoted to the truth, I take it. What then do you hold to be the proper rôle of truth in daily concerns? As, say, between men and women."

"Can there be any question? The truth is, and must be, the foundational tenet of *all* behaviour, regardless of the source or the object of that behaviour."

"Indeed, Sir?" the lady said impishly. "Are you saying, then, that you believe that all people speak the truth at all times? I am well assured that a man of your age and station knows better."

"Of course not, no—of course," Darcy hurriedly corrected himself. "Say then, rather, that the truth is the foundational tenet of all *proper* behaviour."

"And this you really adhere to?" she looked at him enquiringly. "Tell me, then, for example: what truths would you tell one such as our dear Miss Hartsbury? Surely it were a more gentlemanly thing to withhold the mirror of truth from such a one?"

"Would not a sympathetic truth be better than a sympathetic falsehood?"

"'Sympathetic truth', Sir? In my experience the truth is rather harsh. Is not that the trite phrase—'the harsh truth'?"

"Surely there are as many ways of speaking the truth as there are of speaking an untruth."

"Indeed? I do not believe the truth to be so malleable as that. No, it is rigid, angular, and uncomfortable—like a diamond, is not it? It can be beautiful, but it is also hard, cold, and cutting."

"But surely, the lie, once discovered, cuts worse than any truth, does not it, Miss Chesterton?" The ebb and flow of their conversation engrossed Darcy completely; he was sitting forward on the sofa with rapt attention, very close to Miss Chesterton.

She leaned in and spoke gently: "Would you hear a truth from me, Mr. Darcy?" Darcy was very conscious of her proximity. He looked at her, her every feature proven in perfect detail, but he forbore to speak. "Well then," said she, "I would tell you that I should very much wish that our time together to-night need never end."

This brought Darcy to a sudden awareness of his surroundings; aside from the servants, no one was left but the two of them; Miss Chesterton was gently, and with great delicacy, informing him that the evening had ended for the others some time before. The great impropriety of his being there, alone at night with a lady, came crashing in upon him; it was made all the worse for knowing how much he had been enjoying her attentions, and her person; the whole situation was ripe for mischief, or at least, mischievous interpretation: he had placed the lady's reputation in grave jeopardy. "Great Heavens, Miss Chesterton!" cried he as he hastened to his feet, "I do apologise. I had no idea...thank you for your consideration in mentioning—I had quite lost sight of the time; do please accept my apologies. I am leaving immediately. I do hope I have not materially injured you in the eyes of our hosts. And, please, do offer my apologies to Mrs. Johnson for my inexcusable behaviour." He was by this time at the main hall; Miss Chesterton's somewhat cool and distant countenance gave clear indication of how awkwardly he was managing the situation, but there was nothing he could do now to improve matters. Taking up his hat and coat he hurried out the door.

Out in the drive, Perkins, sagging but watchful, met his master with signs of relief. "Perkins, I do apologise. I had no notion the evening had drawn on so long."

"Thank you, Sir, it is nothing. I'm sure I am only too glad we'll be sleeping in our own beds to-night, Sir." So saying, he shut the door of the coach and climbed up with the coachman. Darcy wondered briefly about this odd pronouncement, but his worry and embarrassment over his disgraceful performance at the Johnsons overwhelmed his thoughts, and kept him fully occupied on the brief trip to Grosvenor Square.

Chapter Thirteen

*A*fter a late breakfast the next morning, Darcy had taken refuge in his library; he was giving careful consideration to the question of whether a note of apology was necessary to be sent Mrs. Johnson, but he could not be sure whether it would help or hurt Miss Chesterton's reputation; it might, perhaps, be best to let Miss Chesterton explain things to her friend without his interference. On the other hand, he had more than over-stepped the bounds of propriety, and an apology was certainly due his hostess; but if there was to be an apology, would not it best be made in person?

As he pondered, there was a brief knock on the door, and, uncharacteristically, Perkins entered unbidden, to come and stand across the desk from him. "Yes, Perkins, what is it?" asked his master in surprise.

Perkins hesitated, bracing himself to speak. "Mr. Darcy, Sir, I heard something below stairs last night that I think you should know."

"Oh? Go on, man."

Perkins appeared extremely uncomfortable and had trouble meeting Darcy's eye. "Well, Sir, Miss Chesterton's maid had a bit more to drink last night than she ought— more than a bit, to say the truth."

"Indeed? She will likely lose her place, then; I cannot imagine Miss Chesterton would abide being attended by a drunken maid."

"Yes, Sir; actually, that is the point." Perkins hesitated still more before saying: "The maid said that her mistress expected to entertain certain of her guests late into the night; so she, the maid, Sir, had the night to herself."

"Miss Chesterton would still need the girl to help her undress, no matter what the hour," Darcy pointed out. Perkins's discomfort puzzled Darcy: he could not imagine what he might have found so personally disturbing in the matter.

"Yes, Sir... that is the thing, Sir; she was very sure that...that that part of the business would have been taken care of by the guest," said Perkins woodenly, his ears red and his eyes fixed rigidly on the floor.

As the import of this became clear to Darcy, he said in shocked tones, "Perkins, we are speaking of a lady!"

Perkins said hurriedly, "Yes, Sir, and I beg your pardon, and I should never have given it any credit if the housekeeper had not agreed with her. The two of them had quite a laugh over it, Sir."

Darcy was taken aback; of course, one hears of such things among certain circles of fashionable Society, but he had generally dismissed these reports as merely part of the ill-spirited intrigues and whisperings that were honey-mead to the *ton*. To encounter it directly was deeply shocking to him: he could not imagine it actually occurring within his own acquaintance. He said in disbelief, "I can scarcely credit this, Perkins; are you quite certain?"

"Sir, neither of the two of them were what I might call discreet; and this sort of thing seems to have happened more than once—I should never have dared to breathe a word of it, otherwise. Mr. Darcy, you must believe I would never carry idle gossip to you," said Perkins earnestly. He could not hide his discomfort and was quite literally wringing his hands as he stood before Darcy.

"Perkins, calm yourself, man," said Darcy reasonably. By now he had had time to give it consideration, and he said, "This has to be purest invention: Miss Chesterton spent very little time with any gentleman last night other than myself, and I was the last to leave. There could have been no one to stay with her." His man made no comment, and refused to meet his eye. Darcy again gave in to astonishment.

"Perkins! Do you mean to say…are you telling me that *I* was the 'guest' in question?"

"Forgive me, Mr. Darcy; yes, Sir, you were the gentleman under discussion."

"Good Lord!" Almost too dumbfounded to speak, he stared at his man. "Whatever would make her think…? Impossible! …" Poor Perkins, his every line speaking his distress, could only wait miserably in silence. At length Darcy recovered himself and, seeing Perkins was becoming increasingly distressed, told him, "Very well, Perkins, that will do; I appreciate this."

"I do hope, Sir, you're not upset with me…"

Darcy cut him off: "Great Heavens, man, of course not. Be assured—only one person in this room can be held responsible for this imbroglio." He looked kindly at his man. "Go get yourself a cup of tea: I dare say this has upset you as much as myself. Go along, now." Perkins bowed thankfully and left the room.

Darcy's first reaction was to be shocked by Miss Chesterton's audacity; how could she imagine he would be willing to be part of such an infamous scheme? Flirtation was not entirely new to him; but this went far beyond an additional caress of the hand on the dance floor: this was wanton debauchery! Did she have the assurance to believe that she might have sufficient charms to entice any man to…? There was but one aspect which troubled him: had he let his enjoyment in her company mislead her as to the degree of his interest? He was certain he could not possibly have been so completely unguarded. Besides, the evidence of the maid and the housekeeper suggested that this was not an uncommon occurrence. Could any woman really be that licentious? Darcy hardly knew how to believe it; but when he thought back over their association, he could not help but see that, given a certain construction on her actions, she could be seen as a very determined flirt: the way she had charmed him into their first dance, the episode at the pianoforte in the warehouse, and then, last night.... He had to concede that, if one had a mind to look for it, there was ample support to lend credence to what Perkins had heard against her.

His thoughts, which earlier that morning had been so completely focused on Miss Chesterton's reputation, now turned to his own: could his character suffer if this came out? He soon decided that while it might, the possibility of its becoming known was remote. The lady would hardly publish the matter, and, evidently, her servants had more interesting gossip to retail than that of the man who had *not* been taken in by her fascinations.

He next considered how best to cut the acquaintance, which needs must be done immediately. A note would be sufficient in the case, surely, but he always preferred to handle difficult matters in person, and he felt he could not, in fairness and honour, end the acquaintance without giving Miss Chesterton a hearing at least, a chance to refute these allegations against her character. Not willing to brook any delay, he sent a stiffly proper note round to the Johnson's, asking to see Miss Chesterton at her earliest convenience. Her reply came back by immediate return to say that she would be home to him that very afternoon.

When he arrived, he found Miss Chesterton dressed with less fashion and more decorum than he was accustomed to see. She showed him into the drawing-room, apologising with quiet correctness that her hostess was unwell and would be unable to join them. Darcy passed this without comment and entered straight away into the topic that had brought him thither.

"I thank you for seeing me on such late notice, Miss Chesterton. A circumstance has come to my attention that I could not ignore, and required immediate attention."

"Good Heavens, Sir, you unnerve me, quite," said the lady, looking earnestly into his face. "Whatever can have upset you so?"

"An exceedingly disturbing report has reached my ears concerning last night's entertainment: apparently it was much discussed below stairs that...that an inmate of the house contemplated an illicit liaison with one of the guests."

"I *beg* your pardon, Sir! What are you suggesting?" The lady appeared deeply shocked and affronted. Her sober appearance and sincere countenance lessened Darcy's assurance: how could the demur young woman who sat before him be the licentious and irregulated creature imputed by Perkins's history?

Hesitantly, Darcy said, "That I...that is, that you planned...It was expected that we should be..." He found he could not speak the words.

Miss Chesterton stared at him a long moment without speaking, then a spark of indignation flashed in her eyes; but the next moment her eyes softened. "Come, Sir; stories from below stairs? Do you often credit them? Whence originated this tale?"

"I understand your own maid was the source, Madam."

Miss Chesterton appeared puzzled, and sat thinking for a moment. "*My* maid?" she repeated. "My maid is away at present: I gave her leave to attend her mother, who is seriously ill. I am making do with—Ah, perhaps now I begin to understand." She shifted to face him squarely. "Do you remember, Mr. Darcy, when we met at the furnishings warehouse, I mentioned a housemaid had ruined my carpet?" Darcy nodded, puzzled by this apparent change of topic. "Well, as you might imagine, I had words with her. Perhaps I may have spoken more sharply than I realised; that, I imagine, may be the real source of this tale."

"I do not understand."

"That same girl is now attending me in the absence of my own. Obviously she was trying to take some measure of revenge by spreading this base report."

Darcy was quiet as he mulled this. For a housemaid to have fabricated such a slander against her mistress's intimate friend — she would be very lucky if losing her place was the worst that happened to her. He looked at Miss Chesterton uncertainly. "Surely, Mr. Darcy, you cannot believe this of me!" she cried, reading his doubt in his manner. "I pray you, Sir — what have I ever done that could make you suspect me in this way? A rumour, a low, hateful rumour! — you must surely believe me, Mr. Darcy; you cannot think I would actually...that I could possibly contemplate such a monstrous...no, you cannot think me so lost to every proper feeling. Can you?" When he still did not speak, her colour changed, and she actually came to kneel beside his chair; holding onto his arm with both hands, she said in a voice of strong emotion, "No, please — please say it is not so! I could not bear to have *you* think this of me!" Darcy could see tears starting to well in her eyes.

Darcy hardly knew what to say. The lady's countenance, though deeply troubled, was open, and her manner most sincere; it was impossible to believe that this could be artifice. On the other hand, Darcy had never known Perkins to be mistaken before, in the intelligence he had brought to him. But, looking into Miss Chesterton's face, it was beyond Darcy to doubt her. Such earnest emotion could not be feigned, and such deeply affecting supplication could not be denied. His objections evaporated in the face of such sincere distress, and he felt himself to be suddenly and completely in the wrong.

"Madam, I am at a loss." He felt instantly how insufficient was this as an apology, and continued hurriedly: "I do not know how to apologise. I beg you will tell me how I might make amends."

Her eyes lifted to his, and a tremulous smile appeared; she replied: "Oh, Sir, your contrition is unnecessary, I assure you. You must not blame yourself: you could have had no idea of the true origin of such a tale, and, given that it came from within the household…well, yours is not a suspicious nature, surely; and as devoted as you are to the truth, you can have no experience with such malevolent duplicity as this." At this, Wickham's smirking features appeared in Darcy's mind; when he compared it to the sight of Miss Chesterton kneeling by his chair, mortified, frightened to tears that she might have lost his regard, it was abundantly clear to him how unjust he had been.

Under the circumstances it was impossible for Darcy to release himself without some attempt at redemption. "Miss Chesterton," he said, struggling for words to make her understand how much he felt himself to be at fault. "You must allow me to make some recompense for such an atrocious error — such a mistaken belief in low, malicious gossip."

"Sir: while I assure you it is entirely unnecessary, if you insist, I shall endeavour to think of some means — agreeable to us both, I trust — that will allow you to feel you have atoned for this misunderstanding." Her voice was soft, but Darcy could not meet her eye; if he could, however, the cold anger he would have seen there might have given him pause. "For now, I beg you will put it out of your mind completely."

But Darcy had by no means finished apologising; he continued for several minutes more, until, sensible that to go on would be merely a repetition of things he had already said, he took his leave, awkward and embarrassed. His final words were to beg her to be unstinting in her requirements for his atonement.

Arriving back in Grosvenor Square, Darcy found Perkins in his rooms, apparently awaiting his return. A look at Darcy's face told Perkins what had transpired; after waiting a moment for his master to express his censure, which of course was not forthcoming, Perkins hastily and silently left the room.

Darcy did not see Miss Chesterton the next day; he had no engagements to take him into her company, and embarrassment prevented him from seeking her out. He could hardly bear the idea that he had injured her so monstrously; he knew he could not face her until he had, in some small way at least, redeemed himself in her eyes.

While he could not face Miss Chesterton, he did run into their mutual host, Delacroix, at White's, the club they had in common in Town. After Darcy thanked him again for the party before Christmas, the two men sat down together at a window overlooking St. James's Street.

"Did I see you with Miss Susan Chesterton at my little fête, Darcy?" Delacroix asked.

"Indeed, you did; she is a charming woman," said Darcy. Other thoughts directly occurring to him, he added: "Very genteel and good-natured."

"Yes, she is a woman of many fascinations, no doubt," said Delacroix in his usual dry, sardonic tones. Darcy had never been certain as to Delacroix's character; he seemed, at most times, to be nothing other than another of London's intellectual fops—fashionable and *au fait*, but lacking any real depth. But from time to time, Darcy caught a glimpse of something deeper in his character. Then there was his wife, of course: a plain, sober, and good-hearted lady, whose family background was high enough to make it unlikely that hers had been anything other than a disinterested marriage, founded on esteem and affection on both sides. Her character argued more strongly in favour of Delacroix's than did his own public manner.

"How did you happen to meet her?" Delacroix asked Darcy.

"St. Stephens introduced us," Darcy said with a grimace of distaste at the memory of his cousin's entire lack of decorum and propriety: yet another source of embarrassment before Miss Chesterton: his whole family must appear to her as the lowest set of fools ever to inflict themselves upon decent society. If she thought St. Stephens a duckling, what sort of animal must he appear?

"Of course, it would be St. Stephens," Delacroix said in a low voice.

"How do you mean?" asked Darcy curiously.

"Oh, I do not mean anything, old son," Delacroix said lightly. "I never mean anything, really. It is just that St. Stephens has been...interested...in Miss Chesterton for some time. I can imagine it would amuse him to bring her to your notice. Or perhaps he might only have been doing the lady a favour—after all, Darcy, I have watched half the women in London throw themselves at you." He winked at Darcy.

"Do not be absurd, Delacroix," Darcy chided him. "A lady like Miss Chesterton would never 'throw herself' at any one." His own ill-advised misconstruction of her character made him all the more guarding of her reputation.

Delacroix looked at him blankly for a moment. "No, of course not; have you seen her since?" he asked in an off-handed manner.

"Several times," Darcy acknowledged. "And how did *you* meet Miss Chesterton?" he enquired.

"We met when I was up at Balliol. Her father's a Master: Wadham, I think...or was it Worcester? Met her at the Commemoration Ball, you know."

"Was that one of the nights you were gated for being out after curfew?"

"That catastrophe never occurred, I assure you—in spite what you might have heard. No, at the time there was a most obliging set of revolving spikes that had rusted fast on the wall of the rear quad: a handily placed vine for a toe-hold and, up-and-over you went." Delacroix eyes twinkled at the memory.

Darcy said with mild collegial loyalty, "Lord—Balliol! You would never find such goings on at Christ Church."

Delacroix gave him an amused smile. "Of *course* not, Darcy," he said with very evident insincerity. "No one would have the temerity to *ever* suggest such a thing about Christ Church." Delacroix's manner changed, becoming more serious and less affected. "Darcy, old man, I wonder...how much do you know about Miss Chesterton?"

"Only that she is charming, a fine dancer, and an excellent conversationalist," Darcy said; as he spoke, Mr. Delacroix's manner seemed almost embarrassed. "Why? What are you suggesting? Delacroix, I met her in your own home, you recall."

"Indeed you did — it is nothing, really — only wondered if you had heard of her before."

"Heard of her in what context?" Darcy asked pointedly.

Mr. Delacroix seemed to undergo another change of heart; in more his usual manner, he said, "Well, a woman with her many fascinations *does* get talked about, that's all." He stood and extended a languid hand. "I must be off, Darcy: delighted, as always. My best to Miss Darcy."

Chapter Fourteen

S everal days later, Darcy was taken back into Town on his affairs; his business complete and finding himself in Holborn Street, he was wondering whether to go straight back to Grosvenor Square or treat himself to a visit to the bookseller's, when a nearby shop door opened and carried to him the smell of fresh coffee and baked goods. He followed the scents through the door and found himself in a fashionable little place, filled with warmth, intriguing smells, and quiet conversations. He sat down behind a little partition at a table next to a window and ordered a coffee and a small tart. He had finished his refreshments and was idly watching the passers-by, when his attention was drawn away from the window by the sound of his own name—extremely unexpected in that time and place. Voices came from the table on the other side of the partition to his back: a woman was saying, "…with Mr. Darcy? Or are you ready to vary the tune with…was his name Manwarren? The other gentleman at Delacroix's."

"No, No—things are going very well, Alicia. He came to me after your party, all indignant and full of himself because that besotted slattern of a maid of mine couldn't keep her mouth shut in front of his man. But, oh, Alicia! —I wish you could've seen me! I was decorum itself—I looked, and sounded, just like my grandmother! —I taught him whom to believe. I have sufficiently punished her, the wretch, but I am still deciding how to punish Mr. Darcy—he should never have allowed a doubt of my character to enter his mind, no matter what he heard; but he is well in hand." Darcy recognised the two voices: they were Miss Chesterton and her friend, Mrs. Johnson. "No, you may believe me: the Bingley woman will know in future not to abuse my name in public — and certainly not in front of a man as eligible as Mr. Darcy."

"Are you serious then, about the man?"

Miss Chesterton laughed. "Hardly. I might've been, if he were more amusing: he has money, and is not ill-looking, but he is stiff as a poker and has no notion at all of how to talk to a woman. Besides, while he may be easily subdued, he is far too young for convenience." She went on in derision: "I've never met a clumsier flirt, Alicia — the man actually believes a woman is interested in hearing the truth about herself! But I'll make certain little Miss Caroline doesn't have him, at any rate."

At this point Darcy's incredulity and astonishment gave way to his breeding, and he was compelled to announce himself. He stood and turned to face the two ladies. "I thank you, Madam, for making your feelings so clear, although I might regret the very public manner in which you chose to make your declaration."

Miss Chesterton started and stared. "Mr. Darcy! ...What do you here, Sir?"

"The same as you, I should imagine: I came seeking refreshment. But instead, I found enlightenment."

Recovering herself quickly, Miss Chesterton rose, and, placing a pleading hand on his arm, spoke with utmost sincerity: "Sir, you cannot imagine that I was serious just now. Do you know women so little as to believe that we speak our hearts thus freely?" she smiled winningly up at him, her eyes glowing as they sought his. "Nay, Sir, surely you know better. Rather, you must know that it is our nature to hide our true sentiments; indeed, it is our duty to do so, to protect our reputations, to say nothing of our hearts. Society would surely shun us, and what man would not take advantage if he were somehow to hear a woman declare her true feelings for him?" As Darcy was silent, she went on with greater assurance: "I know you will forgive me for saying in public that which can have no other purpose than to hide surer emotions, which the most common sense of delicacy demands that any woman must keep locked in her secret heart, until she is secure of...the object of her desire." At this she cast her eyes downward modestly, a blush rising to her cheeks.

Darcy stared at her for a long moment, his thoughts automatically tracing the logical flaws in her argument. He was frankly amazed that the woman believed herself capable of subjugating his reason again, after what he had just heard. He found himself once again transported in mind to his father's study, listening to Wickham tell lie after lie — but this time, he was the one seated across the desk, and the deceitfulness before him was almost palpable. While wholly disgusted by this display, he had to acknowledge to himself that it was very convincingly done: to blush on command was a far higher degree of accomplishment than ever Wickham had achieved. He thought wryly to himself that this level of achievement must be the difference between the Town liar and the Country liar.

The lady, misinterpreting his silence, permitted a faint smile to appear on her lips. She was on the point of relaxing her grip on his arm and inviting him to join them when he surprised her with: "You are saying then, I take it, that it is a woman's duty to tell untruths. That a proper feminine delicacy demands that she lies. What a *fascinating* conundrum!"

"Sir," Miss Chesterton said, shaking her head in confusion. "That is a most unkind interpretation of my words. Are you determined to be so very ungallant, then? I had thought we were done with suspicion."

Darcy ignored this, adhering to the subject at hand: "Your argument begs the question, then, of whether you were being untruthful to me, when you demonstrated a regard for me, or to your intimate friend, just now, in renouncing that regard?" At this Darcy saw the lady's friend mouth a small, pained "O!" in sympathy with Miss Chesterton. He kept his countenance carefully neutral while he awaited her reply.

Miss Chesterton shook her head again, a pretty frown creasing her brow. "Sir, you mistake me, indeed. A woman's thoughts do not walk a straight line like a man's…"

But Darcy was not attending to her artifice; he was wielding logic as a rapier, as he had learned under Pender's tutelage. "You are saying then, Madam, that a woman simply cannot help but say untruths? I thank you for this most valuable lesson. If that be the case, out of concern for my own reputation, I must feel that I am better off avoiding all such persons as yourself entirely in future."

With barely a nod, he turned to leave; the lady, stunned, seemed unable to respond. He had almost reached the door when Miss Chesterton hissed angrily at his back: "Go back to the Bingley woman, then, Sir! You deserve no better. Share your truths with *her*, if you will. But do not imagine, Mr. Darcy, that the truth will bring you happiness in *this* life." Darcy turned and stared through her for a moment, then left without saying a word. As he walked out into the chilly afternoon, he reflected that the time he had spent at University might not be very useful in winning a woman, but it was decidedly useful in knowing when and how to cut one.

Chapter Fifteen

*T*he publicity of his *eclaircissement* with Miss Chesterton gave Darcy great distress; he knew it would not take long to make the rounds amongst the wagging tongues of the *ton*. It was exactly the sort of scandal that the people of fashion in Town would find intoxicatingly delightful, and that he, as master of Pemberley, always sought to avoid. And, indeed, only a day later he received early notice that his name had suddenly become the talk of London: his cousin, St. Stephens, sought him out Friday evening, on returning from an afternoon at his club. He came to find Darcy in his library. "I say, Darcy," said he in an agitated manner, "I've just heard the most extraordinary thing at Boodles: is it true you've given Miss Chesterton the cut direct—no…worse—a public dressing down?"

"Not that I see it is any of your affair, St. Stephens, but yes, I have. May I ask what your interest is in the matter?"

"Well, for God's sake, man, I introduced you—and for your own good! Some one had to blast you out of your shell; and if any one could do it, it would have to be Miss Susan Chesterton."

"And what does that mean, pray tell?" asked Darcy.

"Lord, man, are you blind? She could make a dead man shoot out of his coffin with the crook of a finger! And, if she had any reason, she's probably the woman who'd give it a try," he added in an aside. "At any rate, she's a lady I've been after for years, but she won't have me. She would have done you, though, and what do you do? You give her a tongue lashing in some shop, if I got the story right from Cavendish! Scolded her like a scullery maid in front of the whole world! Who would believe it? What were you thinking, man? You cannot treat a woman like Miss

Chesterton this way; half the men in Parliament have taken a run at her. I have personal knowledge of two duels fought over her, and young Carruthers blew his brains out when she left him! She'll have none of *me* now, that's certain." He turned to leave, but stopped at the door: "Hate to say it of me own blood, but you're an idiot, Darcy — that's all: a complete idiot."

With that he swept out, leaving Darcy to stare blankly at the door and shake his head — but whether at his cousin, or at his own folly, was debateable. What had he been thinking, indeed? Looking back, he could only admit to himself that there had been very little thinking involved; and after he had chided Bingley for failing to use his "higher powers"! His spirits sank lower each time he thought of it; he turned back to his book and attempted to read, but he could not keep his mind in order: his thoughts kept returning to the affair with Miss Chesterton. His reputation must suffer, there could be no doubt of that. And certainly, if his name was the subject of conversation at one club, it could not fail to be mentioned at others — including his own, no doubt; this early example of how his misjudgement of Miss Chesterton would sink his standing added itself to his general torment over the affair.

He cursed himself again and again for having been so blind: from the very first evening, the reactions of both Miss Bingley and Miss Hartsbury should have warned him — and the assurance of Miss Chesterton's putting herself forward to ask for a dance was certainly untoward, if not actually improper; and it now occurred to him to realise that there was also a decided indelicacy in her enquiries about his relations with Miss Bingley; yet she had spoken of modesty! At every turn he could now see signs and portents as to her character: the meeting — was it accidental? — at the furniture warehouse, and the merchant's obvious dislike of the lady, now brought into focus by subsequent events; her brazen attempt to be alone with him at the pianoforte; being so forward as to invite him to her hosts' party, and, God above! —her attempt at outright seduction that evening! Then her lies to "subdue" him the day after! Even Delacroix had tried to warn him, although he had not seen it at the time. He could not excuse himself for his blindness. And now, his name was being bandied about by men of George's stripe—in disdain! —his cousin George, looking down on *him*!

The only good that did come out of it was that it cleared the air between Perkins and himself; yet his man hardly knew how to be happy for it: he felt for Darcy's disgrace almost as if it were his own.

Some of his worst distress during this trying time involved Miss Elizabeth Bennet: in his afflictions, his thoughts repeatedly turned to her, with deepest mortification at how she must view this debacle if it were known to her; he was very sensible of having dishonoured his feelings for her, even if she could have no knowledge of it. How he ever could have thought Miss Chesterton resembled Elizabeth in any way was now beyond his comprehension; the two women were so far distant in character, in honesty, in decency—in all those things, in fact, most violated by even the slight interest he had shown Miss Chesterton—that his heart railed at him when he demanded of himself how he could have fallen prey to a creature such as Susan Chesterton, after having known a lady such as Elizabeth. He could only hope that no whisper of his disgrace would ever reach her ears.

Yet again, he saw how little to be trusted was the heart, and the realisation that even *he* was not beyond being taken in, while it allowed him to forgive his father to a degree, still frustrated and angered him. His heart did whisper to him that Elizabeth would not have deceived him so, but his rational side directly retorted that, as she was not to be his either, her superiority could offer no comfort; indeed, it only made his frustration the worse, from knowing the cure to be beyond reach.

A day or two afterwards, he happened to overhear his Aunt Eleanor in a low-voiced conversation with an old friend who had stopped in to visit; the words "Susan Chesterton" came to his ears, and he hastened away down the hallway. Later in the day, though, Lady Andover came by his library, merely to pat his shoulder and kiss the top of his head with a murmured: "My dear Fitzwilliam: you are a good boy." Her approving tone confused Darcy, but she never mentioned it again. There were few such moments of reprieve, however; Darcy's revulsion at suddenly finding himself the darling of the *ton* was beyond expression; he received dozens of invitations from people he had never heard of, and not a few from people of whom he had heard far too much. He abhorred the degenerate fascination implicit in these invitations; the only reason these people had any interest in him now, was because of the scandal he had embroiled himself in; and this worst sort of celebrity was exactly the kind of indignity from which he had always sought to hold himself aloof.

Such were the gentle murmurs of Darcy's heart, and he had little else to divert himself with through the long nights of that dark winter month: the men of his family had gone their separate ways on the Monday following his *contretemps* in the coffee house; Georgiana had gone with her Aunt Eleanor to Bath to visit relatives from Lady Andover's side of the family; and Bingley returned to his house in Manchester Square to spare his friend from constant worry over his low spirits — with the avowed reason being "to attend to the details of my bankruptcy". There was little business to attend to, and Darcy's temper was not such as to tempt him to accept social engagements from his acquaintance; and certainly he had little impetus to seek out new friends. With nothing to do, and no one for whom he need keep up appearances, the weeks passed with him becoming more and more reclusive, and whole days would go by wherein he would scarcely stir out of his library. He was glad Georgiana was absent, for he had no wish for her to see him thus. She would fret, and would probably try to offer assistance he could as well do without. But the long days of silence eventually began to wear on him, and, with Georgiana expected to return the second week of February, he knew he needed to be in better control of himself before her arrival.

He decided he was in need of a change of scene: he therefore determined to venture out to see Pender in Oxford; he left London on a clear Wednesday morning in the last week of January. On his arrival, the Christ Church porter greeted him with the deference and pleasure due a respected Member, and directly showed him to lodgings that were little different from the ones he had occupied as an undergraduate. He enquired whether Pender might be in College.

"Aye, Sir, the Master is in—would you be wantin' 'im?"

"Yes, Conyers, I should be obliged if you could let me know when I might be able to go round to see him."

"Aye, Sir, that I shall."

Rather than receive any message, however, Darcy was agreeably surprised by Pender himself appearing at his door shortly later that afternoon.

"Darcy, my dear fellow!" cried Pender, "What a pleasant surprise! What brings you here? Have you come to improve your knowledge of women and beer?" he asked, recollecting his jest at Delacroix's.

Shaking hands with his friend, Darcy made a derisive noise and said, "I *wish* you might help with my understanding of the former—but I am certain I can count on your assistance with the latter."

"That you can, my boy, that you can." Pender laughed, clapping a hand on Darcy's shoulder. He looked quizzically into Darcy's face, adding: "But I can see that you are in need of enlightenment on *something*; well, if it is women, I am confident that improving your acquaintance with beer will give the impression that your understanding of women is improved."

"Doubtless — but what about something more than just an impression?"

"Ah — There, I fear, we are at a loss. One might as well expect to grasp the mind of God as to understand the other sex."

"Well, then, what use are you?" Darcy grumbled with feigned disgust.

"None whatsoever, in this matter," Pender admitted cheerfully. "But I *will* stand you the first round."

They left through the lodge, where Pender told the porter he might be back late and not to keep the gates open. Pender took Darcy some little way into town, to a pub visited infrequently by any but Senior Members. They settled into a back corner and Darcy's mentor ordered food and two large pitchers of ale. Darcy looked at him in some surprise, but Pender said, "Nothing induces thirst like a discussion involving women — nor requires more...liquidity of thought." Pender smiled brightly and raised his glass. "A toast?"

"Well, then...To understanding women."

Pender shook his head dubiously, but said, "Well enough. — To understanding women...God help all men. Now then, Darcy, tell us a tale: what has brought you all this way to see a broken-down old schoolteacher?"

"Merely that said supernumerary, superannuated academic has one of the finest minds I know."

"Then you had best cultivate a larger acquaintance," scoffed Pender.

"Nonsense; and who was it taught me about the deception inherent in false modesty?" the older man shrugged sheepishly, and let the impeachment stand.

"And some one also once told me that the most efficient way to learn, was to ask the one who knows the most."

"Good Lord, boy, if you think I know much about this, you are very much mistaken. The only men I have ever known who claimed to understand women, knew even less about that topic than they did about themselves. But never mind; we shall give it our best." He topped off their mugs. "And to that end, toss that off and let me hear your story."

Darcy launched into his topic: his difficulties with the previous Season in London, his meeting with Elizabeth in Hertfordshire (although he carefully held back her name), and finishing with his recent embarrassment with Miss Chesterton. They were beginning on their third mugs by the time he had finished.

When he had done, Pender said, "Well, Darcy, you *have* had quite the time...hold on, though—would you by any chance be speaking of Miss *Susan* Chesterton? Light hair, grey eyes, devilishly attractive smile?"

"Yes; you know her?" Darcy was surprised.

"Knew her," Pender corrected. "Her father is Master of Wadham."

"Yes," Darcy confirmed, "So Delacroix said. Have you had difficulties with her, too?"

His friend nodded with a wry expression. "Lord, yes; I should have known she would end up in Town—if not *on* the town. Yes, I did: the little beast even tried to climb into my lap once," he said.

"Where's the harm in that? Darcy asked, mystified.

"She was fifteen at the time, and I was standing up," Pender said dryly. He shook his head. "You got off easily, Darcy. Her father nearly had to drive her away at sword's point, before she ruined his reputation completely and got him thrown out of his post. She even flirted with the old Provost, and he was fourscore and three—the old dog."

The two were silent a time, reflecting on their respective associations with Miss Chesterton. Pender came to himself first: thumping the table with his hand, he said, "To start with, you may put your mind at ease concerning the Chesterton woman; as the man who turned her down, and gave her a good, public basting, your reputation can only increase; women will adore you for it, and men will wonder with great envy who you have in your pocket that could make you reject such a morsel."

Darcy, who had never before seen any possible good in the affair, now allowed a smile to appear. His aunt's gentle benediction in the library suddenly made sense. "That might be true, might it not? Heavens, Vincent...that does make me feel better."

"Good lad," said the older gentleman, taking a healthy swig from his mug. "But, here now, let me understand this Hertfordshire lass of yours; if I understand you, you feel that, while beyond reproach personally, she cannot be considered as marriageable on the basis that her mother is less than desirable?"

"'Less than desirable'?" Darcy answered back. "A carthorse is 'less than desirable' as a hunter — this is asking a pony to jump a grown man over an eight-foot fence."

"Methinks you might exaggerate, there, old son. But, if I mistake not, your concern is that it would be unwise to bring her blood into your family, yes? — but whatever makes you think that heritability works amongst mankind?"

Surprised, Darcy looked at him questioningly.

"Come, come, boy; how many breeding trials have you seen?"

"Using the modern Dishley methods? Dozens, I should say — possibly hundreds: sheep, horses, dogs, cattle... But husbandry has always been practiced at Pemberley; I have seen notes from my grandfather's time..."

Pender broke in: "Yes, yes — now, how many of the offspring were actually superior stock? Half? A quarter?"

"Usually less," Darcy acknowledged.

"And that was where the sire and dam were each carefully selected to produce all the desired traits, was it not?"

"Certainly."

"Then how do you imagine that mankind, so much richer in nature and complex in behaviour, can be expected to follow the patterns of heredity more closely than farm animals?"

Darcy, startled, stopped to consider. "But our entire society is based on family lines," he objected. "Heraldry, bloodlines, successions and heirs of the body: how does one overlook that?"

"Darcy, can you truly be that blind?" Darcy again looked at his mentor in surprise. Pender went on: "Can you really imagine for an instant that our beloved King George is the pinnacle of all mankind? Yet the Hanoverian line is one of the most ancient noble lines in Europe. And do but consider for a moment the ruination the Hapsburgs have brought upon themselves — ugliest people in Christendom, and entirely lacking certain of the most fundamental biological functions required to sustain life!"

Darcy was taken aback. "I had never followed that particular line of reasoning," he admitted. "But it should follow, should not it? If bloodlines are the controlling factor in man's abilities and accomplishments, then the most carefully conserved bloodlines — like the royal lines — ought to produce the most accomplished persons."

"Yes, undoubtedly," Pender said dryly. "But before we wander off into anything that might smack of treason, let us go back to livestock: now, what happens when dogs are bred too closely to their own pedigree?"

"You usually start to see weaknesses in the line: nervy animals, debility in the joints, decreased lifespan — that sort of thing."

"Precisely. And what does one do when this occurs?"

"One breeds from out of the line to reintroduce strength. It is the most common way to improve the breed..." Darcy's voice trailed off.

"The light begins to dawn, does it?" Pender asked, sitting back in his chair. "Now, if we speak of larger groups of animals — herds, say — how are they best improved?"

"By introducing superior stock over and over," Darcy mused, thinking back over the years he had been doing just that, and his father before that, and his father before him..."Over the years the whole herd improves in all manner of ways."

Pender said nothing further for some moments while Darcy was silent, thinking over what his mentor had said; there was undoubtedly much truth in what he was proposing, but... "What you are suggesting is all well and good, Pender, and I concede that I rather agree, now you have given me the idea, but the fact remains that society is what it is; for me to marry Elizabeth...the lady...would disgrace my family."

"So your lady has a name, has she? Well, the name at least is a royal one."

Darcy fixed his friend with an admonitory gaze: if one were to stand in any hamlet in the kingdom and shout the name, it would bring no less than three females of varying ages out of their cottages. "Yes, Vincent, I thank you; terribly helpful."

"One does one's best," said that gentleman with a grin.

"But still," Darcy went on more seriously, "as I am the head of the Darcy family now, it is particularly incumbent on me to protect the family name."

"Of course; but are you certain you have properly assessed the damage your marriage to the lady would entail? After all, you would hardly be the first, or the highest in standing, to have married 'beneath' him. If the lady has brains enough and bowels, which I am sure she does, I do not think you need worry."

Darcy wished he could be convinced, but there was, in addition, one other argument that he fought with in his private struggles: "Pender…do you know the tale of King Cophetua and the beggar maid?"

"Of course: he rejects every noble lady in his kingdom only to fall hopelessly in love with a beggar woman, naked and starving, and marries her. Your point being, then, that your Elizabeth is a beggar lady?"

"Hardly," said Darcy in driest tones. "No—ever since I first heard the story, though, I always felt that the girl must have got pretty short shrift from every one around her, and for the rest of her life."

Pender tilted his head, considering. "You have a point, there," he said. "And a sharp, nasty one, I admit."

"So what should we do, if we were to marry? —go abroad and live like pariahs, or try to face down all of London? My own family would have difficulty countenancing her: what about the rest of "good" society? How might she fare in London? Constantly having to excuse her family and defend herself against snobs, fops, and fools: there would be no end to it."

"Come, Darcy, it is not as bad as all that; there *are* good-hearted people in Society, you know."

"Not many, in my experience," Darcy said bitterly.

"And you know, I *have* met your uncle, Lord Andover; I can hardly imagine he would snub a girl of your choosing."

"True—but you have *not* met my Aunt Catherine; she would make our lives as damnable as she could." Darcy ran down the list again in his mind; Georgiana, Edmund, and likely Uncle Jonathan and Aunt Eleanor—he trusted he might count on their support, but would that be enough to face down all of Society? He could not very well bury Elizabeth in Derbyshire for the rest of her life. There was

Charles, of course; and his marriage to Elizabeth would probably lead to another, making them brothers; but that would also mean a near and constant relation with his sisters; and while Miss Bingley would never be disobliging to *him*, what might not she say to Elizabeth when he was absent? As Bingley had said himself, no one was safe from her tongue. He was sure Elizabeth could stand up to her, of course, but how would her connections fare, with their constant improprieties...?

In spite of his wishes to the contrary, Darcy could not contrive to convince himself: for one thing, his belief in proper behaviour as the only acceptable behaviour was a cornerstone of his existence and a cornerstone of his family's standing—it was beyond him to disregard it in this matter; for another, he would be offering Elizabeth a poor future, indeed, if all she could look forward to was prejudice and disapprobation. He shook his head despairingly. "No, Pender, I have been through it a thousand times, and I still cannot see it. The Beggar Queen had no one to defend but herself; the lady in question needs no defence—in fact, I pity the man, or the woman, indeed, who could actually stir her to anger—but there *is* no defending her mother, not to mention some of her sisters; and then, my own family...no, it is impossible." He stared morosely into his nearly empty mug.

Pender looked at his young friend silently for some moments. "So, having arrived at this same conclusion a thousand times, why do you yet ponder the problem?" he asked, not unfeelingly. "Could it be that your heart will not listen to reason? How extraordinary!"

"Do not mock me, I pray you Vincent," Darcy said unhappily. "I find I cannot jest on this subject."

"I know, lad...I know," Pender said with sincere sympathy. "T'were better an' you could: then there might be hope."

"How do you mean?"

141

"Because, as any one who reads Shakespeare knows, comedies end in marriage." He stood and brought Darcy to his feet, saying, "Come along then, lad; let us home to bed."

Chapter Sixteen

*D*arcy spent the next day in college, renewing acquaintance with some of the Fellows he had known when he was up, but aside from two hours wandering dispiritedly through the Bodleian in search of inspiration, he did not pursue the topic which had brought him thither. In his quarters in the afternoon, however, Pender came again to visit, bringing with him a student named William Ackerman; Mr. Ackerman was currently at the top of his class and set to graduate in May. Pender presented him as a very worthy candidate for a position, should Darcy happen to have one, or know of one. After Mr. Ackerman, whom Darcy found a very pleasing young scholar, had left, Pender staid behind for a word with Darcy.

"Well, Darcy, what do you make of the lad?"

"He seems very able—brilliant, in fact. I am sure I can find something for him."

"Excellent," Pender beamed. He looked at Darcy a moment. "Truthfully, that was not the only reason I wished for you to meet him."

Darcy looked the question, and Pender continued: "His history is most illuminating: his parents were drunkards; they died in a spunging house when he was but a child."

"Indeed? Amazing."

"Yes. The rector in his parish took pity on the boy and brought him up at his expense. But when he discovered the lad's abilities—the boy had taught himself to read before going to the rector, and was keeping the parish books at twelve—he contacted us; I found the boy a sponsor, and here we are."

"A fascinating story, but I had no real need to hear it; his abilities speak for themselves."

"They do indeed: that is the point, my boy." Pender looked expectantly at Darcy.

"Ah, another facet of our debate," said Darcy. "That brilliance is to be made useful, no matter where found."

The older gentleman shrugged. "Can you deny it? As you said, his abilities speak for themselves—and who would gainsay them?"

"I know, Pender, and I should be the very last person to deny Miss B...Elizabeth's worth, but still, her connections..."

"Actually, Darcy, I was thinking about that, too: a repellent mother-in-law would do wonders for your reputation, you know; as it is, your life is just a little too golden to suit the notions of most people, and some disobliging relations would make you a much more approachable figure amongst your acquaintance."

"An embarrassing mother-in-law would *improve* my reputation, is that what you are saying? Fascinating, Pender—truly: a superb and novel thesis. But, at any rate, I am not afraid for *my* reputation; it is the lady I fear for most."

"So your deepest concern is for how she might fare as your wife? Darcy, do you really think the lady would object to the match on the grounds that she would have a difficult life?" Darcy made no answer; when one looked at it from that angle, it did seem to make less sense.

"Are you certain this has nothing to do with you?" his friend queried. "After all, you, too, would be called on to excuse your choice of wife. You could, when it comes down to it, marry easily enough among our first families: your own family does have high standing and a proud history, and your connections would enable you to marry wherever you wished."

"...pride will always be under good regulation." The words echoed in Darcy's mind: was he regulating his pride, or was it contrariwise? He found no answer to the question. He said, "Yes, we do have a proud history, and one I am loath to sully."

"Then why have you not married any of the women who have doubtless crossed your path, or even thrown themselves at you?"

Rather than answer the question, Darcy asked one in return: "Well, what about you, Vincent? Why have you never married?"

"I simply never met the right girl."

"And I can but answer the same."

He returned to London early the following day, little better than when he had left it. The trip seemed long: long enough that he had time to add considerably to his tally of the times he tried to come to some resolution of his problem. It must be said that in this endeavour Darcy was not as fully cognizant of his own habits of thought as he wished to believe; the one factor that he consistently failed to account for in all his deliberations and debates was his devotion to logic: it rendered him incapable of accepting *opinions* in support of his own inclination, or the reverse; opinions and convention could not be argued either for or against. What he wanted, what he sought—although he could not realise it—was a logical, well-reasoned argument as to why he *could not* marry Elizabeth, that he might shred it and prove it wrong; he required a solid, rational position he could defeat in a clear, definitive manner, and be done; as he could find none, he was unable to reach the conclusion he wished, or, indeed, any conclusion at all.

Finally, as he was pulling into Grosvenor Square, Darcy left off his inner soliloquy, and reminded himself of his own advice to Georgiana: even the deepest wounds must heal in time.

Yet there was surely too little time for healing before Georgiana returned home on a Tuesday in the middle of February. Darcy did most diligently try to hide from his sister how low were his spirits, but her customary concern and attention to him made it impossible to keep it from her it completely. She tried not to trouble him with her solicitude, but she was most considerate of his needs: indeed, had she been able, she would have arranged matters so that he would never have had to turn a hand; but Darcy was insistent that she attend to her own cares, and let him sort through his own. With her great respect for him, she did as he bade, but she conspired frequently with Perkins and Mrs. Annesley to determine if they might not be able to do something to ease his days.

Darcy was not blind to this, and, while he appreciated the attempt from his heart, he earnestly endeavoured to persuade her to desist. "I know you mean well, Dearest," he told her, "but surely you have better uses for your time than to try to cosset and cozen me out of my ill-humours."

Georgiana smiled gently and told him, "Once, in a letter written by someone on whose opinions I feel I can rely, I was told that one of the most important things a family does is to help its members when they have been ill-treated by the world. I believe the phrase he used was 'pernicious influences.' He also said there could be no imposition or obligation from such assistance. So, if you will allow me, I shall continue to be family to you." Darcy took her hand and kissed it, and no longer sought to resist her efforts to bring him ease. But while she could soothe, she could not cure; his heart continued to wound him, and his thoughts could light on nothing that brought him peace.

To his misfortune, his conversation with Pender had served mostly to bring Elizabeth to mind with even greater frequency, making him all the more sensible of her virtues, and the perfection of her features. He was daily plagued by her absence: never in his life had his mind been so little his own; he had heard of one losing one's heart, and thought he had understood its meaning; but he now discovered what our best minds and most prolific writers on the subject have conspicuously failed to mention: that losing one's heart and losing one's mind were one and the same.

In his deliberations he would take occasional excursions to Bingley and *his* wounded heart. The outings of the two friends had grown fewer as the weeks passed, but Darcy's sense of duty towards Bingley would as often force him to carry his friend off to some social affair as Bingley's did for him. Neither of them, however, seemed to benefit much from these diversions, and nothing but his obligations towards his friend would have induced Darcy to engage in any kind of entertainment.

The following is illustrative of their respective moods during this trying period: early in March, Darcy had accepted an invitation for the two of them to attend an evening gathering at Miss Hartsbury's home; a small ball and cold collation was the sum total of the scheme, but Darcy knew from previous experience that it would be executed in the highest style, and with complete propriety, which appealed to him especially at that time. It is a telling point that the friends decided to walk the short distance from Grosvenor Square to Hill Street, where Miss Hartsbury lived, rather than take the carriage; the weather was fine for the time of year, it is true, but the consideration that privately prompted each was that it would be faster to walk home, than to wait for their carriage to be brought round from the mews, which was small for the neighbourhood and likely to be crowded and slow. They elected to go down South Audley, rather than cut through St. George's in the dark. As they walked along, neither had a great deal to say; each one, likely, imagining how much more agreeable the evening might be if the lady of his choosing were by his side.

Miss Hartsbury greeted them with her usual effusive energy, and seemed particularly glad of Darcy's presence; he had not seen her since Delacroix's party in December.

"Mr. Darcy! And Mr. Bingley! So delighted to see you!" said she, laying a hand on Darcy's arm after his bow; she drew breath to launch into one of her accustomed fusillades of speech, but brought herself up short as she recalled her duties as hostess. "We shall talk later," she assured them, and turned her smiles to the next guest.

Later, shortly before the ball was to begin, she came to find them. The two were standing off to one side, as Darcy often did; but Bingley's presence next to him was a new and rather worrisome development. "Here you are!" Miss Hartsbury cried, coming up to them. "Do you dance? Not you, Mr. Darcy, of course, but Mr. Bingley: can I find you a partner? I am to open the dancing with my uncle. It is to be Sir Roger de Coverly, as we all know it, you know. I like a reel to begin, myself; so lively and amusing: do not you agree?" at this she stopped, beaming at them and blinking.

"Indeed," Darcy replied. "But you need not trouble yourself; we shall be perfectly all right…"

"No, but please, I insist," cried Miss Hartsbury.

Darcy, who was suffering particularly that evening from a maudlin distemper that left him wishing to help any one and every one, given he could not help himself, determined within himself that he would see his friend enjoy the evening. He looked out over the company; spying one particularly lovely lady, he gently took Miss Hartsbury's arm and turned her from Bingley. "Might I ask you to introduce my friend to that young lady?" he said, speaking softly. "She in the pink gown, and pearls." Miss Hartsbury, seeing to whom he referred, turned instantly and linked her arm though his friend's; Bingley, surprised at this sudden attack, could not but consent to her carrying him across the room. Darcy watched as the introduction was made, and as his hostess led the couple to the dance floor, placing them just below herself and her uncle.

He continued to watch, and, to his pleasure, he saw Bingley dance with increasing spirit. He also noticed a young gentleman, of undistinguished bearing but an intelligent expression, of an age between Bingley and himself, watching the dance intently. At first Darcy thought the gentleman was watching Bingley and his partner, but came to realise he was, instead, observing their hostess with considerable attention.

At the end of the dance, Bingley remained with his partner, which relieved Darcy's mind considerably; the more so when, as the musicians struck up for the second, he saw Bingley ask the lady's hand again. Miss Hartsbury stood to one side as the set was forming, smiling encouragingly to all her friends: Darcy saw the young man he had noted before, move as though in her direction, but his nerve appeared to fail him and he stepped back away. Darcy was then prompted, both out of gratitude to Miss Hartsbury for introducing his friend so obligingly, and out of a sympathetic compassion from having seen his hostess stand out of many dances in the past, to step to her and ask her hand for this one. She accepted delightedly, and with no little surprise; Darcy could not help but see that the young man looked at them both with interest, and something like alarm. As he observed the gentleman's expression of discontent, he decided to make an attempt to see if there might be cause to help the two young people along, moved by that same peculiar distemper which led him to propose a partner for Bingley.

"Mr. Darcy," his hostess said happily as they took their places, "you have made my reputation this night! Every one knows how you dislike dancing."

"My dear Miss Hartsbury," Darcy demurred, "I must believe that a substantial exaggeration: why on Earth would any one know or care whether I like to dance or not?"

"I fear, Sir, you do not do yourself justice; people *will* notice these things, and if for no other reason, your position assures that you will be remarked upon particularly."

Darcy smiled ruefully with a deprecating gesture. "I have certainly been made aware that those interested in such things might like to gossip about my activities around Town; but surely only my friends would care about something so trivial as my predilection for dancing, or its reverse."

"I assure you, Mr. Darcy, that to those among my own sex, dancing is no trivial affair. Who dances with whom, how often, and which dances, occupies a good deal of our energies the day after a dance, you may believe me. You must not think dancing trivial at all, you know; indeed, this dance with you will have given me a material advantage over my friends for the next twelvemonth, at least."

Darcy laughed, "Well, if that be so, I am delighted that you will have benefitted from our dance to such a degree; for myself, I am content to enjoy it for what it is: a pleasant interlude with my hostess." Just then the musicians began the dance, and they were forced to break off their conversation for the opening. During the first movements, Darcy caught sight of the same young gentleman looking at him rather apprehensively, reminding him of his intended object for the dance. When next they had a chance to speak, Darcy enquired of his partner, "Miss Hartsbury, may I ask: who is that young man?" he nodded in the gentleman's direction. "The gentleman seated behind, to your left."

Miss Hartsbury peered around, squinting in the direction Darcy had indicated. She turned back, blinking rapidly. "Oh! That is Sir Neville...Sir Neville Canham."

"He seems an upright sort," Darcy offered tentatively.

"Do you think so, Mr. Darcy? Yes, I believe him to be...I have had that thought...that is, I do not know him well, of course, but he does have an air, do not you think?"

"I do," said Darcy in an approving tone. "He carries himself well." He allowed himself this slight overstatement as the gentleman was, at that moment, seated very alertly as he sought to observe the dancing, and Darcy's partner in particular.

"Yes," agreed Miss Hartsbury, looking back around to view Sir Neville again. "Yes he does, does he not?"

"Where does he come from?"

"We met in Bath…that is, I was in company with his sister last autumn, and we were introduced, you know; we may have even danced once—though I cannot really recall; he dances but seldom, I know," she said, looking away. Given the fact that her countenance and air were usually so open and easy of interpretation, Darcy construed this studied ambivalence to be a definite sign of approval, and possibly even interest. And, to his eye, Sir Neville certainly did not view his appropriation of Miss Hartsbury's time with equanimity. Darcy considered: if there was in fact a mutual attraction between them, he was sure that Miss Hartsbury would not be timid about pursuing it, were she made aware of it. But from what he could tell of Sir Neville, that awareness might never be forthcoming; he therefore determined to stir the gentleman to action. The better to spur him, as the set swept them up again, Darcy put on his best airs for the dance, and he flattered himself that he did not acquit himself poorly; his partner, to be sure, seemed quite pleased with his efforts. Darcy could see Sir Neville's concern rising through the dance, and believed his scheme to be proceeding well. Unsuspecting, Miss Hartsbury's enjoyment of their dance together was very evident on her face, which Darcy hoped would prove an additional provocation, and compel Sir Neville to act upon his inclinations.

Mid-way through the set, after an unusually long pause in the conversation, by Miss Hartsbury's standards, during which she seemed to be resolving some measure within herself, she took the opportunity to address him in a serious manner: "Mr. Darcy, I have wanted to say...I feel I should ask your forgiveness."

"*My* forgiveness?" asked he in wonder. "Whatever for?"

"For not having given you warning—about Miss Chesterton."

Darcy, startled by this, hastily gave her his assurance: "Goodness, no—My dear Miss Hartsbury, please: I berate myself almost daily for having failed to benefit from the very obvious distaste you displayed on finding yourself in her presence; if I had any wit at all, I could have needed nothing further."

Miss Hartsbury's countenance fairly shone with pleasure and relief. "Then you do not blame me?"

"It would never cross my mind, I promise you" he said.

"I heard something of what passed between you at *Fortuno's*," she ventured, her expression one of anxious concern compounded with curiosity.

"*Fortuno's*? Oh, the coffee house; yes, I dare say all of London heard something of that day," Darcy acknowledged with some embarrassment. "That gossip I mentioned..."

Miss Hartsbury nodded sympathetically. "I have to say," she informed him in a reassuring tone, "you are quite the hero with some of the ladies of my acquaintance, you know. With every one, in fact, who ever knew Miss Chesterton. They quite envy me your coming here to-night, as you have declined invitations from several of them this Season: imagine it—they envy *me*" she marvelled artlessly. "And when they hear you asked me to dance..." She stopped; then, colouring, she said, "Well, I believe you have secured my reputation for life; on my honour, you have."

Darcy smiled at this, amused that she should imagine a dance with him could be the means of affording her any sort of distinction amongst her acquaintance. He scoffed good naturedly, "I am sure you cannot be serious, but I thank you; if this be heroism, though, you may have it. Every titled reprobate in London, *and* his wife, are panting after my acquaintance now."

Miss Hartsbury sniggered in a candid, if somewhat indecorous manner. "Well, I believe I *was* serious, you know, but you have cured me of that. And, my dear Sir, be assured: you will always find refuge here; my door is always open to you—and they unquestionably do not wish *my* acquaintance." She gave Darcy a little *moue* of self-pity, then laughed at herself. Darcy bowed his thanks for this gentle indication of her friendship. The dance at this point caught them up once more, postponing their conversation yet again.

They danced amicably for some time without saying much of import. But towards the end of the set, Darcy, noticing the young gentleman from Bath looking at them with an altogether discontented look, observed to his partner: "Do you know, Miss Hartsbury, I believe Sir Neville Canham has been watching us; is that at all likely, do you think, or do I imagine it?"

Miss Hartsbury glanced Sir Neville's way, who, starting, instantly turned his gaze from her; Miss Hartsbury turned back, blushing. "I am sure you must be mistaken, Mr. Darcy: I can think of no reason whatever why he might be observing our dance."

"No, of course," Darcy assured her, privately amused. "I was undoubtedly mistaken." On seeing her look slightly disappointed at this, however, he said as if musing to himself: "I would have taken my oath he was, though." Miss Hartsbury brightened again, and Darcy was persuaded he had fulfilled his charge to himself.

At the end of the dance, after releasing Miss Hartsbury, he was highly gratified to see the young gentleman approach their hostess; that he asked her hand for the next was apparent, and Darcy was rewarded by seeing the elated look that crossed her face as he left her. The warmth this private moment of tenderness provided was, however, short lived: it was soon replaced by a subdued and wistful envy; he did not wish their happiness less, of course, but he would have risen to a similar elevation of spirit, if he could.

He looked round for Bingley, and found him once again standing by a corner of the room, deeply engaged, or so it appeared, in studying the musician's feet. He secured two glasses from a footman and took one to his friend, they drank in silence for a bit; as the musicians struck up for the next set, Bingley said, "I suppose it would look bad if we left as early as this?"

Darcy looked around in time to see Sir Neville arrive to claim their hostess's hand; her happy smile and faint blush told him all he needed to know, and all he thought he could support; he turned back to Bingley, saying, "I am sure Miss Hartsbury will forgive us for taking an early leave. I, too, should be just as well pleased to be on our way." So saying, the two unobtrusively gathered up their coats and began the quiet walk home.

Chapter Seventeen

*M*arch passed slowly away. Darcy's struggles continued, his thoughts chasing a weary circle from Elizabeth, to the demands of propriety, and back to Elizabeth, but at least his fears for his reputation where Miss Chesterton was concerned were gone: Pender had done that much for him. But the damage done his self-esteem, and the deep and lasting doubts as to the reliance he might place on the heart as a guide, made his ruminations tiresome in the extreme. His loathing of Miss Chesterton increased each time he revisited the matter: as dishonesty was always a source of abhorrence to him, such calculated dishonesty, on such trivial provocation, angered him all the more; Elizabeth's generous, forthright, and open temperament was rendered almost sublime in comparison with Miss Chesterton's deceitful, licentious, and contemptible character.

Over time, however, Darcy gradually learnt to quell his sentiments and school his thoughts. By the end of March his regard for Elizabeth, while neither gone nor forgotten, was become submerged in his daily activities, a part of his normal existence. His life settled back into its accustomed rhythms of family and affairs, duties and diversions. Only when his attention would fix on Elizabeth would his regrets expand to discompose him: but he was becoming better able to avoid those moments, consciously turning his thoughts aside when they would threaten to remain too long on her.

Miss Bingley contrived to keep Manchester Square lively and full of entertainments, in spite of her brother's marked lack of enthusiasm; she even managed to persuade her brother to dance occasionally at her gatherings, although Darcy had largely fallen back into his former disgust of the pastime. Aside from these gatherings, however, Darcy was very little seen in company.

Bingley was, seemingly, mostly returned to his former good humour, but Darcy's narrow observation of his friend enabled him to see the occasional symptom of unhappiness: moments wherein Bingley experienced a fleeting lowness of spirit that he worked hard to keep hidden. Seeing this through the lens of his own regrets, Darcy knew how to pity his friend, but not how to mend him.

In April Darcy was required to visit his Aunt Catherine in Kent, accompanied as usual by his cousin, Colonel Fitzwilliam. It was a yearly visit, begun when the gentlemen were quite young; in the beginning it was a family custom, a chance made for them by their elders to be with their cousin Anne. Since his father's death, it had fallen to Darcy to oversee his aunt's affairs, and he spent some weeks each spring reviewing Rosings' books prior to the planting season. This year he was of two minds about his visit: what he was accustomed to seeing as no more than a duty, now at least offered some diversion from being in Town; yet diverting was not a term one normally associated with his Aunt Catherine. He hardly knew whether he should be glad to go, or to regret that his life was become such that he could see this journey as anything other than a most disagreeable chore.

Early in the morning on the first Monday of April, therefore, Darcy went to pick Colonel Fitzwilliam up at his barracks in Knightsbridge. Colonel Fitzwilliam waved as he emerged from the Governor's House, turned to give some instructions to the corporal on duty, and strode over to join Darcy in the coach.

'Well, cousin, say good-bye to the joys of Town life," Darcy told him lightly. "It will be some time before we will know good company again."

"I thank you for the reminder," Colonel Fitzwilliam replied dryly. "I had nearly forgotten."

"At least Aunt Catherine does not view you as Cousin Anne's intended," Darcy responded with some asperity. For the last five years, since his cousin Anne had turned eighteen, Lady Catherine had every year been more pressing on the subject of their nuptials; when her daughter was born, she and Darcy's mother had fixed it between them that their children should marry, and Lady Catherine never wavered from that intention.

"True—very true," grinned the Colonel. "I do feel better, indeed. My thanks."

Darcy snorted. "So glad to be of service," said he. "Where is your mount?" Colonel Fitzwilliam was accustomed to bringing one or two horses with him into Kent, as Lady Catherine's manor afforded several outstanding chases, which offered the Colonel a good excuse to be out of the house.

Colonel Fitzwilliam's face hardened: "Poor brute came up lame two days ago—near-fore hoof is hot. I *told* the Stable Master there was too much grain in the feed—if he founders I shall have that man's hide. Be lucky if he is fit to ride by the time we get back. If that animal is not fully fit by mid-May, I shall have the beef-wit up for court martial!"

It amused Darcy to hear his cousin become so very military in tone; normally there was no more gentle-spoken person in the whole of his acquaintance. "Why mid-May?"

Colonel Fitzwilliam looked up at his cousin with a smile. "I have my orders, Darcy!" he confided. "I go over in June."

"Fitzwilliam, congratulations!" Darcy cried. "Well done! You are sure to do well. Where do you go?"

"To Italy, up near Milan. I am to be Attaché to the Austrians there."

"Attaché?" Darcy asked in mild surprise. "You will be only an observer, then?"

"Well, that is rather vague," his cousin said with a jaunty grin. "My orders do not specify from what distance I am to observe, and it might just happen that I shall be called on to observe from rather close quarters; and if my pistol should happen to discharge accidentally in the direction of the French, well, I can hardly be blamed for that, can I?"

Darcy laughed, then looked at his cousin most seriously, "Only, see here, Edders; do try not to get yourself killed—I should take it amiss." The two friends, when speaking privately, were given to using their boyhood nicknames at times of particular feeling.

"Yes, Mother," Colonel Fitzwilliam answered with a wry expression. "Darcy, do not be an idiot; I shall be safe enough."

"I am in earnest, Fitzwilliam. You do sometimes let your enthusiasms run away with you, you know—especially when you have a good horse under you." Then Darcy's manner grew lighter. "You may allow yourself to be maimed...slightly—it will add distinction to your bearing." Colonel Fitzwilliam scoffed at this. Darcy made a show of considering him thoughtfully for a moment, "And your face could do with a bit of alteration." His cousin thumped him a blow to the chest too quick for Darcy to either block or dodge. Darcy laughed again and went on: "Yes, I think an eye-patch would look well; that would lend a bit of interest. But that is the limit. Agreed?"

The Colonel snorted. "Very well, Darcy, you have my word: I shall attempt nothing more ambitious than a slight maiming and an eye-patch."

"And so now you are off with me to Kent? Are you sure you can be spared?"

"Yes: my training duties have already been handed off, and I am my own master until the last week in May, then two or three weeks studying dispatches at the War Office, to be sure I am abreast of the full situation, and I am off. I shall go home after we leave Kent: I have to break the news to my mother."

"Did your father not do so? I assume he knows."

"Yes, he knows, but I asked him to let me tell her. It were best, coming from me, I think; I am in no great hurry about it, though, I can tell you." The two fell silent momentarily. "And so—Kent," the Colonel continued. "I shall have just time enough to become too soft to ride before going over to spend weeks in the saddle."

"Well, I dare say Lady Catherine's stock can use some exercise."

At this Colonel Fitzwilliam looked disgusted. "Ride *her* cattle? Gad! I do not see why you keep buying her good horses, Darcy; she only ruins them. Last year that hunter you got for her could barely be saddled, he was so fat and lazy. Doubt he had been ridden all year. Lord knows what she has done to him by now."

"Well, at least it will give you occupation, and a reason to be out of doors."

"I dare say that is true," Colonel Fitzwilliam allowed. "With you locked in the library all the day, it gets deucedly tiresome wandering about the house, I assure you; but if memory serves, Lady Catherine's library has a fine atlas of Europe that I could spend some time on to good effect. Other than that, I shall have to hope for decent weather, that I may be out of doors a good deal."

As the coach wove the rest of the way through London's streets down to Westminster Bridge, the gentlemen were mostly quiet, each of them occupied with their own thoughts. When they were well out into the country, after an hour or so of aimless and intermittent conversation, Darcy turned to his cousin and said, "Fitzwilliam, there is something on my mind I should like your opinion on; perhaps I had best ask it now, as you will not be so ready to hand for much longer."

"Certainly, Darcy. What is that?"

"Frankly, it is the question of making a proper marriage; does one, in this day and age, need to observe the same delicacy of generations past, when it comes to making a fitting alliance, marrying into the proper family?"

"Is this a personal concern, Darcy?" his cousin asked teazingly.

"In a manner of speaking, yes," Darcy allowed; not being prepared to introduce the subject of Elizabeth to his cousin, he had thought he might use Bingley's situation to test his cousin's thoughts on the question. "I recently secured a friend from a most unfortunate marriage; I have been congratulating myself on having saved him; but I should be glad to know that I did the right thing."

"What were your objections to the match?"

"The lady was not right for him, in many ways; I was sure his marriage would be highly injurious to his happiness, and his standing."

"He is a man of standing, then?"

"Yes, I should consider him so—about Town, at least."

"Well, I have to say I probably should have done the same. Indeed, if the lady is wrong for him, I cannot see how standing comes into it. I should have done as much for any friend, no matter his station." The Colonel, at much the same time of life as his cousin, had never had his affections seriously tried; his avowal was therefore based on the assurance inherent in the want of experience, and ignorance of how such interference was likely to be met with. Most men of any experience, of course, would sooner try to saddle and ride a mad bull than to attempt to persuade another to abandon his lady-love. Had he realised, the acceptance of such interference by Darcy's friend would have struck him as a wonderful demonstration of his regard for Darcy; Colonel Fitzwilliam, however, saw it as no more than the response any rational man would have had to such objections.

"True," Darcy agreed with equally untried innocence. He went on: "But what about the larger question of misalliances: what are the constraints, the defining factors, for passing judgement? How, precisely, is one to know which marriages are acceptable, and which are not?"

Colonel Fitzwilliam nodded as understanding dawned: "I see—this is, then, an exercise of the mind: you wish to logically define how to decide which ladies are allowable as one's spouse, and which are not?"

"Yes, if you will."

The Colonel was accustomed to his cousin's way of thinking, and, as Darcy had asked the question seriously, he gave it serious consideration. "At first glance," said he, after a moment's reflection, "there seem to be several factors: first, I suppose, there is the wealth and standing of the two families—what you might call the issues of Society: does a baronet marry a tradesman's daughter, for example. Then the issues of family—does a Whig marry into a Tory family? And, finally, the more personal issues of understanding, opinions, education, and so forth, which I would lump together as the issues of breeding."

"Excellent—well put; I agree. Now: which, if any, of the three takes precedence over the others as the first consideration for accepting, or rejecting, a given union?"

The Colonel made no immediate reply as he sought to give one priority over the others. "I am not sure," he answered at length. "Each time I ask the question, I arrive at the same problem: what if one does not care?"

"What do you mean?"

"Well, take the issue of family: your family are Whig, and hers are Tory; what if you do not care?"

"Well, of course, the couple themselves might not care; probably would not, I should think. But what of the families, their connections?"

"Again, what if one does not care? Is it one's father who objects, or a second cousin twice removed?"

"Well, say it is the father."

"Even there the same thing applies: what if the old man is a crusty, disobliging cur one would not cross the street to give greeting to?"

"But under threat of disinheritance?"

"That is rather an indelicate question to put to a second son," Fitzwilliam said sardonically. "But I stand by my answer. It all depends on how one feels about it. There does not seem to be any firm ground to stand on, in order to reach a secure position."

Darcy, in his personal debates, had been rather inclined to take the position that one's obligations to family and standing took precedence, and were quite nearly absolute. To cast aside one's responsibilities on these points would be to discredit the family's history, position, and honour; how could one injure so many others, merely for the sake of one's personal gratification? Especially if one were head of that family?

"You do not see the need to maintain the family's standing as demanding the highest sacrifice of personal inclination?" he objected. "The demands of being head of family can be of the first importance, I think. Is not that very nearly a principle—at least in English society?"

"That, of course, depends on the family, and who is its head—take my father, and his heir: with my father there could be no doubt, but we can only pray that George is spared making any personal sacrifices in the name of his family's honour. Yet who could stop him from following his inclination, if it came to the point? And that is the problem, Darcy, when seeking an absolute—one can hardly call a thing a principle when it is flouted so often and with so little ill-consequence. In the particular instance of marriage, we would have no word for a misalliance if it did not happen—and with some regularity, I might add."

This was one of the reasons Darcy enjoyed his cousin's company so; his was a sharp mind, and he was nearly as devoted to logic as Darcy was. Unfortunately, this discussion had not got Darcy much farther in his quest for a resolution to his dilemma; by Fitzwilliam's reasoning, the question could not be resolved on the basis of first principles and logic: it remained a matter of mere choice and convention, so he was left pretty much as he started. "That still does not make it proper behaviour!" he protested, coming all the way back around to his own beginning, from as far back as Netherfield.

"Well, true — but to what degree is it improper?" Colonel Fitzwilliam replied. "Does not civilisation ascribe degrees of impropriety? An act of murder is so improper as to be punishable by death: what is the punishment for an imprudent marriage, besides having to eat breakfast with one's mistake for the rest of one's life? Marrying beneath one is not illegal, after all. Eating with the fingers is improper, too, and will likely leave one wanting for dinner invitations, but I should not think any one so uncouth would be troubled by that; my meaning is, if the consequences are not sufficiently dire, there is little to deter one from following one's inclination."

"So, marrying beneath you is somewhere between murder and eating with one's fingers! Well, that certainly narrows the field of discussion." Darcy said with a wry expression.

Colonel Fitzwilliam laughed. "Very well, what would be the penalty? Say my brother marries some glazier's daughter, or the scullery maid — which, God knows, given his taste and sense of decorum, is not wholly out of the realm of possibility — what would happen?"

Darcy saw this as being somewhat akin to his own situation; he put aside his frustration to consider. "Well, the family would cast him out, I should imagine."

"Probably, as it is George — Father is close to throwing him out almost all the time; that would just about push the matter far enough. And as long as my father lived, he would likely be denied the estate, I dare say. But given that he hardly ever leaves London, I should not imagine that he would much care. And after Father's death, he would still inherit. But this is all conjecture: George is far too conceited to marry a nobody. No, my point was this: irrespective of how foolish the marriage might be, very little of import would result from it."

"I doubt his great friend Mr. Fox, and the rest of them at Boodles, would continue his acquaintance."

Colonel Fitzwilliam gave his cousin a look indicative of great disbelief, but said mildly enough, "Oh, I doubt that would be an issue, Darcy. Even the highest-placed of his friends have…well, let us say they have rather broad-minded attitudes towards the ladies. In their eyes, his only real impropriety would be to ask them to countenance the girl; if he kept her safely away from their notice, I doubt any of them would pass on his very liberal friendship. If he went on and kept mistresses, as so many among them do, they might even congratulate him on choosing a wife whose family could scarcely object to his infidelity."

Darcy's sense of propriety was highly offended by this representation of the society to which they both belonged, notwithstanding his generally poor opinion of London morals. "Good Lord, Edmund; what a cold way you have of seeing these things!"

"I spend rather more of my time in Town than you, Darcy, and may know more of its workings, I think; and the army is a favourite place for families to hide ne'er-do-well sons, so I have got to know more about that sort than I might wish."

"Hmmph…Aunt Catherine would never countenance the marriage," said Darcy pensively. This was something he had mulled on his own account.

Colonel Fitzwilliam gave a snort: "Is that a punishment? Seems rather a boon, to me." The two men laughed, but Darcy's laughter ended too soon, and he made a grimace of frustration. The Colonel, noticing, asked, "Darcy, is all well? What is wrong?"

Darcy shook his head; he knew not what to say. "It is nothing, Fitzwilliam; you must not mind me; I have not been myself of late."

"I have been aware of the fact," his cousin said. "Ever since you came back from Hertfordshire..." understanding lit his countenance. "Dirks, you *are* thinking of offering for some one, are you not?"

Darcy did not answer immediately. After staring out the window a moment, he said, "I do not know, Edders; not precisely — more like wishing I could offer."

"How do you mean?"

"I mean there is some one whom I would consider offering for, but who is too far from me in standing to be a match."

"Really?" the Colonel was puzzled. "You surprise me, Darcy. How could you have come to know a lady from outside our own circles well enough to wish to offer for her?"

"Oh, she is a gentleman's daughter, but still..."

"How bad could it be, then? I cannot imagine how any gentleman's daughter could be so far out of reach."

"Well, it is more her relations than herself."

Fitzwilliam considered. "So all this has been about you?" he surmised.

"Edmund," Darcy admonished him, "do you imagine I would offer you a fabrication? The situation I described was perfectly real; but, I must own, the question has been on my mind."

"So what will you do?" his cousin asked, echoing his father.

"Heaven knows; I certainly do not."

The Colonel gave a quiet laugh. "Well, for my part I suggest you marry the girl and be damned. At least you would be softening the blow for the rest of us when George brings home whatever beast of a woman his choice will be."

Darcy laughed as well, and the two gentlemen fell silent. Darcy continued his thoughts; by now, having run through every path and by-path he could think of to traverse his difficulty, he very quickly came to the crux: could he, as head of the Darcy family, put his wishes before the good of the family name? His notions of propriety told him that there could be no argument—that to put one's private interests in front of the well-being of an entire family, dishonouring even one's ancestors, could never be supported. Even under his cousin's more forgiving calculation, he had rather come down on Lord Andover's side than on Lord St. Stephens's. His father had always admonished him to "remember, you are a Darcy!"—such a deep-laid imperative, reaching all the way back to childhood, could not be lightly cast aside. His musings carried him the rest of the way to Hunsford village.

Chapter Eighteen

*A*s the carriage turned past the lodge guarding the entrance to Rosings, Darcy spied a figure standing in the Parsonage garden, making an ostentatious and excessively formal bow towards the carriage; in a moment his memory supplied him with a rather disgusting recollection of that same bow being made him in Bingley's ball-room at Netherfield. The new parson! — Elizabeth's cousin, who had so thoroughly embarrassed her and repulsed Darcy at Bingley's ball. He had quite forgotten this individual, but now it came back to him: the parson's dance with Elizabeth, and his presumptuous introduction…Collins was his name. They would probably have to put up with his company during their time at Rosings, Darcy realised; this did not augur well for their stay; he would have to be quick about his duties.

The trip from the Lodge to the house was a short one, and, as Kent was not Derbyshire, had little to offer the eye beyond a well-kept greensward. Composed on classical lines, Lady Catherine's home was a large, newer edifice, with a sharp symmetry echoed by an extensive, rigidly formal garden set directly in front of the house; nor were there any trees or shrubs set near the building that would detract from its precise mathematical splendour; this made the house excessively warm in summer, but then, Lady Catherine was always one to favour appearance over comfort.

Lady Catherine de Bourgh was the sister of Darcy's mother; she too, was a woman of some strength of character, but unfortunately lacked Mrs. Darcy's good sense and forbearance with the faults of others. While Darcy did not consider her a foolish woman by any means, in his estimation she tended to ignore those things she ought to attend to, and attend to those things she ought not. A deep and abiding regard for her own dignity and consequence, and a decidedly lesser regard for nearly every thing else, were the leading aspects of her character; her favourite pursuits, therefore, were those which gave her leave to issue commands to her fellow beings, while those affairs which involved regulating her own actions, held only a passing and easily extinguished interest for her. Darcy's father had made a yearly pilgrimage to Rosings, which usually coincided with the visits of the two young cousins, for the purpose of keeping the guidance of her estate from resting exclusively in the hands of her steward; it was now become Darcy's place to administer this duty.

Lady Catherine and the gentlemen's cousin Anne spent almost all of their time in Kent, rarely coming up to London. The excuse Lady Catherine offered was that the London air did not suit Anne, although Darcy rather suspected that she herself preferred the country, where her undisputed precedence of place was assured, and she could inflict her opinions and edicts on all and sundry without fear of challenge.

Their aunt and their cousin met them at the front entrance, outside of which all the servants had been arrayed in great state down the steps, to pay their tribute to the two young gentlemen. "Darcy! And Fitzwilliam!" cried Lady Catherine. "Such a pleasure to see you both! Anne, say hello to your cousin Darcy." Miss de Bourgh made a curtsey to her cousin, stiff, awkward, and silent; Darcy was exceedingly startled to see every one of the servants emulate this compliment, bowing or curtseying in concert with Miss de Bourgh: such an orchestrated display was a new, breathtakingly eccentric feature to his arrival; indeed, he could hardly imagine it could occur on any other estate, any where. While taken aback, he bowed with formal reserve to his cousin Anne, careful to avoid the Colonel's eye lest his composure fail him. Lady Catherine beamed down upon the whole scene, with the air of an artist admiring her work. They were invited in directly; they passed through the entry hall, lined with pictures of widely varying subject, taste, and colour—but perfectly matched in size—and into the antechamber of fine, inlaid Italian marble, which Darcy, after a trip abroad some years ago, had recognised as having been copied from the tomb of the Medicis. They followed Lady Catherine as she led them to the stairs with her stately, almost regal, bearing.

"You will want to change, of course, before we sit down," said she. "Hollister will show you to your rooms."

Darcy and his cousin ascended to the landing; there they parted, as Darcy was to be in the west wing, near the library wherein he spent much of his time at Rosings, and Colonel Fitzwilliam was staying in the rear wing: while smaller, it was also quieter, more removed from the household, and nearer the courtyard and stables. Darcy's room was at the front facing south, making it brighter and warmer for the fresh spring weather; it also afforded a pleasing prospect of the grove that stretched along the palings bordering the lane to the turnpike road.

After settling into their respective apartments and cleaning off the dust of travel, Colonel Fitzwilliam and Darcy met at the landing. The Colonel was beforehand of Darcy, and was dawdling at the top of the stairs, waiting for his friend. As Darcy approached, Colonel Fitzwilliam said, "I thought I might as well wait here, so we could go down together."

"Quite so," agreed Darcy, "better to wear out the carpet here than face Aunt Catherine alone."

The Colonel snorted, "It is not her—it is that chatterbox, Anne. A man can never find a moment's peace with that one around." Darcy chuckled, and the two friends went to assail the drawing-room where their aunt presided.

That great lady, overcome by the joy of having her favourite relations about her, actually rose to greet them. "I am so glad to see you both; it has been far too long! No, no, Fitzwilliam, sit here," she told the Colonel as he was about to sit in the chair next to his Cousin Anne. "Darcy, you sit there." The gentlemen did as they were bid; that Miss de Bourgh noticed the alteration was not immediately obvious.

"Was your journey tolerable? Not too cold? The evenings here have been quite brisk; I must remember to instruct your menservants to lay out warm clothes for this evening. Anne, have not the evenings been surprisingly cold for the time of year? I worry about you when you go out." To Darcy she said, "Anne has a very cunning new phaeton, and makes a point of taking an hour's drive each day. I am convinced, and Dr. Lampley quite agrees, that it has improved her health very decidedly." Miss De Bourgh shifted in her seat, but to Darcy's eye this was the only sign of vigour about his cousin's air or person. Mrs. Jenkinson, who was Miss de Bourgh's companion, apparently took this fit of activity as a signal to wrap a shawl around her charge's shoulders, though to Darcy the room felt rather warm than otherwise.

Darcy had never been sure what to make of Cousin Anne: he had never been able to tell whether she truly was as dull as she seemed, or whether her protracted illnesses had depressed her spirits, or whether perhaps her withdrawn manner was the natural consequence of living with a mother whose personality was so much stronger than her own. Whatever the reason, she had ever kept to herself, and, when in company, spoke but rarely. Even as a child, she had never been truly animated. Over the years he had tried to draw her out on various occasions, but had never seen anything resembling real character in her. When he was younger it had been a point of some interest, as both his mother and his aunt had spoken of his marriage to his cousin as an established fact. But with his mother's death, his own maturing years, and his father's perfect indifference to any such nuptial, by the time Anne had reached a marriageable age he no longer considered their union as at all likely, let alone a certainty.

Not so Lady Catherine. She said, "Darcy, is not your cousin Anne looking well? At this rate we shall see her at St. James's by autumn, or November at the latest; what say you — would not a betrothal party be a first-rate start to next year's Season?"

To Colonel Fitzwilliam this was the signal to intercede; the two cousins had long before arranged that it fell to the Colonel, during these visits, to redirect Lady Catherine's conversation whenever the topic of Darcy's marriage to Cousin Anne should come up.

"How does that hunter do, Ma'am?" Fitzwilliam asked quickly. "I was planning on putting him through his paces while I am here." Lady Catherine turned away from Darcy to the Colonel; Darcy, also per arrangement, then relieved his cousin of the need to continue, saying to her directly, "Lady Catherine, I believe I met your new parson while in Hertfordshire last November. Mr. Collins, is it not?"

The lady was momentarily distracted between her two nephews, but she answered Darcy's question, and let the Colonel's wait. "Indeed, yes; I had forgotten that you had met. He has his new wife with him, too."

Darcy, who had been congratulating himself once again on the successfulness of their simple tactic, now felt his heart still: remembering Collins' attentions to Elizabeth at Bingley's ball, he asked: "'His wife'? Who is the lady?" He tried not to let the concern he felt reveal itself in his tone.

"You know her as well, I believe; they met while he was in Hertfordshire." To Colonel Fitzwilliam she said, "The hunter? I have no idea, Fitzwilliam, you must speak to the groom." She then instructed Mrs. Jenkinson on the correct placement of a screen for Miss de Bourgh. To Darcy, this pause was very trying to his anxious apprehension; the thought of meeting Elizabeth again under such circumstances was dreadful to consider. He held in his alarm as best he could through it, until at length he was forced to prompt her with: "Yes? The lady—Mrs. Collins?"

"Oh...her maiden name was Lucas; her father was knighted not long ago, but I do believe he had been in trade. But she is a good girl, notwithstanding—not handsome, of course, and her bearing is quite common, but she has some sense about her."

Darcy hoped his relief did not show, as he asked, "A Miss Charlotte Lucas?"

"Yes, that is she."

"Ah...I did know her; her father and mother, as well. I agree; she struck me as being a lady possessing some sense." He did not voice his surprise at her choice of husband; he supposed that Mrs. Bennet's "four-and-twenty families" had failed to produce a more suitable match. And, his thoughts pursuing the topic a little farther, he wondered at how such a sudden transference of interest had come about: in November Mr. Collins had given every appearance of paying court to Elizabeth, and by March he was married to Miss Lucas. Further proof, if any were needed, of Collins' oddity.

"They have some others of your Hertfordshire acquaintance staying with them at present," said Lady Catherine.

"Indeed? She has some of her family with her, I presume?" said Darcy, hardly caring, but happy still to divert the conversation away from Cousin Anne and himself.

Lady Catherine nodded. "Her sister, Miss Maria Lucas; and a friend—a Miss Elizabeth Bennet."

Once again Darcy's heart stilled: Elizabeth—here? "I beg your pardon; did you say Miss *Elizabeth* Bennet?"

"Yes—Pleasant sort of girl: surprisingly genteel, although certainly nothing to Anne," said Lady Catherine. "She mentioned you had met."

Darcy nodded, but his thoughts were running far ahead and he did not speak. He was perfectly divided between delight and despair. He had been chiding himself five times a day for months, when his thoughts sought to dwell too long on his memories of her, all the while certain that he should never see her again—and here she was, almost in the same house with him! So near they would, or could, see each other daily. Nothing has changed, he reminded himself firmly. You must not allow yourself to make your estimation known to her. But his mind immediately began presenting him with schemes and notions involving Elizabeth and himself, which he just as immediately sought to suppress.

Fortunately for Darcy, conversation at dinner was always dominated by Lady Catherine, and she had planned a simple evening of cards for their first night together; no conversation was wanted on his part, therefore, which was as well, as his thoughts were thoroughly occupied by Elizabeth, and what her being in the neighbourhood must mean to him.

There was no denying that his principal sentiment had swung towards delight; to see her, hear her wit, and receive her smiles once more, to be the object of her attentions: these were pleasures he had been certain he would never again experience. But hard on the heels of his anticipation came all the old cautions and distress, strengthened the more by her nearness. He was highly distracted by the unruly clash of such thoughts throughout the evening—so much so that Colonel Fitzwilliam reproached him for his stupidity and inattention at cards. Nor was he able to shake his preoccupation on retiring—his first night at Rosings was a long one, indeed.

In the morning, after a late and leisurely breakfast, at which Lady Catherine alluded to the nuptials of her daughter and Darcy not less than half a dozen times—severely testing the gentlemen's ingenuity in turning aside her thoughts—at last they were offered an interesting diversion in the form of a visit from Lady Catherine's new parson. On being introduced, he bowed deeply to Colonel Fitzwilliam, and deeper still to Darcy; but this was nothing compared to the obeisance he made Lady Catherine on entering the drawing-room: he very nearly prostrated himself before her. Colonel Fitzwilliam looked at his cousin Darcy in amazement; that gentleman held up an admonishing finger and said quietly, "Wait—his speech is better still."

Mr. Collins did not disappoint: after the initial introductions were made, he offered his fulsome and protracted compliments to each member of the company, not excepting Miss de Bourgh, whose return curtsey was a marvel of restraint. When he came to address the Colonel, he said, "Colonel Fitzwilliam, I am *deeply* honoured to make your acquaintance; your revered aunt has often spoken of you in the *highest* of terms."

"I thank you," the Colonel replied briefly, looking at the parson curiously.

"No, Sir, it is I who must thank you; for, to be in the presence of a man who has devoted his life to the service of the King, and, indeed, to all of us fortunate enough to be English, I can only compare to being before one of the knights of old: for surely your calling falls in a direct line from theirs!"

At this, Lady Catherine smiled approvingly; but Colonel Fitzwilliam found his self-possession temporarily suspended: for a moment he could do no more than stare. Darcy, too, was taken aback, not so much by the folly of the speech, but by his instant conviction of its having been carefully rehearsed.

But Colonel Fitzwilliam, recovering quickly, was up to the challenge of meeting this extraordinary compliment: "But what of your own calling, my dear Sir? From Whom does *it* fall in a direct line? Doubtless He is the only One who must out-rank the King?"

As Mr. Collins thought his way through to the meaning of this, he fairly blushed and simpered like a schoolgirl. "Colonel Fitzwilliam," said he, stammering, "Sir, I can hardly...you are too kind, really...I...well." Darcy could scarcely believe it: the parson, rendered speechless: well done, Fitzwilliam! he thought.

"How do the ladies to-day, Mr. Collins?" asked Lady Catherine. "I trust Mrs. Collins took my advice about yesterday's dinner: that bird had not been hung long enough: it would not have been healthful to eat for at least another three days."

"They are well, indeed, Your Ladyship," Mr. Collins answered, "My wife had the lamb prepared, instead, and very wholesome it was."

"Well..." Lady Catherine said, as if trying to find aught to object to; but apparently the lamb passed her approval. She then enquired: "And has Mrs. Collins finished sewing up the rent in her work-bag? I have mentioned it to her twice, now."

"She has, Your Ladyship," the parson replied with a slight bow. "I regret that she did not attend to it sooner: I know she fully intended to do so as soon as she could find a moment; but what with our guest, and the Spring Festival to prepare for, she has been hard pressed to keep up, I'm sure."

"Very well: I understand—you may tell her I said so," Lady Catherine sniffed.

"Your Ladyship is all kindness and condescension," Collins said with another, and possibly even deeper bow. Darcy and the Colonel shared a knowing look off to one side of this scene; it always amazed them that Lady Catherine's dependants tolerated such liberties of manner, but, while this newest member of her little ensemble seemed to enter into it more whole-heartedly than some, it was no more than they had been accustomed to seeing in the past.

At this point there was a general pause, and Mr. Collins began to apologise for his intrusion; he was working himself up to taking his leave when Darcy heard himself say: "Is Mrs. Collins at home? And do I understand that Miss Elizabeth Bennet is staying with you?"

"Indeed, Sir, the ladies are all at the Parsonage at this moment."

"Fitzwilliam, perhaps we should go pay our compliments," suggested Darcy. "Lady Catherine, you would not mind?"

"Of course not Darcy; you two run along. It is time for Anne's outing, in any event: you will find her back home in an hour's time."

Darcy's cousin was looking at him in alarm and wonder, but Darcy made him a subtle calming gesture, to which his cousin shrugged: it was, at least, an escape from Rosings, if only for an hour. Mr. Collins, however, was beside himself: "Mr. Darcy! *Such* an honour! I hardly know...but I hope you will pardon my humble circumstances. Lady Catherine has, of course, generously supported me in every effort to make it all that is charming, but I fear such gentlemen as yourselves might find it very humble, indeed."

Cutting short his effusions, Lady Catherine said with some sharpness of manner, "Mr. Collins, if *I* may visit without loss of dignity, surely my nephews might, also."

"Yes, of *course*, Lady Catherine; I do apologise, *most* sincerely. I hope you know I meant no disrespect, and I beg you will forgive the implication..."

Darcy caught his cousin's arm and took him away to find their coats. "Lord knows how long this might last if we were to give it free rein," he cautioned quietly.

"Why are we going to the Parsonage, Darcy?" Colonel Fitzwilliam whispered.

"Because I have met the ladies there, and I assure you they make for far better company than the two here."

"This Miss Bennet: what sort of looking girl is she?"

"I shall leave it to yourself to determine," Darcy said; he was unwilling to be so disrespectful of her as to discuss her looks with his cousin.

Colonel Fitzwilliam, interpreting this instead to mean that his cousin was amusing himself at his expense, said, "Darcy, please—say she is not hideous; I know you would not do that to me, after dragging me out to Kent just so I might deflect Aunt Catherine's many courtesies."

Darcy, realising the misunderstanding, reassured his cousin: "Never fear, Fitzwilliam; you may trust your cousin Darcy—the lady will not disappoint."

Collecting Mr. Collins on the way to the door, they bade their aunt adieu. On the walk to the Parsonage, Darcy kept silent and left his cousin to deal with Mr. Collins. What *had* possessed him to invite himself to see Elizabeth? The answer came too easily to mind: he had had no choice. "Possessed" was the right word, indeed. He had known from the moment he heard her name that he could have no hope of keeping from her. It had been over four months since he had last seen her, yet her smile had been before him the whole of last night; he could no more avoid her than he could avoid food and drink. But, he reminded himself firmly, you must still protect her; you must not permit yourself to give way to your wishes in her presence. That was the one thing he demanded of himself; he might lack the resolve to stay away, but he was honour-bound not to injure her happiness. Nor did he neglect to remind himself that he could hardly deserve her attentions, after having been so completely taken in by Miss Chesterton.

Chapter Nineteen

*T*he Parsonage was a neat, well-designed little house: set cosily amidst a well-pruned garden, with a laurel hedge and a bordered walk to the door, it had struck Darcy so whenever he came to Kent, although he had never had reason to visit before. As they approached the house, he felt some misgivings at being face-to-face with Elizabeth again; not wishing to be first through the door, to encounter her without sufficient preparation, he tarried behind and let his cousin enter before he did, that he might more slowly accustom himself to being in her presence again. As his cousin was being introduced to Mrs. Collins, her sister Maria, and Elizabeth, he stood to the rear and fixed his eyes on the woman he could never have; she was lovelier even than memory had made her, and her smile even more captivating. When he was called on to greet the other two ladies, he forced his attention away from Elizabeth long enough to bow and say, "It is a pleasure to see you both again; and Mrs. Collins, please accept my congratulations on your marriage."

"I thank you, Sir; and also for being so good as to call so soon after your arrival."

"Not at all; we were delighted to come." Holding himself in very carefully, he then gave his greetings to Elizabeth; his emotions were too high for him even to know what he said: some perfectly tame formula, doubtless. She simply curtseyed in return without speaking, but he did not care: being in her company was difficult enough, without calling on his resources for conversation. Then, his obligations fulfilled for the time being, he gave himself over to the exquisite misery of being in her presence again.

Colonel Fitzwilliam was his usual, charming self, and Darcy could see he was not unaffected by Elizabeth's beauty. Like Bingley, Fitzwilliam never seemed to be out of his element, and was capable of engaging any one in polite discourse; Darcy was persuaded that if the Colonel should ever find himself about to go under the hangman's noose, he would engage his executioner in pleasantries right up until the floor dropt, and bid him a good day at the end. Of course, talking to Elizabeth was no hardship, and Darcy could have envied his cousin were it not for the emotions he was attempting to govern. Whenever he looked at Elizabeth he had a great tendency to lowness. Every word, every gesture of hers, made him feel how much he was being denied, how much happiness might have been his. To take his thoughts away from her, he turned to his hostess and offered the uninspired remark: "I have always admired this house, and its lovely garden."

She thanked him briefly, and Darcy was again silent. Oppressed by his feelings, he sat quietly for quite some time, merely listening to what was passing without trying to take part; when he felt he could no longer sit without speaking, he made what effort he could: "I trust, Miss e Bennet, your family are well?" Another empty formula — but it was safe, and came readily to his tongue.

"Yes, Sir, I thank you." She hesitated a moment, then added: "My eldest sister has been in Town these three months. Have you never happened to see her there?"

This, of course, brought forth a host of memories, and none of them comfortable. To her question he could but answer truthfully: "No, I was never so fortunate as to meet her." His consciousness, both her having been in Town and of his rôle in Bingley's unhappiness, stopt up his tongue; he could say no more. Fortunately, his cousin shortly thereafter decided that they had stayed long enough for an unannounced visit, and the two gentlemen took their leave.

"Well, well, Darcy," his cousin said with relish on the short walk back to Rosings, "This *is* a delightful surprise! I confess I had been worried, but Miss Bennet is both lovely

179

and charming! I must say, this bodes well for our time here."

Darcy could not disagree, but he was not sorry to have left: he knew he had been behaving boorishly, as his disappointed longing for her left him tongue-tied in her presence. If that was the best the present situation could offer, he told himself resolutely, then rather than sit by like an unmannered dolt and make a fool of himself, he would do better to avoid her whenever possible.

On returning to his apartments, he wrote to Georgiana to tell her they were safely arrived, but, though it felt disingenuous to hold back the whole truth, he did not inform her of Elizabeth's presence. It were better, he thought, to avoid the topic altogether, than to open his sister to additional injury. His letter was therefore short; but as his stay away from home was also to be short, an extensive correspondence did not seem particularly called for.

He held to his intention of avoiding Elizabeth's presence for nearly the whole week, although it cost him something to have Colonel Fitzwilliam come back to Rosings after a visit to the Parsonage and relate what a marvellous conversation he had had with "the charming Miss Bennet". His cousin also dropt frequent hints to his aunt that they ought to invite the Parsonage to tea, or to dinner, or to an evening of cards; he upbraided Darcy privately for not supporting him. Mr. and Mrs. Collins came to Rosings nearly every day, but Elizabeth Darcy saw only at services on Good Friday; the family left promptly, however, and did not speak to any one. On Sunday, though, his aunt lingered after church, and with mild alarm he heard her invite the Collinses and their guests to Rosings for the evening.

Darcy spent the afternoon in his rooms, preparing himself for the trial to come. Over the course of the week he had worked hard to gain strength, and, by dint of serious effort, flattered himself that he had got used to the idea of

Elizabeth being in the neighbourhood; he was now per-suaded that he could spend three hours in her company without danger. His confidence was high, largely because his strength was untested.

So, when the company from the Parsonage arrived af-ter tea, he felt prepared to meet Elizabeth with a passable degree of equanimity. Lady Catherine gave them brief greeting: "Mrs. Collins, Mr. Collins…Miss Lucas, Miss Ben-net: welcome. You know every one, of course. Do be seated. Darcy, you sit here." She indicated a seat between herself and his cousin Anne. The company exchanged greetings and compliments, then seated themselves wherever fancy or convenience led them. Elizabeth found a chair some dis-tance from Lady Catherine, and Colonel Fitzwilliam, rising directly, moved to be nearer to her; he was obviously pleased to see her again, and greeted her with an easy fa-miliarity that Darcy rather envied him. Darcy, who had been standing by the fire so as not to be too close to Eliza-beth on her arrival, hesitated before deciding that the chair his aunt had indicated was as safe as any.

Without regard for their new guests, his aunt picked up a topic she had broached with Darcy earlier: "Darcy, what have you decided about Mr. Turner? I have warned him before that I would take a hand in this myself if he did not settle it properly."

Each year it fell to Darcy to clear up any local disputes that might be extant during his stay, as Lady Catherine was wont to interject her judgement into just about every thing that went on within the reach of her intelligence. Although she was not, of course, the magistrate for the county, the fact that her decisions and commands had no legal force dissuaded neither her from issuing them, nor her tenants from complying with them. This portion of his visits was one which Darcy felt he was peculiarly better-suited to per-form than she. He differed from his father in that the late Mr. Darcy, while all that was benevolent and charitable, had never made himself very accessible to those who worked his lands. The present master of the Pemberley estates took a more active hand. The practice had yielded good results at Pemberley, and he had put the abilities he had learnt there to good use at Rosings during his visits; his interests here, however, were aimed less at justice and harmony amongst the estate's tenants, than towards the more modest goal of keeping the degree of discontentment with his aunt at a level short of armed rebellion; he had no desire to see the enthusiasms of the French Revolution visited upon Kent.

He usually made some attempt to deflect her from her self-appointed magisterial duties, and so he replied, "Frankly, Ma'am, I cannot see why you should wish to concern yourself in the affair."

"Really, Darcy! Of course it is my concern! The men live on my lands, and that means they are my responsibility; it is my duty to see to it that these matters are attended to." Darcy had had this discussion with his aunt often enough in years prior, and so forbore to argue further; it was beyond his ability to convince his aunt that she did not live in the sixteenth century.

"Are you certain it is true, then?" he asked.

"Yes; Mr. Collins drove out and confirmed it with his own eyes. The fence was down and Turner was watering his sheep at Tilden's pond again."

"Indeed, Mr. Darcy," Collins took it upon himself to spare Lady Catherine from having to fatigue herself with further explanation, "I myself have represented to the men in question, in the strongest of terms, how discreditable it is that they should fail to resolve their dispute. That they should have the assurance to ignore Her Ladyship's explicit instructions, and to oblige her to spend even more of her time on the issue, is so inconsiderate as to be unchristian, in my opinion." To this Lady Catherine nodded her solemn agreement.

The facts of the case were these: Mr. Turner kept a flock of sheep in a particular field; his neighbour, Mr. Tilden, had a pond nearby in an adjoining field. As there was no other source of water ready to hand, Mr. Turner would take his sheep to the pond on Mr. Tilden's land. For as far back as any one could remember, the business had presented no difficulties, but on one occasion recently, Turner had slightly damaged Mr. Tilden's fence, and the practise had become an issue of dispute between the two farmers, with bad blood and threats from both sides. "Mr. Tilden makes no objection to Turner's using the water—it is only the fence?" he enquired.

"Indeed, Mr. Darcy," Mr. Collins said. "The two men were known to be good friends before this falling-out. While they were previously unknown to me, I took upon myself the commission of seeing them both, on Lady Catherine's behalf; I stressed to each the desirability of displaying proper Christian forgiveness and humility. I fear my efforts were not well received: indeed, I regret to say that Mr. Turner forgot himself so far as to offer me violence, and warn me off his farm." Mr. Collins placed a hand ruminatively on his hindquarters, making Darcy smile so broadly that he was forced to turn his face away. This relation seemed to him rather an indication of the farmer's good sense, and his hope of a resolution improved.

"Yes, yes," said his aunt with some exasperation. "But the point is that Turner should have mended the fence after he damaged it. It is no less than criminal trespass, compounded by vandalism, and now, assault on a Church official. He is fortunate indeed not to have been taken in charge." Darcy's expression might have told his aunt his opinion of this bit of homespun jurisprudence, but just then his attention was drawn off by laughter coming from the direction of Elizabeth and the Colonel. He looked over, and saw the two of them engaged in what appeared to be a most congenial conversation. He watched them a moment until his aunt reclaimed his attention: "Now Tilden is at daggers-drawn every time he sees Turner. It must stop, Darcy. I will not have such goings-on amongst my people."

Darcy drew his attention away from Elizabeth and the Colonel, saying briefly to his aunt, "I shall attend to it, Lady Catherine."

"Splendid," the lady patted his arm in thanks. "I was sure I could count on you: you are just like your dear father; I envied my sister her husband, you know, quite envied her. And you are himself all over again."

Another burst of laughter drew his eyes back to Elizabeth and the Colonel, who were so thoroughly engaged in what they were saying that they paid hardly any attention to the others in the room. After a moment, Lady Catherine called out, "What is that you are saying, Fitzwilliam? What is it you are talking of? What are you telling Miss Bennet? Let me hear what it is."

"We are speaking of music, Madam," the Colonel replied, with some reluctance.

"Of music!" said Lady Catherine with a sedate and dignified display of enthusiasm. "Then pray speak aloud. It is of all subjects my delight." Darcy saw his cousin make a martyred sigh towards Elizabeth, to which she responded with a smile, although it was tinged with embarrassment. Lady Catherine continued: "I must have my share in the conversation, if you are speaking of music. There are few people in England, I suppose, who have more true enjoyment of music than myself, or a better natural taste. If I had ever learnt, I should have been a great proficient. And so would Anne, if her health had allowed her to apply. I am confident that she would have performed delightfully. How does Georgiana get on, Darcy?"

"She plays so well I admit to feeling some guilt that only I hear her," Darcy replied.

"I am very glad to hear such a good account of her," said Lady Catherine, "and pray tell her from me, that she cannot expect to excel, if she does not practise a great deal."

"I assure you, Madam," Darcy informed her firmly, "that she does not need such advice. She practises very constantly." He waged a continual, undeclared war against his aunt's interference where Georgiana was concerned.

"So much the better. It cannot be done too much; and when I next write to her, I shall charge her not to neglect it on any account. I often tell young ladies, that no excellence in music is to be acquired, without constant practise. I have told Miss Bennet several times, that she will never play really well, unless she practises more; and though Mrs. Collins has no instrument, she is very welcome, as I have often told her, to come to Rosings every day, and play on the pianoforte in Mrs. Jenkinson's room. She would be in nobody's way, you know, in that part of the house."

Wincing slightly, Darcy glanced fearfully Elizabeth's way, embarrassed by his aunt's shocking want of tact; an awkward, pained look came over Elizabeth's countenance for the briefest moment: clearly, she had felt the affront, but was too well-mannered to let it appear to the room. Darcy remembered having seen that same look on her face before—she had looked that same way whenever her mother had said something of which she might be ashamed: he had seen it often enough to recognise it. He was dismayed to realise that his aunt's lack of propriety had created the same sensations in Elizabeth as did her mother's. He now understood somewhat of Elizabeth's difficulties in having embarrassing relations, but even more, it was highly upsetting to think that there could be any such similarity between the two women. In Elizabeth's response to this present offence, however, so untaught and immediate, he could see the flaws in his aunt's behaviour mirrored very clearly. To help direct Elizabeth's thoughts away from his aunt's unthinking affront, the Colonel promptly turned her attention to a new topic in their discussion.

"Mr. Collins," Her Ladyship went on, unheeding, "What is this I hear about Haycock and Aylward?"

Mr. Collins, his countenance darkening as though he were about to announce the Judgement Day come upon us, recounted: "Mr. Haycock...who is a tenant on Her Ladyship's estate," this, an aside to Mr. Darcy, "has had cause to deny payment to Mr. Aylward for the shoeing of one of his horses, as the shoes hold no longer than two weeks, at best. And now Mr. Aylward refuses to shoe any of Haycock's horses at all; it is a matter of some concern and discussion in the village."

"One would think that after twelve years here, Mr. Aylward would know his trade better," Lady Catherine said disapprovingly.

"Indeed, Your Ladyship," Collins agreed solemnly. "And so says Mr. Haycock."

"Well, I consider it a scandalous business," said Her Ladyship, "and you may tell them both I have said so. Mr. Haycock has worked my land his whole life and is never behind in his rents; that he should be thus treated by a village smithy is insupportable."

Darcy enquired of the parson, "How many others have had occasion to complain?"

"I beg your pardon, Mr. Darcy?" asked Mr. Collins.

"Who else among this Aylward's custom have had a similar experience?"

"I have heard of none others, Sir," said the parson.

"And what does Aylward say in the matter?"

"That the horse throws the shoes a-purpose," Mr. Collins said with a disparaging smirk.

Darcy considered. "How many horses do you keep, Mr. Collins?" he asked.

"Just the one," replied the parson in an apologetic tone, as though embarrassed by living in such modest circumstances.

"Spend much time in the stables, do you?"

"Why, no, Sir. Never."

"What is it you are after, Darcy?" enquired his aunt.

"Well, Ma'am, I know the depth of your knowledge on the care of horses, but I was previously ignorant of Mr. Collins': I wished to ascertain if he might have heard of a horse pecking, and now I have my answer."

"Horses peck? As birds do?" Lady Catherine asked dubiously. Darcy looked around to see Colonel Fitzwilliam's response to this, but he was wholly engrossed by his conversation with Elizabeth.

As a boy Darcy had enjoyed visiting the Pemberley stables, and especially watching the smith at work: the bright iron from the forge and the sparks as they flew from the hammer had fascinated him, and he had been impressed by the steady, unhurried manner in which the smith had got so much accomplished in a day's time. The smith's son, some years older than Darcy, had taken the opportunity of displaying his knowledge to the heir of the estate, and had informed Darcy, among other things, of how some horses pecked at their shoes, kicking the outer edge on the ground until the shoe loosened and fell off.

"Not precisely," Darcy answered his aunt. "But I would wager that Mr. Haycock's horse is given to the practice, and that Mr. Aylward is in the right; and you may tell them both I have said so," he added mischievously. Mr. Collins and Lady Catherine looked at each other uncomprehendingly; Darcy looked around for his cousin again, but that gentleman still was not attending to anything beyond his discussion with Elizabeth.

The next half-hour Darcy spent listening to his aunt exposing her lack of understanding by speaking her mind, and trying not to listen to his cousin and Elizabeth enjoying each other's company. Their coffee finished, the latter two eventually moved to the pianoforte, the Colonel seating Elizabeth and then pulling a chair near her for himself. She began to play, and Darcy could feel her performance pulling at his attention; Lady Catherine listened briefly and then returned to her prattle. Darcy's interest in Elizabeth's performance outlasted Lady Catherine's, in spite of his relative lack of true enjoyment and natural taste; at length, weary of his aunt's conversation and continually attracted by the amiable sounds issuing from the direction of the instrument, he felt compelled to join his cousin and Elizabeth; telling himself that he could surely venture near her if he let his cousin attend to whatever conversation was wanted, he stood and excused himself to Lady Catherine. Making sure to regulate his features, he walked to the instrument and stood facing the two of them. Unfortunately, his intention of leaving the conversation to his cousin was thwarted by the lady herself. With the delightfully playful smile that Darcy had imagined in every room of Pemberley, she accosted him with one of those charming attacks that always beguiled him: "You mean to frighten me, Mr. Darcy, by coming in all this state to hear me? But I will not be alarmed though your sister *does* play so well. There is a stubbornness about me that never can bear to be frightened at the will of others. My courage always rises with every attempt to intimidate me."

Darcy, on being thus the object of her charms once again, felt his all his hard-earned strength leave him in an instant, and his feelings for her swept up in a rush; his embarrassment at the suddenness and depth of his attraction was acute, and he was all too aware that his cousin was looking on; hoping his face did not reflect as much emotion as he feared it must, and very conscious of maintaining his dignity before his cousin, he engaged her thus: "I shall not say that you are mistaken, because you could not really believe me to entertain any design of alarming you; and I have had the pleasure of your acquaintance long enough to know, that you find great enjoyment in occasionally professing opinions which in fact are not your own."

Elizabeth laughed with good-humoured ease at this, saying to Colonel Fitzwilliam, "Your cousin will give you a very pretty notion of me, and teach you not to believe a word I say. I am particularly unlucky in meeting with a person so well able to expose my real character, in a part of the world where I had hoped to pass myself off with some degree of credit. Indeed, Mr. Darcy, it is very ungenerous in you to mention all that you knew to my disadvantage in Hertfordshire," said she with mock gravity, "and, give me leave to say, very impolitic too—for it is provoking me to retaliate, and such things may come out, as will shock your relations to hear."

It had been months since Darcy had been the target of Elizabeth's attentions—she could teaze him as long as she wished. So long as she was teazing and playful, he believed himself safe; said he with a smile, "I am not afraid of you."

His cousin joined in: "Pray let me hear what you have to accuse him of: I should like to know how he behaves among strangers."

With a stern look at Darcy, softened by a first, fleeting smile, the lady said with greatest solemnity, "You shall hear then—but prepare yourself for something very dreadful. The first time of my ever seeing him in Hertfordshire, you must know, was at a ball—and at this ball, what do you think he did? He danced only four dances! I am sorry to pain you—but so it was. He danced only four dances, though gentlemen were scarce; and, to my certain knowledge, more than one young lady was sitting down in want of a partner. Mr. Darcy, you cannot deny the fact."

Darcy, while thoroughly amused, recollected the evening with perfect clarity, and made her the same excuse he had made to himself that evening: "I had not at that time the honour of knowing any lady in the assembly beyond my own party."

"True; and nobody can ever be introduced in a ball-room," Elizabeth chided him, but the look she gave him was bright and appealing; again he was struck by the fact that she reserved this mischievous side of her conversation to him alone. "Well, Colonel Fitzwilliam, what do I play next?" she asked, turning to his cousin. "My fingers wait your orders."

But Darcy could not let go her attentions so soon—and he wanted to make some kind of apology, to make her understand that his disinclination to dance that night at the assembly was in no way a slight on her. "Perhaps I should have judged better, had I sought an introduction, but I am ill qualified to recommend myself to strangers."

"Shall we ask your cousin the reason of this?" said Elizabeth, still addressing Colonel Fitzwilliam. "Shall we ask him why a man of sense and education, and who has lived in the world, is ill qualified to recommend himself to strangers?"

"I can answer your question," said Fitzwilliam, happily entering with her into baiting Darcy, "without applying to him. It is because he will not give himself the trouble."

Darcy ignored his cousin's attack. As he had done once before at Netherfield, he answered Elizabeth's teazing with candour: "I certainly have not the talent which some people possess, of conversing easily with those I have never seen before," he confessed. "I cannot catch their tone of conversation, or appear interested in their concerns, as I often see done." He looked at her earnestly as he spoke, hoping for understanding at the least, and perhaps even forgiveness, for not having sought her out those many months before.

Elizabeth did not, as she had done once months before, reply to his truth with more playfulness. "My fingers," said she, "do not move over this instrument in the masterly manner which I see so many women's do. They have not the same force or rapidity, and do not produce the same expression. But then I have always supposed it to be my own fault—because I would not take the trouble of practising. It is not that I do not believe *my* fingers as capable as any other woman's of superior execution."

She understood him—or so it seemed to Darcy: in divulging her own weakness she acknowledged, and in some measure forgave, his own; he was satisfied. He was perfectly aware that Elizabeth could have been a fine performer, had she devoted herself to it; that she had not, he felt, was an indication of her superior understanding: she preferred to improve her mind, rather than her ability to charm, and had apportioned her studies accordingly. He smiled, and complimented both her choice of study and her performance, by saying, "You are perfectly right. You have employed your time much better. No one admitted to the privilege of hearing you, can think anything wanting." A thought then struck him—something which he believed brought their similarities into view; he added: "We neither of us perform to strangers." Elizabeth turned her face to look at him, and Darcy believed he saw a degree of interest there, which more than rewarded his candour. Nor could he fail to notice that she never spoke with such openness to any but him: that she singled him out for her most heart-felt discourse spoke as directly to his heart as her wit did to his intellect; looking down into her eyes, he could hardly imagine how she might be improved on, in any particular.

Here they were joined by Lady Catherine, who immediately took command of the conversation, thus relieving Darcy of the need to speak at all, for which he was not sorry; it removed him from the focus of Elizabeth's attention, and allowed him to reclaim governance of his emotions. He drew breath, not remembering having done so for some minutes. Was this like control? he demanded angrily of himself. No sooner had he spoken three words to her than he was opening his heart to her, and hoping for her to do the same. He railed at his weakness: Come to stand staring at her like a dog begging at table—where is your strength, man? He remonstrated with himself at considerable length, and stood thus by the instrument for as long as the evening lasted, watching her play and scolding his feelings.

Chapter Twenty

The next morning Darcy wrote again to his sister, then roamed irresolutely about Rosings after breakfast for an hour or two, having resolved that he would not wait on Elizabeth that day. Finally, however, ignoring his own loud and crowding reproaches, he followed his feet to the Parsonage; the door was answered, not by the housekeeper, but by a young girl Darcy took to be the scullery maid. "Are the ladies in?" he asked, gently, because the poor creature looked terrified to find herself addressed by a gentleman. She bobbed quickly and pointed down the hallway to the drawing-room, too shy to speak. He thanked her with a smile and turned into the hall, only to hear her running feet behind him carrying her back to the kitchen.

On reaching the drawing-room, however, he was surprised to find only Elizabeth. This was a circumstance he had been half dreading, half hoping for, ever since he heard that she was at Hunsford. Although disconcerted, he recovered quickly, his manners coming to his rescue: "Miss Bennet—Good morning; I do apologise—I had thought to find all the ladies within."

Elizabeth politely forgave his error and invited him to sit, informing him that the others had gone into the village. When she had made the usual enquiries after every one at Rosings, she was content to sit without speaking. "My gracious silence," quoted Darcy to himself: who had called his wife so? Coriolanus—there was another poor, tortured brute, indeed, Darcy reflected; but at least he was not at war with himself—how does one win that war?

After some little while Elizabeth broke her silence to ask after their friends in London; Darcy answered several questions from her in a desultory fashion, content to let her lead the conversation where she would, satisfied simply to be in her company; when she paused and looked at him expectantly, however, he realised that he was not holding up his side of the conversation; casting about for a topic, he began with the first thing to come to mind: "This seems a very comfortable house. Lady Catherine, I believe, did a great deal to it when Mr. Collins first came to Hunsford." This he knew from his review of Rosings' books for the year preceding; it had been a substantial figure in the last year's expense.

"I believe she did—and I am sure she could not have bestowed her kindness on a more grateful object."

This exhausted his ideas concerning the house; he therefore started a new thought: since arriving at Rosings he had often wondered at Mr. Collins' substitution of Miss Lucas for Elizabeth in his affairs of the heart, and he invited the history of it by observing, "Mr. Collins appears very fortunate in his choice of a wife."

"Yes, indeed; his friends may well rejoice in his having met with one of the very few sensible women who would have accepted him, or have made him happy if they had. My friend has an excellent understanding—though I am not certain that I consider her marrying Mr. Collins as the wisest thing she ever did. She seems perfectly happy, however, and in a prudential light, it is certainly a very good match for her."

It was not the answer he had in view, but in her unreserved answer concerning her close friend and her relation, Darcy saw an obvious indication of increasing intimacy between them; he knew not how to feel about it—or, rather, his feelings were clear, but his rational side was warning him against encouraging such communications. As was usual in the perplexing and ambivalent internal struggle in which he was trapped, neither half of him could gain a clear mastery and force a decision. He was satisfied to continue the general topic, however: it felt safe from undue emotion.

He therefore observed: "It must be very agreeable to her to be settled within so easy a distance of her own family and friends."

"An easy distance do you call it?" Elizabeth demanded. "It is nearly fifty miles."

Thinking of his own frequent trips between Derbyshire and London, a journey of more than thrice that distance, Darcy replied: "And what is fifty miles of good road? Little more than half a day's journey. Yes, I call it a *very* easy distance."

"I should never have considered the distance as one of the *advantages* of the match," Elizabeth cried in protest. "I should never have said Mrs. Collins was settled *near* her family."

Pleased to have finally found an opening for wit—no matter how slight—after having been the recipient of her lively teazing so many times, Darcy now teazed her in return: "It is a proof of your own attachment to Hertfordshire. Anything beyond the very neighbourhood of Longbourn, I suppose, would appear far." Convinced as he was that she had been educated elsewhere, he was sure that the accusation of being too attached to a simple country life would pique her. He smiled his challenge at her.

The lady coloured at this and hesitated, but in her reply she avoided his challenge, speaking instead to the literal meaning of his words: "I do not mean to say that a woman may not be settled too near her family. The far and the near must be relative, and depend on many varying circumstances. Where there is fortune to make the expense of travelling unimportant, distance becomes no evil. But that is not the case *here*. Mr. and Mrs. Collins have a comfortable income, but not such a one as will allow of frequent journeys—and I am persuaded my friend would not call herself *near* her family under less than *half* the present distance."

Her air seemed to indicate to Darcy that there was something of peculiar meaning behind her words, and her

answer seemed directed at some different meaning altogether: speaking of how a lady might be willing to settle
farther or nearer her family, based on her husband's fortune, rather than addressing her attachment—or lack
thereof—to Hertfordshire. Is this for me? Darcy asked himself. It certainly seemed that she might be taking the
opportunity to tell him that, had one resources such as his,
the distance between Pemberley and Meryton were no object; is that why she blushed? He considered, and was
inclined to think that this was indeed the case; she was taking advantage of their time alone to inform him of her
interest. He was perhaps a little surprised by such a direct
reference to a potential union, if indeed he had divined her
true meaning, but he was by no means offended. He did not
feel himself prepared to pursue so highly charged a topic,
but neither did he wish for a complete change of subject,
nor in the openness of their discourse; as she seemed to be
willing to speak with him on diverse matters, he drew closer to her and instead took up again the question which was
the original subject of his teazing: "*You* cannot have a right
to such very strong local attachment. *You* cannot have been
always at Longbourn."

Darcy could see surprise and embarrassment in her
face, and realised he must have pressed her too closely on
her personal history—or, perhaps he had wounded her by
not responding to her true meaning? No, more likely she
was thinking he *was* answering her: saying that, having
been out in the world, she could have no objection to living
away from Longbourn, either in Town or at Pemberley, and
her embarrassment must then mean that her thoughts ran
along those same lines. He followed the train of logic again
in his mind, and felt that he had hit the truth of the matter.
Regardless, to spare her discomfiture, he quickly turned the
conversation onto less personal topics—but he treasured up
the ideas that had presented themselves during this most
interesting discussion. He kept the conversation on com-

mon and indifferent subjects until they were interrupted by the return of Mrs. Collins and her sister, who were come back from their errands. After exchanging the usual civilities, he found his thoughts too much occupied with what had passed, either to offer any conversation, or to be able to enter into theirs; so, true to his promise to himself to avoid any appearance of ill-manners, with no better excuse than being in Elizabeth's presence, he returned to Rosings.

During his return, his thoughts were, of course, full of what had just taken place; however, as was usually the case with him on this subject, by the time he was half-way to the manor he had managed to convince himself that his impressions and deductions at the Parsonage were almost certainly wrong; and, even if true, unquestionably ran contrary to the lasting happiness of either party; in consequence of which, his rational side, at least momentarily and in this instance, was able to declare victory. Regaining his rooms, he determinedly took up a book, that he might lose himself for an hour in some one else's difficulties and labours.

Later that afternoon he had arranged with Lady Catherine's steward to have the disputatious farmers, Turner and Tilden, come to Rosings, as he did not know them and wished to hear from each. He thought at first to speak with the two of them out on the drive, where they would be more comfortable than inside the austere elegance of Rosings, but he had then decided having them both a bit unsure of their surroundings might be best; he therefore met with them in the library—a cold and imposing room, and one in which they could not very well be at ease.

Hollister introduced them at the door; the two men entered the library and removed their hats; the taller of the two, Turner, looked as if he were about to set his down on a large open folio, but seemed to think it would perhaps not be suitably set off in such a display: he therefore retained it in his hand. Even though dressed in their best, in their heavy woollens and stout boots they looked decidedly out of place among the gildings and filigree of Lady Catherine's library.

"Mr. Turner," said Darcy, addressing himself to the trespasser in the case, who fidgeted nervously with his hat, "you have been using Mr. Tilden's pond to water your stock for how long?"

"We been doin' that since me father's father's time," the man replied, scowling suspiciously.

"And Mr. Tilden, you have never opposed this arrangement?"

"Not afore people starts tearin' down of other people's fences!" cried he with some heat.

"Call that a fence!" Mr. Turner burst in. "A sneeze would knock it down!"

"With you a-tearin' it down twice day to water yer blessed sheep, 'ow do you suppose I'm to keep it up?" demanded the other.

"You know I've got to 'ave that water, or I'd lose 'alf me stock!"

"It's bad enough you use my land for free..."

"Free! T'ain't free—my granddad give your granddad two full acres o' good land for the right to use that pond."

"Where's yer proof o' that?" sneered Tilden.

"Proof! I'll gi' ye proof!" Turner began rolling up his sleeves.

"Enough!" Darcy shouted, slamming his palm on the desk to get their attention. The two farmers looked over at him, as if surprised to see any one sitting there. "Let me to remind you gentlemen where you are standing. Mr. Turner, are you planning to start a brawl in Lady Catherine's library?" Turner looked about him, his face becoming terrified as he realised the probable outcome of the course he was about to follow.

Darcy turned to face Mr. Tilden. "Tilden, did your family receive land in return for the right for the Turners to use your pond?"

"Well, Sir, that's always been me understandin', but I never seen no..."

Darcy cut him off. "Right. Now, Mr. Turner—the fence you damaged belongs to Mr. Tilden. I do not care if it was made of straw, or was a line of chalk he used to mark his lands: you had no right to damage it."

"Well, Your Honour, Sir, I never meant to, and I'd 'ave fixed her when I could 'ave got the tools out there..."

Darcy stopped him short, saying briskly, "This is what is going to happen. The two of you are going to build a proper gate..."

Both farmers started to protest: "'Oo's to pay for that?" cried Turner.

"I got better things to do wi' me time..." began Tilden.

Darcy stood to his full height from behind the desk, glowering fiercely; the two farmers, neither of whom were overly large men, fell silent. "Turner, you will provide the tools, and you will apologise to Mr. Tilden for the damage done his property." He turned to the other man, who, mis-apprehending him, cried out, "See 'ere, you don't mean as I'm to buy..."

Darcy cut him off again. "I could certainly make the case that you should," he said sternly, "Your family was to provide access to that pond; if you did not provide a gate, how else could Turner get to the water but by taking down the fence? But you will be required to provide only labour, you and Turner, both—Lady Catherine will supply the ma-terials." To Darcy it seemed that if Lady Catherine wished to insert herself into the affairs of others, it was only fitting that she should help carry the burden of their resolution.

The men digested this for a bit. "All right with you, Bill?" asked Mr. Turner cautiously.

Mr. Tilden nodded slowly. "I don't see anything wrong with it—you?"

Turner shook his head, then stuck out his hand: "I'm sorry I took on so, Bill—it's just that when you threatened to cut off the pond..."

"Now, Tom, you know I never meant that, did I? That pond ain't no use to me—nothin' but hardscrabble around there: couldn't raise a goat on my side o' that fence." The men shook hands. "Buy you a pint?" asked Turner. "I'll get the next," agreed Tilden, and the two turned to walk out of the library, remembering to stop at the door and tip their hats to Darcy.

"Get on with it, gentlemen," he admonished them brusquely. "If it is not finished within two weeks' time, I shall have left, and you will have Lady Catherine to deal with." The two looked at each other apprehensively, and nodded. Doffing their hats to Darcy again, they took their leave.

Darcy passed a hand across his eyes as he sank back in his chair; would that all ills were so easily cured, he thought.

Chapter Twenty-One

When next he went to the Parsonage, he went with Colonel Fitzwilliam, who had started to find opportunities of visiting there twice daily; the opportunity to escape from Rosings for a time was a very seasonable relief to the Colonel, even though it was scarcely over a week since their arrival; for Darcy, going there with his cousin represented a means of being with Elizabeth, without having to expose himself through conversation.

The Colonel, of course, made himself a very welcome addition to the small gathering at the Parsonage, but, particularly when his rational side was in the ascendant, Darcy could hardly excuse his coming there to himself, let alone to the inhabitants of the house. At times all he could do was sit, engrossing himself in Elizabeth's wit and beauty; at such times he would observe her narrowly for any indication as to her esteem for him, but she was unfailingly proper in the presence of others, in which Darcy found additional correspondence in their natures, and more to admire in hers. At other times all he could think about was the difficulties before him: he then would choose between amusing himself by inwardly condemning the fates, or by casting about for ways to overcome the objections that stood between him and his wishes.

On this morning's visit, as he sat in contemplation of these varied, yet too-familiar topics, he roused himself to find, as often was the case, that his cousin and Elizabeth were once again enjoying a spirited discussion. He rose and drifted over to where the Colonel was holding forth; he was telling Elizabeth some anecdote of Army life. As Darcy came up to them, they both stopped and turned to face him; he gestured for them to continue.

"Upon my soul, Darcy," the Colonel said amiably, "this Kentish air is not good for you; you will surely need a physician when we get you back, for your voice box will have withered away entirely." Elizabeth looked at Colonel Fitzwilliam in astonishment, that he should sport with his cousin's silent dignity in this manner. "But perhaps it is not the voice box, but the brain-pan that has withered," suggested Fitzwilliam with a grin. Elizabeth began a laugh, but, recalling herself, she lowered her eyes and covered her laughter with a hand.

"What has my cousin been telling you, Miss Bennet?" Darcy asked her, passing over his cousin's barbs.

She raised her eyes back to his and, smiling, said, "I asked him to tell me about military life, and he was telling me what it was to live among...what did you call them, Colonel?"

"The great unwashed heroes of the Empire," the Colonel laughed.

"I had thought it '*unsung* heroes'," Darcy said.

"That is just what Miss Bennet said," cried the Colonel.

"And you said," supplied Elizabeth, laughing, "'And they will remain unsung, so long as unwashed'! And that you sometimes went to the stables for a breath of fresh air." She laughed and coloured; Darcy, looking down at her, felt all the power of her perfect loveliness and delicacy.

"Not even to the Officers' Mess?" he asked, forcing his eyes back to his cousin.

"The language there is so coarse and unrefined," the Colonel said with elegant distaste, "that the air in the stables is sweet by comparison." Darcy and Elizabeth both laughed.

"I should have thought, Miss Bennet," said Darcy, his thoughts touching on Wickham, "that you would have had your fill of the military." Turning to his cousin, he asked: "Has she told you that the --shire Militia is currently stationed in Meryton?"

"Forster's lot?" asked the Colonel. "Sound man, there." He laughed and said, "Once, I was invited to inspect his men with him. There were two men in the ranks, though, who looked like they had been through the wars: black eyes, broken lips, great welts all over—a lovely sight, I can assure you. Well, Forster asked his sergeant with perfect innocence, 'What has happened to these men, Sergeant?' 'You 'eard the Colonel', the sergeant said to the first man, "What's become o' ye?" The man could barely speak, as his jaw did not seem to be in working order, but he mumbled: 'Trod on a mop, Sir.' Well, Forster took a close look at him, then at the second man, and said to him 'And I suppose you stepped in the bucket?' So that man managed to say: 'Aye, Sir," though it looked like it cost him something to say even that much, and one of his eyes refused to open. Forster nodded, saying in the most reasonable manner: 'Dangerous implements, indeed.' Then he turned to his sergeant and said: 'Put these men on clean-up duty for a week or two, Sergeant, so they will know better how to avoid injury with such treacherous weapons.' We all three then went down the rest of the line, but none of us could keep a straight face, so we had to cut short the whole affair." The Colonel told the story with great relish, and a fine ear, and Darcy laughed heartily.

Elizabeth, who had been looking shocked through the majority of the tale, asked dubiously: "Had they been fighting?"

Colonel Fitzwilliam looked at her with renewed amusement and answered; "Yes, Miss Bennet; they had."

"And Colonel Forster knew?"

"Yes, Miss Bennet; and every one *knew* that he knew: that was what made the whole of it so entertaining—that, and the woebegone expressions on the two men's faces."

Elizabeth now laughed, but looked a little ashamed of herself for doing so, and coloured ever so slightly; enthralled completely, Darcy stared unabashedly until her renewed blushes told him he was now become the source of her embarrassment. Darcy was careful to school his glances thereafter, and the Colonel went on to entertain them both with more tales of Army life, until the two gentlemen took their leave after perhaps an hour more.

On leaving, he had opportunity to ask himself, not for the first time, what Elizabeth's sentiments towards Wickham were now, and whether she still felt offended by Darcy's supposed treatment of him? He had never got from her any sense of lingering resentment against him on Wickham's behalf; and unquestionably, during their times together at Hunsford and at Rosings, her open unreserve and her willing acceptance of his society, even when there was no conversation offering, argued for interest, if not attachment. But how did things stand between Elizabeth and Wickham? Had he exposed himself at last? —or did he continue to enjoy her regard? Elizabeth gave Darcy no hint either way. Had he recognised the fact, the jealousy revealed by these thoughts might have informed him how far his feelings for the lady had gone; but, as he did not, he entertained them without alarm.

As they walked back to Rosings, he spoke his concerns: "Edmund—George Wickham has joined Colonel Forster's regiment; he is a lieutenant. He has been in Meryton since before Christmas."

The Colonel looked sharply at Darcy. "Lord! Does he know Miss Bennet? He must, I suppose."

"Indeed he does; I found out that much before I left. You know him, Edmund: I am concerned for Miss Bennet's sake. Could you not discover what she knows about him, and if he has any designs on her? I feel it is our duty to give her proper warning, if such be the case; indeed, I tried to hint to that effect when I was with her in Hertfordshire, but Wickham had already insinuated himself into her good graces; she more or less warned me off the subject, which is why I suggest *you* pursue this: you might succeed where I failed."

"It is certainly worth a try. I shall see what I can ascertain."

"Do, please; it would relieve my mind."

"Well, so long as he is stationed in Meryton, at least he cannot get at Georgiana."

"I have had the same thought," Darcy agreed.

"And Forster is no fool: he may be able to keep him in line."

"My father was no fool, either — much good it did him," Darcy said pointedly. The Colonel nodded soberly, and the two gentlemen were quiet the rest of the short trip back to the manor.

Chapter Twenty-Two

*D*arcy's visits to Hunsford were not always dependent on his cousin's pleasure; at times, either when his cousin was occupied by his own affairs, or when Darcy simply ran out of arguments to hold himself back, he would wander off to the Parsonage on his own. One such afternoon, he entered the house to find all four of its inhabitants in the drawing-room.

"Mr. Darcy!" the parson enthused as Darcy was admitted, "we are honoured by your visit, indeed. May I enquire how does my noble...that is, how does your revered aunt?"

"She is well, Mr. Collins, I thank you, as is her daughter. And I trust that all are well within the Parsonage?" He sent a smile around to every one present.

"Very well, Sir, indeed," answered Collins. "You are most condescending to enquire. And your cousin, Sir...how does our esteemed Colonel Fitzwilliam?" Darcy assured him that the Colonel was well, but found it difficult to speak in an even tone; the parson's unusual meekness of address Darcy found grating; it was such an odd combination of humility and parade that Darcy hardly knew what to make of it, or what could be the character of the man who could produce it; and seldom was he in Collins' company but he wished he had a dictionary to hand, as he felt Collins was in need of correction on the application of certain words.

Mrs. Collins here thought it well to intervene and invite her guest to be seated. Darcy sat down by the window in one corner of the room. From this vantage, he knew, while still facing his hosts, he would be able to see Elizabeth without the need to turn his head.

"You seem much occupied, Mr. Darcy, by your aunt's affairs," his hostess began pleasantly.

"Indeed, Mr. Darcy," her husband broke in eagerly, "I have heard in the village how you have resolved instantly the standing feud between Turner and Tilden. Such wisdom! Such judgement! Surely Solomon himself could not surpass such sagacity!"

Darcy saw Elizabeth smile to herself at such fulsome compliments; for his part, Darcy could think of no adequate reply to this description of what was no more than a two-minute affair: he imagined it had taken the parson longer to prepare that little speech, than had the incident itself. Mrs. Collins enquired: "What have you done, Mr. Darcy? When last I heard, the two men were sworn enemies for life!"

"I assure you, Mrs. Collins, it was nothing."

"'Nothing', Mr. Darcy!" cried her husband, "As I had it from the baker's wife, you quelled in a moment a riotous feud of many months' standing." The parson beamed down on Darcy, saying, "'Blessed are the peacemakers', Sir."

"No, truly," Darcy demurred. He looked quickly over at Elizabeth, colouring at being given such a flaming character; he could see the hint of a smile at the corners of her mouth.

"This can be no surprise to those of us who know Mr. Darcy," she commented, looking up at him with an air of mild wickedness. "He is widely celebrated in Hertfordshire as a man without defect."

Darcy gave her a droll look of reproof, as though to say: "Must you?" Aloud he said, "It was a simple misunderstanding between two friends, which, when allowed to fester, will always turn putrid. It would have blown over eventually without my intervention; I have seen it often enough at Pemberley."

"You are far too modest, Sir..." began Mr. Collins.

"My Dear," his wife interrupted his next speech, "You will embarrass our guest."

"Oh! Of course, my Dear," said the parson, reacting, as always, to the least hint of blame with abject humility. "I *do* apologise, Mr. Darcy: I hope you will forgive me!"

Embarrassed, and looking rather at his wife than at Collins, Darcy muttered, "Gladly, if only we might pass on to some other topic." That good lady immediately introduced a new subject, and Darcy was released. Elizabeth, smiling, did look over with one short side-glance for him alone, and his feelings improved.

On the Wednesday morning, Darcy was sitting in his rooms after breakfast, staring vaguely out at the grounds from the window when he spied Elizabeth making her way past the Lodge and into the park. She was briefly obscured by trees, but after a moment he saw her emerge and walk away from Rosings, towards the heart of the grove on this side of the palings. Darcy knew from his youth that there was a pathway that led in the direction she had taken, and, without giving his rational self time for establishing injunctions and filing demurrals, he quickly changed for the out of doors and set off to meet her. He was no more than five minutes behind her, and, as that pathway had no other return, he simply followed along it, confident that they would meet some where along its length. Nor was he wrong: after less than a quarter-hour's walk, he caught up to her; she was standing in a secluded dell with her back to him. "Miss Bennet, good morning!" he called.

She looked round in surprise. "Mr. Darcy!" she cried. "How you startled me!"

"I beg your pardon," was all he could think to say; she was very lovely this morning, framed by the fresh green of the new leaves on the trees behind her, and the sun washing her, too, with the fresh glow of youth. He approached, and they stood together, but neither spoke for a moment. Hesitantly, he asked: "Do you return to the Parsonage, or do you stay?"

"I should have gone back shortly," she said briefly.

"Shall I accompany you?" he asked: always correct, he wished to ensure that she would not be uncomfortable in his company; they were, after all, alone and unchaperoned.

"If you wish," she replied. There was a slight emphasis to her tone as she said this, and in this particular response Darcy saw more than acceptance: her answer was actually a tentative invitation that, depending on his answer, would tell her whether he truly wished to be with her, or would as soon go on his way alone.

"I should be very happy to," said he, answering both the spoken and unspoken question. He smiled at her and turned back the way he had come. She gave him a momentary smile in return, then cast her eyes down at the path.

They walked together some minutes in silence, enjoying the morning and the fresh spring air. Darcy, conscious of her every movement, was careful to observe her silence; she clearly had come out to enjoy a quiet walk, and he did not wish to draw down her disapproval by disturbing her morning with chatter.

"Do you come this way often, Mr. Darcy?" Elizabeth asked after a time.

"Not now, but Colonel Fitzwilliam and I used to play here as children," Darcy smiled at the memory. "We were hunters, castaways, pirates—mostly the latter. All the things boys will get up to when their elders are not there to scold them. I cannot tell you how many sets of clothing I must have ruined." He made an embarrassed laugh: "In fact, this very grove is where I got my nickname. I was 'the Dread Pirate, Dirks-and-Daggers Darcy'. My cousin still calls me 'Dirks' from time to time."

"You, Sir, are Dirks Darcy?' the lady asked in wonder; her face marked her incredulity.

"At your service, Ma'am," Darcy replied, bowing with a flourish.

Elizabeth stared at him for a moment without speaking, then quickly cast her eyes down; a sound like a stifled sneeze issued from her, and Darcy offered a "God bless you!"; she repeated the noise twice again in rapid succession, to which Darcy added: "Goodness! —and bless you again." After walking a bit further without hearing the lady speak, in an attempt at banter he asked, "What seek *you* here amongst the trees? Surely you do not come here to play out *your* girlhood fancies?"

"No, indeed not," she replied shortly. There was a slight hesitation before she supplied with pointed significance: "This grove is a favourite with me; the tranquillity, the picturesque of the woods, the pleasures of nature without alloy of company—I have enjoyed a great many hours here by myself. As it is inside the paling, I feel secure from unwanted visitors."

In this earnest return Darcy could feel that she was sharing something of herself, in answer to his admission of his childhood absurdity; but just what she meant was equivocal; as he thought about it, though, it came to him that she might very well be telling him how they might be together, without interference from 'unwanted visitors'. He glanced quickly down at her; something in her manner, or perhaps how near to him she walked on the narrow path, convinced him: she was inviting his company, here in the grove. He tried to see her face, but her eyes were modestly cast down, no doubt from the consciousness of her daring, in offering such a bold suggestion. When he compared this behaviour with that of another he had recently had occasion to observe, he could not but be struck by Elizabeth's superiority over that lady in every way: indeed, her superiority over any lady he had ever known.

As he considered, Darcy was, at first, very encouraged by this allusion to how much she desired his company, but this was instantly followed by all his accustomed doubts; these he immediately suppressed—he did not wish his time with Elizabeth squandered on such thoughts as these. He turned his mind instead to their dance at Netherfield: the sensation of her hand in his, watching the flow of her form in the graceful lines of the dance; these memories, combined with her quiet loveliness beside him, brought back that coursing warmth to his heart which he had felt at Netherfield. "England's heart is in the country..." he murmured, musing over the particular aptness of the phrase in his present circumstances.

"I beg your pardon?" asked Elizabeth.

"Oh—I *am* sorry," he apologised. "I was merely thinking aloud."

The lady did not press the conversation, and he was content to walk along beside her in silence for most of the way back to the Parsonage.

When they reached the gate in the paling across from the Parsonage, Elizabeth dropt a quick curtsey and hurried away; to Darcy it seemed almost as if she were embarrassed, and he knew not why she should be so, until it occurred to him to realise that he had not answered her daring suggestion with an acceptance, which must naturally have left her embarrassed and uncomfortable in his presence. Recognising in himself the "stiff and clumsy" fellow condemned by Miss Chesterton, he nearly called her back; but she had by then already reached the far side of the lane. He watched her until he was sure she was safely inside the Parsonage, then walked slowly back to Rosings, his thoughts, emotions, and imagination all deeply engaged.

For the next two mornings, Darcy was forced to stay within by affairs. But on the morning of the third, he saw Elizabeth again enter the park and walk down the same path. He directly went to meet her. He found her, as before, not far from the centre of the grove, where she stood quietly watching back along the pathway, almost as if she was expecting some one to come down it. "Mr. Darcy, here you are again," she greeted him, "in this place where I have had so much time to myself." The smile on her face was again difficult of interpretation; Darcy was unsure if she were rebuking him for not having come back the last two days, or simply remarking on the seclusion of the grove.

"I beg your pardon; am I disturbing you?"

"Of course not, Sir—how could you be? I have neither claim nor cause to be here, save by your leave—or Lady Catherine's, perhaps, as the case may be." As she spoke, a satirical smile played on her lips; Darcy was decided: she was teazing, rebuking him for his absence—it was for his cause that she had come, yet he had not been there.

He excused himself as well as he could: "I had much rather have been here myself, but it was necessary to remain within, labouring on Lady Catherine's affairs; and you must know you are free to come and go any where on the grounds without leave," he assured her. "At least the weather has been fine," he finished apologetically.

The lady looked at him pensively a moment. "Indeed, it is more pleasing to be out of doors than within," she said at last, "but should you not rather be riding than walking?"

"Colonel Fitzwilliam has taken upon himself the exercise of Lady Catherine's horses this year," he answered without thinking. "When the Colonel is on a horse, he is not a companionable sort; he is too fine a rider, and is always intent on getting the most out of his mount." Then, realising she must mean she wished to hear him say how he would rather be with her and not riding—if indeed, she meant anything at all—he added, "When one is in want of good company at Rosings, one needs must look elsewhere." He smiled at her to convey his meaning; she smiled back at him briefly before releasing him from her gaze; Darcy was relieved: she had absolved him of the sin of having absented himself the past two days.

He took a spot to stand not far from her, where the sun came from behind her, that she need not face the bright of day. As was her way when they were alone together, she allowed the silence to stretch between them; he thought, at first, perhaps he ought to apologise for having failed to answer her explicitly the last time, when she had hinted at the possibility of their meeting in the grove together; but as his presence now had already made that reply for him, logically there was no point in speaking the words. The lady being preoccupied with her thoughts, he was content to respect the tranquillity of her morning retreat; indeed, he preferred the quiet himself: coming as he did to enjoy the morning by her side, he did not wish to waste his time with her on empty formulæ. "Where words are scarce they are seldom spent in vain, for they breathe truth that breathe their words in pain," Darcy quoted silently to himself. Certainly this must apply to him, he thought ironically. His feelings towards Elizabeth were becoming more Shakespearean by the day. Would Pender laugh at his comedy, or sympathise with his tragedy? He shook free from these thoughts and devoted his attentions to Elizabeth.

Being very sensible of her nearness, he stood observing the sunlight play on the tendrils of hair which escaped to trail delicately down her neck; his eyes found the soft curve of her lips, and his memory carried him back to the first real kiss he had ever known: when he was quite a young man, an associate of his father's had come to stay at Pemberley, bringing with him his daughter, who was almost of an age with Darcy. Towards the end of their short stay, she had come upon Darcy in the shrubbery, and to his very great surprise, had directly stood on tiptoe to kiss him once, slowly, her hand laid softly on his cheek, before running off down the winding pathway. He had never forgotten how sweet and soft were her lips on his; he smiled gently at this cherished memory, and could not but indulge his fancy in imagining how Elizabeth's lips might feel on his.

Realising he had probably been silent—and had certainly been staring—too long, he roused himself to say, "The quiet here is remarkable, is not it? I find it exceedingly refreshing, after the clamour of London."

"Indeed," the lady replied. "I have found nothing here of more value than its silence."

Darcy smiled and nodded, then stood without speaking for a time, listening to the sounds of nature; after a while, though, he was moved to say, "I hope, Miss Bennet, the time you have spent at Rosings has not been unpleasant." He wished to know that his aunt had not been too *very* vexing during her visits.

"Certainly not, Mr. Darcy. How could you think so?"

"Well, as you are a guest of the Collinses and cannot choose the coming and the going, perhaps you would have as soon stayed at the Parsonage, as to call upon my aunt."

"I assure you, Sir, in the main the company at Rosings is every bit as pleasant as that at the Parsonage. I will confess, though, that the last week or so has seen an improvement in each."

"I am very glad you should have found it so," Darcy answered, much flattered. Such a very open compliment made him look at her with a degree of favour he could not hide.

"Not at all," said Elizabeth, "your cousin is a delightful conversationalist." She spoke with a slight emphasis and Darcy saw something of a challenge in her look; he understood, of course: she was teazing him again, and perhaps playing for a show of jealousy.

"I am so pleased to have been the means of bringing him to your notice," said he with a playfully formal bow. That same equivocal smile reappeared; then, returning to the study of the verdure surrounding them, she permitted the silence to fall yet again. Darcy had come to value these moments of silence between them very highly: that two people would be content to be silent together, that they could feel sufficient ease and...*trust*, withal, to allow each other into their silences, seemed to him a very strong indication of their mutual esteem. They stood without speaking for a long while, until at length Elizabeth made to leave, with a brief: "I fear I must be getting back." She moved quickly past him back up the path, nearly brushing up against him; he moved with alacrity to accompany her. He was disappointed that they could not spend more time together, but she was right, of course. Should their absence be noted, the coincidence of their return must be seen as a very noteworthy circumstance, so prudence argued for an early return. The lady spoke but little on the way back, and they parted quietly at the gate.

Returning to Rosings, Darcy sought out the Colonel. "Fitzwilliam, I have been thinking: I should like to delay our departure another week; I find that my work here is taking rather longer than I expected. This will not inconvenience you, I hope?"

"Not in the least," the Colonel replied. "Another week with Miss Bennet will be no trouble at all!"

"Yes…by the way, Fitzwilliam, have you had any chance to discover Miss Bennet's thoughts on Wickham as yet?"

"I have; that is, I have made the attempt: it is difficult to know without baldly asking outright, but I could not detect anything resembling a deep regard, certainly."

"What did she say?"

"Well, I asked her about Forster's militia, and how the townspeople felt about them, and whatnot: you know, just in general. Then, over the course of a few minutes conversation, I dragged the subject of his officers into the conversation by the heels several times; she never said anything particular about any of them, or showed any sensibility on the subject at all. Of course, I could not mention him by name…"

"No, of course not," Darcy agreed. "But this seems to tally with what I know, as well. Moreover, I cannot help but believe that Miss Bennet has too much sense to be taken in by Wickham for long."

"We might certainly hope so," agreed his cousin, "the fellow does not seem capable of keeping his sins hidden for very long—that is certain."

Darcy, satisfied, nodded and let the matter drop from his mind.

Chapter Twenty-Three

*S*unday varied the scene at Rosings, offering Lady Catherine an opportunity to display her solemn dignity to the admiration of the assembled tenantry and cottagers of Rosings and Hunsford, at church. To Colonel Fitzwilliam, the morning service meant a respite from Lady Catherine's conversation for a period of two hours; but to Darcy, especially now, knowing Elizabeth to be nearby, the family pew, with its ornate carvings and gildings, served rather to accentuate the gulf that stood between them. Caught as he was between his aunt and her daughter, and altogether incapable of listening to Mr. Collins' exceedingly grave and excruciatingly unimaginative sermon, his mind was left wholly free to wander. As he ran his fingers vaguely over the freshly applied gold leaf on the railing, and heard the vacuous platitudes issuing from the pulpit, it occurred to him that this was a reflection of his entire stay there at Rosings: splendour and gilding covering over an utter want of substance.

This conceit staid with Darcy through the rest of that day and evening—spent trying to read and being pulled away time and again by his aunt's need to express her opinions to an audience; the Colonel remained most studiously affixed to his correspondence, although Darcy was reasonably sure that he had seen his cousin open some of the letters at least two times over; and his cousin Anne sat silently by the fire being fussed over by her companion. The lack of all reasonable discourse was wearying, indeed; Darcy would have given anything to have Elizabeth walk in to join them, or to be able to justify to himself a trip to the Parsonage. His ruminations eventually led him, with more than a degree of self-contempt, to find another unsettling parallel: this between his circumstances here at Rosings and his life in

London—both were what was called "good society", yet neither was very good, nor very social.

The next Tuesday morning Darcy once more spied Elizabeth setting out along the path through the grove, and, his time being his own again that morning, he started off to meet her without hesitation. He found her this time seated, facing back up the path in the direction of the manor, obviously awaiting his arrival. "Miss Bennet, good morning," he greeted her with a smile.

"Good morning, Mr. Darcy; here you are again."

"Yes…another lovely morning, is it not?"

"Indeed: so quiet and still—the perfect morning for solitude, surrounded by Nature's beauties."

Darcy did not need this warning to tell him how Elizabeth enjoyed the serenity of the grove without conversation; he therefore smiled and held his tongue. He found a place to sit facing her. After some minutes the lady spoke again: "And so, Mr. Darcy, do you come to Rosings merely to visit this grove and be silent?"

Darcy smiled again at her teazing. "No; each year I come in the spring to look over the plans for the estate going forward. My father was accustomed to do so, and after his passing it more or less fell to me to keep up the practice."

Silence descended once more. Darcy opened a new topic: "How do you enjoy Hunsford?"

"Quite well. Mrs. Collins is an old and dear friend; she is very much missed in Hertfordshire. We enjoy many hours together while Mr. Collins is occupied in his study, or in the garden."

The manner in which she spoke of Mr. Collins plainly suggested her pleasure in her cousin's company was far less than in her friend's; this could hardly be a surprise, of course. But a most worrying thought occurred to him: Collins could not be the most agreeable husband in the world; perhaps some discord had surfaced within the Parsonage?

Did Elizabeth come here, *not* to take an opportunity to meet with him, as he supposed, but rather to escape the house of her cousin? Nothing had suggested it before, but the possibility was unsettling to Darcy in his anxious and minute construction of Elizabeth's intentions. "How do the Collinses get on?" he enquired with interest. "Mrs. Collins seems to have a most even and gentle temper."

"Indeed she does. That has always been her way — and I am sure she has need of it, at times."

"But I think I recall you saying she seemed happy?"

"She does, strange as that must appear to those who know them both."

Again, Darcy felt the compliment of her sharing such very direct observations, and spoke candidly in return. "Indeed: Mr. Collins cannot be an easy man to be married to."

"Perhaps not," the lady agreed. "But one must not judge. No one can know a couple's happiness but the couple themselves, and I must say she seems perfectly content."

Here was the intelligence he looked for: her friend was content: there was no discord from which to escape. His mind relieved, he offered: "To each his own, then?"

"Yes. Of course, Mr. Collins would not be the man of my choosing, but we are told that every one has a mate some where, are we not, Mr. Darcy?" She turned her gaze to him.

In her look Darcy saw such meaning as captured his most peculiar notice. "That is the established wisdom," he replied carefully; he was all attentiveness, and he felt a tension in his chest not unlike that at the culmination of a long hunt. With a certain emphasis, he said, "Of course, some of us must look longer than others."

"This is undoubtedly true: but surely, in this matter, the wait is more than rewarded, if one truly finds the right person. Failing that, of course, one might just as well marry the odd parson who might happen by and express an interest."

As she spoke, Darcy felt she again looked at him with pointed meaning. He smiled at her clever turn on Mr. Collins' character, but his interest was aroused most decidedly by the statement itself: she seemed to be telling him she had refused Collins for his sake. Was that the reason Mr. Collins' interests had shifted to another object? Had Elizabeth, in spite of every thing, been aware of his own interest at Netherfield? After all, both his sister and Miss Bingley, he knew not how, had been able to penetrate his regard for her: why not Elizabeth, too? He was silent, pondering her words and her air; she had never spoken of it directly, to be sure, but if he was not mistaken it placed an entirely new light on their time together here at Rosings; if she were aware of his feelings, his long-continued silence must surely have pained her greatly, and his heart sank at the thought. He was very tempted to say straight away that he understood her, and how much he agreed—how well assured he was that she was the one he had waited for through nine weary Seasons, a full third of his life: in her presence he was far less sensible of the objections that plagued him in his solitude. But his lingering doubts, especially on his having correctly read the lady's estimation for him, held him in check; and so, while longing to speak, he simply smiled and nodded with a certain wistfulness—but he did give his eyes license to hold hers for a long moment.

Another long silence ensued. This time the lady broke it, asking: "I never see Colonel Fitzwilliam in the grove, Mr. Darcy: does he not care to walk?"

"I believe he likes the exercise quite well, but his rooms on this present visit are in the rear wing, and so he is more likely to walk north from the house. But he has been preoccupied with affairs, and with keeping Lady Catherine's hunters from a life of complete senescence, so I believe he has taken little opportunity to walk. But he will, I am sure; he always does."

"I do not know that I was aware the house had a rear wing."

"It is not much used, but he requested it especially, as it is quiet, and close to the stables. I like it too, but it is rather removed from the library, where I spend most of my time. I have no doubt you will find it answers your ideas of comfort, in future." As he spoke the words, Darcy realised with a start that he had formed the unconscious expectation that they would be coming there again together — and that he had now given it away! — for she *could* only assume that he meant she would be coming there with him. He hoped his embarrassment did not show, and held his tongue, watching Elizabeth's reaction carefully. She offered no reply, but Darcy could see in her momentary expression of surprise and confusion that his words had not passed unnoticed; as had happened before at Netherfield, however, her delicacy and regard for him made her act to spare his feelings, and she forbore to speak her own. He, on the other hand, knew not how to chastise himself too much for injuring her in this way, making it so very clear that his silence concerning his sentiments came from nothing but want of resolution on his side; what must she think of a man whose lack of decision and will would thus force her to endure months of pain and suspense? In his embarrassment he could say little after this, and after a little while spent without hearing anything further from him, or finding anything to say herself, Elizabeth kindly released him by standing and announcing her intention to return; Darcy followed dismally along behind her like a scolded pup; on parting from her at the Parsonage, mortified and repentant, he went to sit by himself in the library to worry at this crisis; he deliberated on both the assumption that had made him speak so, and the lady's reaction to it: she had understood his meaning, of course; but what heavenly disposition would let words of such import to pass off unchallenged? To spare him, when her own interests must urge the severest reprimands—surely only the deepest regard could explain such an act of forbearance.

Or—and this possibility struck him with particular force—might not she be disguising her own sentiments for much the same reason he did his? —recognizing the difficulties that must attend their union, perhaps she concealed her attraction from *her* sense of propriety. That she hesitated to relieve her feelings and speak her mind on *these* grounds, rather than out of concern for his peace, was certainly credible; she was undeniably a very proper lady, for all her playfulness; indeed, that was part of her special charm—her ability to maintain the strictest propriety while managing still to be lively and fascinating. She was infinitely more captivating than Miss Susan Chesterton, but, unlike the latter, Elizabeth never failed to heed the demands of civility and decorum, regardless of any warmth for him she might be harbouring. Of course she would have concealed her feelings for him: her delicacy and propriety would demand it.

As to her having discovered his attachment, there could scarcely be any doubt: whether she knew of his attraction in Hertfordshire or not, he had often enough been unguarded; fool that he was, she surely must have been aware of how he struggled not to stare, and how difficult he found it to speak in her presence. Could any mooncalf be more obvious than he had been? Add to that to-day's slip of the tongue, and it was impossible that she should remain unaware of his interest. He found, however, that the conviction that she understood his heart did not release him and enable him to speak; rather, it rendered speech more difficult still, and at the same time made his silence all the more inexcusable. He longed to rise up and go out to Elizabeth, wherever she might presently be, to declare himself and offer his most heart-felt apologies; but his doubt and mortification held him back.

The following evening the Parsonage once again came to Rosings. Embarrassment and indecision do little to stimulate conversation, and Darcy was even less talkative than usual. He held a book, and would occasionally refer to it, but it could not hold his attention. Very much occupied by his wavering inclinations, he sat quietly in a deep chair by the low fire, content to let the evening unfold around him whilst he sought to bring some clarity to his mind. Elizabeth had nothing to say to him, nor could he blame her, but he could contrive no adequate means of mending the rift he had created between them.

As his thoughts drifted about, his attention was captured by Mr. Collins, who was trailing after his aunt as she walked here and there in search of a conversation to command, or a behaviour to correct. As was his habit, the parson took a place behind her to the left; Darcy caught the Colonel's eye and directed his glance to Mr. Collins with a nod; the two shared a grin, as the Colonel had some days previously whispered "Heel!" as they had watched a similar procession.

"Mr. Collins, how do the preparations for the Spring Festival get on?" asked Lady Catherine as she swept a disdainful finger across the dust on the base of a lamp.

Collins clasped his hands happily in front of his chest and, smiling happily, replied, "The suggestions Your Ladyship so condescendingly offered regarding the decorations have made every thing easy." Darcy gave a discouraged shake of his head; five days prior he had left the dictionary in Lady Catherine's library open to the definition of "condescending", and had done the same with one he had found in the Parsonage: evidently Mr. Collins was not one to trouble himself with such matters.

"And who is to ring the peal?" Lady Catherine enquired.

Mr. Collins now turned his beaming countenance upon Mr. Darcy. "We have two new ringers, Your Ladyship: Turner and Tilden! They have joined together, in a show of fellowship. And we have but one man to thank for this blessing," he finished with enthusiasm, looking pointedly at Darcy.

"How is this?" enquired the Colonel.

"Have you not heard?" asked Collins in surprise. "Why, your honoured cousin has shown himself to be possessed of the wisdom of the ages." Darcy winced, and winced again when his cousin asked delightedly for the tale. It had lost nothing during its residence in the parson's memory, and Darcy, embarrassed and annoyed, had to bear with his cousin's merry grin as the tale unfolded; Elizabeth, on the other hand, registered no particular interest. When the parson had done, Colonel Fitzwilliam chafed Darcy happily and mercilessly, and at some length, before Elizabeth finally stepped in, coolly urging the Colonel to desist in the name of civility. Darcy could not be insensible to the change in the lady's manner towards him: her intervention on this occasion was an urging on the strength of her good breeding, not of her esteem.

To avoid reflection on this uncomfortable observation, Darcy chose instead to consider Mr. Collins: the absurdity of his retelling of the story, his generally repulsive demeanour, together with his fawning obedience to Lady Catherine's every whim, gave Darcy to contemplate how wholly unjust were society's rules; this man, though no longer a rival, of course, had made himself free to court Elizabeth in Hertfordshire, yet to Darcy she was denied by what society deemed "proper". As he listened on and on to Collins' speech, the notion that the parson, whose personal deity appeared to be Darcy's sometimes nonsensical Aunt Catherine, could have the right to wed a lady of Elizabeth's character, but that she was forbidden to Darcy, deeply offended his sense of justice, and provided him a more convenient object on which to turn the annoyance which resulted from his own self-condemnation.

Contemplating Mr. Collins and the absurdities and inequities associated with him, watching him trail behind his aunt like a puppy on a lead, brought to mind his cousin, St. Stephens, the duckling. On the heels of that diverting thought came the memory of whence it originated, and he stole an embarrassed look at Elizabeth. There were so many points on which she might, very understandably, feel resentment against him, had she but known, and surely she was entirely justified in her present coldness. He could only hope that she would come to allow that the retarding weight that held him back from declaring himself was not unreasonable, at least insofar as to acknowledge the certain disapprobation their nuptial would earn from Society; as she was clearly aware of her family's oft-demonstrated lack of decorum, he hoped that he might rely on this for his future redemption.

But in the next moment his mind stopped abruptly at the notion of Collins being a duckling, like St. Stephens; first Lady Catherine and Mrs. Bennet, and now Mr. Collins and Cousin George; that there should be two such notable instances of correspondence between his family and that of Elizabeth was more than unsettling. Looking about the room, he saw only two truly superior persons: Elizabeth and his cousin, Colonel Fitzwilliam. Very few men Darcy had ever met could compare to the Colonel when it came to honour, ability, and breeding, and he knew Elizabeth to be far above the other ladies of his acquaintance in her merits as a sister, as a daughter, and as an exemplar of her sex. The implications of these points on the connections that each party would be bringing to an union between Elizabeth and himself, gave him much to think on, and he turned it over slowly in his mind while watching his cousin entertain Elizabeth.

It was clear that Darcy's emotions had quite escaped his control, and were now colouring his every thought; but unlike Netherfield, where his rage at Wickham had had an object and sharpened his mind, the present confluence of warm esteem, excessive embarrassment, and a deep sense of injustice and frustration, had mired Darcy in a tangle of indecision that bewildered him, and made rational thought nearly impossible. After their guests had departed, he took himself upstairs to write to Georgiana; his letter, a convoluted affair that commingled his ideas of Society, Pender's discussion of human heredity, and St. Stephens's being a duckling, must have puzzled his sister on reading it, but it quite accurately reflected Darcy's own disordered state of mind.

Throughout the next day, determined to see it through to a conclusion, he devoted all his energies to the problem. At length, however, with greatest dissatisfaction, he was forced to acknowledge that it was simply beyond him to end this on his own: try as he might, he simply could not force it to a resolution. Without additional intelligence there never would be a final determination; he needs must hear from Elizabeth—on her feelings he must rely to break this stalemate. The Collinses and their guests were to come to Rosings that evening for tea; he hoped to find some opportunity of speaking to her, perhaps to arrange another meeting in the grove, where he might speak more openly, and discover the true nature of her disposition, both towards himself and as to a potential union. Without more information, he was certain, he would never find his way free of this impossible quandary, and be released.

When evening came, however, and the company from Hunsford arrived, Elizabeth was not among them. He immediately enquired, and heard from Mrs. Collins that Elizabeth was unwell, and had stayed home in consequence. His apprehensions awakened, he considered this through the hour they drank their tea; the longer he thought, the stronger his concerns became for her health. His fears grew greater as the others sat by, idly talking; and when the card tables came out, he excused himself, pleading indisposition—as he was certainly indisposed towards sitting there playing at cards, while Elizabeth lay ill and unattended at the Parsonage. Rather than to go to his chambers, of course, he hurried directly to her.

Darcy had by this time worked himself into a state of immoderate anxiety and alarm at the possibility Elizabeth might be seriously unwell; as he hastened across the darkened grounds, he forgot his embarrassment and misgivings: his only thoughts were for her well-being. Should she be seriously ill, he would ride that night himself to London, and fetch his own personal physician to attend her. Soon arriving at the Parsonage and being ushered into her presence, however, his urgent enquiries as to her health were answered favourably: she was not seriously ill. He sat down in relief, and assured himself it was so by seeing her look well, although her ailment had seemingly left her spirits low. His apprehensions over her illness, however unnecessary they had proven to be, now turned to an even deeper unease: what if she had been lost to him? What if, having found her truly ill, he had ridden off immediately to London, only to return too late? These terrors, coupled with the altogether repellent notion of leaving her, to return alone to the insipid elegance of Rosings, held him there with her in spite of the hour, and the fact that they were alone.

With high-wrought emotion, he rose and began pacing the room; the possibility that he might have lost her, and that he might never have spoken, he could not face. He paced across the floor in silence some minutes; the lady—his lady, his dearest Elizabeth—sat quietly watching; she understood him, he knew: his silences did not offend her any more than hers did him. He thought back warmly over the many instances when she had honoured him by sharing the recesses of her heart and mind, in consenting that he might enter into her silences.

Looking up and finding Elizabeth's eyes on his, he found himself suddenly and shockingly overset; it was not the moment he would have chosen, nor was he at all prepared, but her gaze stopt him where he stood, and his long-withheld emotion burst forth without preamble: "In vain have I struggled. It will not do. My feelings will not be repressed. You must allow me to tell you how ardently I admire and love you."

He saw her start and blush, but it was not to be expected that her modesty would permit her to speak.

He hurried on, carried along on the surge of his passion as it fought free of its bonds: "I have loved you ever since Netherfield, I think — but this I am sure you must know already; indeed, you must have been aware of my feelings, even before I was. But I hope you will believe me when I say I had not the slightest intention, at any moment, of trifling with your heart; I did, most earnestly, endeavour to protect you from knowing how I felt; but all my efforts have come to nought. I cannot tell you how you have haunted my thoughts, every where I have gone: in Town, at Pemberley — you are ever with me in my mind, and in my heart; I cannot look any where, but I see your smile. I was a fool to think I could deny you that place in my heart which is so completely yours, and that I could accept any sort of existence without you as part of it. Every cherished good that I can ever hope for, descends from you; I have come at last to recognise that you are as life itself to me.

"For so long I have wished to speak; but you must know the difficulties I have had to overcome: your family, your connections — the inferiority of their standing seemed an unconquerable barrier to our happiness. No matter with what exertions my heart would rail against it, the demands of character and judgement always stood opposed to my inclination. As I am head of the Darcy family now, I must of course be all the more vigilant to avoid any hint of degradation in a possible alliance, and if I could have stopt up my emotions, I would; but here, being with you, the passionate admiration I hold for you has prevailed over every feeling, overthrown every argument set against it—by comparison with my love for you, these considerations count for nought. I know I must look a fool to you, to have wasted so many months of our happiness on idle, vain debate; yet I hope you will not think me weak, or irresolute in my love for you, as I am certain you must recognise the duty I had to my family's honour to avoid any misalliance, and will forgive me that delay and indecision which must have injured you ever since Netherfield.

"I hope, and I pray, that you will accept these present measures by way of amendment, and reward that attachment I have found so impossible to overcome, through all the anxious days and months that have separated us, by accepting my hand in marriage."

At his conclusion, leaning an arm on the mantle of the hearth, Darcy thought he had expressed himself creditably, regardless of the extemporaneous manner of his beginning; all in all, he felt a great relief: all his endless deliberation, all that he had tormented himself with, was now behind him. He had found speaking his heart to Elizabeth much easier than he could have imagined; his faith in her was complete, and in openly speaking his feelings, it seemed to him that he was doing no more than confirming to her what she already knew—what they had already shared together in the quiet recesses of their hearts. His trials were over, and, from this night, he hoped never to be separated from her more. He turned to his beloved to accept her reply.

The lady spoke thus in return: "In such cases as this, it is, I believe, the established mode to express a sense of obligation for the sentiments avowed, however unequally they may be returned. It is natural that obligation should be felt, and if I could *feel* gratitude, I would now thank you. But I cannot—I have never desired your good opinion, and you have certainly bestowed it most unwillingly. I am sorry to have occasioned pain to any one. It has been most unconsciously done, however, and I hope will be of short duration. The feelings which, you tell me, have long prevented the acknowledgment of your regard, can have little difficulty in overcoming it after this explanation."

As Elizabeth began to speak, Darcy at first heard her words with greatest confusion: her manner expressed anger: could she still be angry with him? —he had just asked her for her hand in *marriage*. He had told her that he wished to join their lives together forever, that he would do anything for her—had already done much for her, indeed—and desired to share every thing life could offer: joys and sorrows, triumphs and defeats—how should her anger be so complete that it stood proof against such sincere application? But as the lady continued, he gradually became aware that in her response she was beyond curt—she was, in fact, being altogether rude; in her manner there was nothing but ire and resentment. Elizabeth, rude? Darcy thought incredulously. She is *never* rude—not to Miss Bingley, not even to Aunt Catherine! He heard her say "...never desired your good opinion..." with utmost bewilderment; after all the time they had spent together, after all the attentions she had shown him, both in Hertfordshire and here at Rosings, how was he to understand this?

He stood by the mantelpiece some moments, attempting to bring his thoughts into order, and to make sense of what she was saying. When he arrived at the cold and uncaring rejection at the end of her speech, he felt the stirrings of that anger that presaged an outburst of emotion. He strove against it, and, when certain he had risen above it, he said, "And this is all the reply which I am to have the honour of expecting! I might, perhaps, wish to be informed why, with so little *endeavour* at civility, I am thus rejected. But it is of small importance."

"I might as well enquire," she retorted heatedly, "why, with so evident a design of offending and insulting me, you chose to tell me that you liked me against your will, against your reason, and even against your character? Was not this some excuse for incivility, if I *was* uncivil? But I have other provocations. You know I have. Had not my own feelings decided against you, had they been indifferent, or had they even been favourable, do you think that any consideration would tempt me to accept the man, who has been the means of ruining, perhaps forever, the happiness of a most beloved sister?"

Again, Darcy was at a loss to understand her: "offend and insult"? thought he in wonder. How have I done that? "...against your will..." — He had never said that! But in the next moment, it was borne in upon him that she must somehow have learnt of his involvement in her sister's affairs — Edmund: blast! This, he then apprehended, was the true source of her anger, the reason behind her coldness. That she should be angry at his interference he could understand; but, in all honesty, he still could feel no remorse: even now, she had never stated as fact that her sister loved his friend; he was secure in knowing that this was because, in truth, she could not, and her delicacy and probity would not authorise her to misrepresent the case. That he had been right at the time, he doubted not — and still was, indeed: her sister did not love Bingley, and, fine person though she might be, he deserved some one who would return his love equally, regardless of any other consideration.

But Elizabeth had not done: "I have every reason in the world to think ill of you. No motive can excuse the unjust and ungenerous part you acted *there*. You dare not, you cannot deny that you have been the principal, if not the only means of dividing them from each other, of exposing one to the censure of the world for caprice and instability, the other to its derision for disappointed hopes, and involving them both in misery of the acutest kind."

Darcy looked at her in disbelief: he was astounded she could so misinterpret his actions; he had done no more than what was right, and necessary. In the absence of an over-powering affection for his friend on her sister's part, how could he *not* act to preserve his friend from such an alliance? And, her partiality to her sister notwithstanding, he knew her to be entirely sensible of her family's indiscretions and improprieties: had he not seen her embarrassed looks, time and again, in the face of her mother's ill-bred improprieties? Moreover, if not in justice to his friend, to what purpose did he follow him to London? If it was not a generous act to step in, to save his friend and support him through his heartache, when his own heart was wounded, then he did not know how to call it.

"Can you deny that you have done it?" she demanded, piqued by his silence.

Darcy, still amazed, answered back directly, "I have no wish of denying that I did every thing in my power to separate my friend from your sister, or that I rejoice in my success. Towards *him* I have been kinder than towards myself." While he had no wish to antagonise Elizabeth further, he could not forbear to express somewhat of the anger he felt towards the unfeeling rejection she had offered him, in the irritation of her temper.

"But it is not merely this affair," she continued, her eyes fixed hard upon him, "on which my dislike is founded. Long before it had taken place, my opinion of you was decided. Your character was unfolded in the recital which I received many months ago from Mr. Wickham. On this subject, what can you have to say? In what imaginary act of friendship can you here defend yourself? or under what misrepresentation, can you here impose upon others?"

Wickham – dear God above! Still, and again? Darcy felt his control beginning to slip away at the sound of that accursed name, and all his anger came to the fore. With greatest effort did he maintain his control, and manage to say, though in heated accents, "You take an eager interest in that gentleman's concerns."

"Who that knows what his misfortunes have been, can help feeling an interest in him?" demanded Elizabeth.

"His misfortunes!" Darcy spat out in aggravation and disgust, as his self-command gave way. "Yes, his misfortunes have been great indeed." His abhorrence at having to speak of this individual, to defend himself against him, when he had thought by now to be rejoicing in his betrothal, was beyond all endurance.

Elizabeth would not wait for him to continue. "And of your infliction," she accused him angrily. "You have reduced him to his present state of poverty, comparative poverty. You have withheld the advantages, which you must know to have been designed for him. You have deprived the best years of his life, of that independence which was no less his due than his desert. You have done all this! and yet you can treat the mention of his misfortunes with contempt and ridicule."

This was Darcy's end; he could do no more: that she still — even now, after knowing him and knowing Wickham, and after having listened to his proposal of *marriage* — that she still would take Wickham's part and give him preference; that she would still believe Darcy could somehow throw the man over without cause, could act in complete disregard of all that was right and honourable, was intolerably offensive. His tolerance overborne, he was done; and with the lady of his heart casting her despite in his face, nearly three decades of pent up anger reared its head and released its strength: "And this is your opinion of me! This is the estimation in which you hold me! I thank you for explaining it so fully. My faults, according to this calculation, are heavy indeed!" As his anger took possession of him, he turned his back that he might not show all that he felt, and stepped away from her for a moment. She had never said anything, not a single thing! — to prove his actions wrong, or to support her low opinion of him, as in all honesty she could not; he was convinced that she must now be speaking merely from anger—both on her own account, and on her sister's. But he was well assured that Elizabeth did, in fact, know perfectly well the difficulties that must attend their marriage, and could no longer tolerate accepting any blame on that account; or on *any* account, in fact. These thoughts taking no more than three steps to run through his mind, he spun to face her, and his vaulting anger answered hers: "But perhaps these offences might have been overlooked, had not your pride been hurt by my honest confession of the scruples that had long prevented my forming any serious design. These bitter accusations might have been suppressed, had I with greater policy concealed my struggles, and flattered you into the belief of my being impelled by unqualified, unalloyed inclination—by reason, by reflection, by every thing. But disguise of every sort is my abhorrence. Nor am I ashamed of the feelings I related. They were natural and just." Unhappily, his tongue was at this point running his affairs without reference to those powers he might, under kinder circumstances, have used to moderate his expressions. With hardly a pause for breath, he drove on: "Could you expect me to rejoice in the inferiority of your connections? To congratulate myself on the hope of relations, whose condition in life is so decidedly beneath my own?"

Beneath his high resentment and unfettered emotion, Darcy was immediately ashamed of having spoken the words; but, in the heat of his wrath, he could not allow them to be unjust—they were no more than the regrettable truth. But he saw anger rise in Elizabeth's eyes, and a momentary foreboding entered his heart.

"You are mistaken, Mr. Darcy, if you suppose that the mode of your declaration affected me in any other way, than as it spared me the concern which I might have felt in refusing you, had you behaved in a more gentleman-like manner."

She could not have chosen better: this last accusation, above all others, struck Darcy the hardest blow. To have behaved in an ungentlemanly fashion would have been a violation of every thing he believed to be right, all that he demanded of himself; but it was not he who had begun the incivilities; it was rather she who had set the heated, quarrelsome tone of their exchange, when she had rebuffed the offer of his heart so callously. He was formulating a stinging rebuttal when the import of the former portion of her statement struck heavily upon his consciousness.

When Darcy had been a young boy learning to shoot, the very first time he had fired on a living creature, a curious circumstance had occurred: his intended prey had been a rabbit, and just as he had laid his finger on the trigger, the small thing had turned to look full at him. He felt those rôles now reversed, as he looked into the burning contempt in Elizabeth's eyes.

With cold precision she said, "You could not have made me the offer of your hand in any possible way that would have tempted me to accept it."

Darcy felt the impact of this statement as it struck him; yet, as with many mortal wounds, he did not at first know its power. His first thought was merely confusion, then a mortified rejection of what his ears were telling him. Elizabeth, her face fully registering her wrath and scorn, went on, "From the very beginning, from the first moment I may almost say, of my acquaintance with you, your manners, impressing me with the fullest belief of your arrogance, your conceit, and your selfish disdain of the feelings of others, were such as to form that ground-work of disapprobation, on which succeeding events have built so immoveable a dislike; and I had not known you a month before I felt that you were the last man in the world whom I could ever be prevailed on to marry."

Only then did the truth illume Darcy to his core: this was neither a momentary pique over his delay in confessing his love, nor for his interference in her sister's life — no; Elizabeth had never *concealed* her love: she had *felt* none, none at all. Nay, infinitely worse — she despised him entirely, and had done, all the time he was imagining she held a regard for him. Deep, deep within him, something failed — something vital and singular; but, still protected by the armour of his anger, he contained his injury and mortification. Their intimacy, the intimacy he had imagined, lay broken and twisted at his feet; he did not meet with her at any point, did not share any coincidence of esteem, hope, or intention; they were as strangers, and it was now absolutely necessary to keep the harm she had done him from showing on his face. With a dazed detachment that sprang from his shock, he felt himself to be standing on one edge of a vast divide, and she, far distant, on the opposing; between them stretched a threatening void that pulled at him, compelling him forward towards ruination. In the crushing confusion and passion of the moment, his rational powers utterly renounced their sovereign control, but his manners — dull, plodding, and dependable — came once more to his rescue: "You have said quite enough, Madam. I perfectly comprehend your feelings, and have now only to be ashamed of what my own have been. Forgive me for having taken up so much of your time, and accept my best wishes for your health and happiness." Hardly knowing what he was saying or doing, he bowed and walked quickly from the room, holding back hard against his fevered emotions.

He walked away from the Parsonage; once freed from Elizabeth's restraining influence, his anger emerged to fill his entire being; it supplanted his shame and sustained him on the uncommonly brief journey back to Rosings. Wickham's treachery and Elizabeth's wilful complicity in it enraged him with all the frustration and sense of injury he had suffered throughout his childhood; it was no less bitter now to experience such want of faith and credence than it had been when he was a boy. He let himself in through the west wing, that he might not encounter any one of the household; on gaining his rooms, he instantly set himself the task of accepting and adjusting to this new understanding, and re-establishing his self-command; but in this he was not able to bring his accustomed discretion and judgement to bear — these were denied him. This was not the precision of logic and discrimination, but rather a brutal, maddened bashing of any traitorous emotions that beset him and sought to bring alloy to the purity of his rage. His savage and resentful temper having broken free with transcendent force, he was powerless to contain it; each time such disloyal sentiments as loss or humiliation would break free, he would contemptuously smite them down and cast them back into the darkness, there to await another season. He returned again and again to the revelations at the Parsonage, reviewing every thing that had been said; under the sway of his rage and immoderate condemnation, he could not allow Elizabeth to be justified to the slightest degree; neither in the rancour she had displayed, nor in her uncaring refusal of his love; even though Wickham had perverted her heart and turned it against him, still — she had known them both, and had chosen Wickham over him. He went back over every instance of peculiar favour she had shown him; it was not possible she could have been insensible of his growing admiration and attachment. His resentment grew apace as he reflected on how she must have seen his rising affection for her, yet had done nothing to warn him, nothing to discourage him — how *could* she be so aloof and uncaring? He hardly knew how to believe Elizabeth would treat him so unfeelingly.

Perkins came and went silently at times, leaving first food, then brandy; Darcy scarcely noticed him, and when he did, dismissed him to his bed. Darcy had no need of food, and he scorned the weakness of drink.

Anger gives strength to endure, but not wisdom to change; through that long night, Darcy's anger enabled him to vanquish the humiliation and grief that would occasionally seek to overset him — but it did not sanction him to examine them, or credit them in any way. Any time his sense of justice tried to give Elizabeth the right to her feelings, or give credit to any of her assertions, his inflamed sensibilities would strike it down again immediately.

He could, at least, comfort himself on one point: he had rightly interpreted her character. Any one of a dozen women he knew in London would have taken him gladly, regardless of their attraction to him — but Elizabeth had turned him down without a thought. He could almost feel a grudging pride in the disinterested sentiments and delicate sense of honour that motivated her; but in them he saw an uncomfortable reflection of himself, from which he instantly turned away.

Chapter Twenty-Four

*W*hen the darkest watches of the night wrapped the house in perfect stillness, Darcy began to feel his honour commanding him to seek redress against Elizabeth's accusations: he must correct her information — to have her think him a wanton meddler and heartless blackguard was intolerable. Having once allowed a misapprehension to stand between them to his regret, he would not allow it again; there were two points on which he could — must — defend himself: Miss Bennet and Wickham. His character must be retrieved from the damage Wickham had done it; and he could not let Elizabeth believe that his influencing his friend was mere officiousness, or pride of position. Therefore, as soon as his passion had waned to the point he felt capable of composing a cold and coherent statement in his defence, he began to write[1]:

> "Be not alarmed, Madam, on receiving this letter, by the apprehension of its containing any repetition of those sentiments, or renewal of those offers, which were last night so disgusting to you. I write without any intention of paining you, or humbling myself, by dwelling on wishes, which, for the happiness of both, cannot be too soon forgotten…

That *he* felt the anger behind his words might be argued; but he was persuaded that the words themselves were cool and collected. With something like his accustomed precision of thought, he decided he ought to deal

---

[1] The full text is to be found in Correspondence: Darcy, April 25th.

with the first thing first: her sister's sentiments towards Bingley, and its effect on his actions in London. Not only had it been the first accusation levelled at him, but it was the most important argument driving his actions in December. Having reviewed each point many times before broaching the subject with Bingley, his arguments came easily to mind; reassured by this evidence of his self-command, he continued:

> I had not been long in Hertfordshire, before I saw, in common with others, that Bingley preferred your eldest sister to any other young woman in the country. — But it was not till the evening of the dance at Netherfield that I had any apprehension of his feeling a serious attachment...I observed my friend's behaviour attentively; and I could then perceive that his partiality for Miss Bennet was beyond what I had ever witnessed in him. Your sister I also watched. — Her look and manners were open, cheerful, and engaging as ever, but without any symptom of peculiar regard, and I remained convinced from the evening's scrutiny, that though she received his attentions with pleasure, she did not invite them by any participation of sentiment... I shall not scruple to assert that the serenity of your sister's countenance and air was such as might have given the most acute observer a conviction that, however amiable her temper, her heart was not likely to be easily touched.

He hoped that this might protect his friend from the disapprobation of both Elizabeth and her sister. But, while Miss Bennet's indifference was the most important reason for his interference, there were others: he could not, in truth and in justice, pass over the many indiscretions of her family.

> My objections to the marriage were not merely those which I last night acknowledged to have required the utmost force of passion to put aside in my own case; the want of connection could not be so great an evil to my friend as to me. — But there were other causes of repugnance; — causes which, though still existing, and existing to an equal degree in both instances, I had myself endeavoured to forget, because they were not immediately before me...

While these arguments, he believed, were forceful, Darcy knew that Elizabeth would doubtless see a blameable degree of complaisance in Bingley's willingness to give over her sister; he wished to inform her that his friend was in no way at fault, and did not do so without struggle. He continued:

> The part which I acted is now to be explained. — His sisters' uneasiness had been equally excited with my own; our coincidence of feeling was soon discovered; and, alike sensible that no time was to be lost in detaching their brother, we shortly resolved on joining him directly in London...

This, then, would account for Bingley being persuaded that his belief in Miss Bennet's attachment was in error. He was careful to recall that, even though she had certainly been thoroughly unreserved last night, Elizabeth had never come out and attested to her sister's love for his friend. That being the case, he could not but hold to his original conclusion regarding Miss Bennet's sentiments. But he felt he must allow for the possibility of error on his part, although he could see but little possibility of being mistaken in his observations of the couple; he therefore addressed these issues as well. But neither could he give himself permission to pass over his one true fault: the use of artifice and obfuscation to keep his friend from Miss Bennet's company in London. It was wrong, and he had felt it to be so at the time, but the sacrifice of principle had been made to spare his friend, and he would abide by its consequences. After having dealt with Bingley's concerns, and his own contributions to the measures taken in December, he wrote in summation:

> ...done for the best. — On this subject I have nothing more to say, no other apology to offer. If I have wounded your sister's feelings, it was unknowingly done; and though the motives which governed me may to you very naturally appear insufficient, I have not yet learnt to condemn them...

But now, he had Wickham to deal with: as he set out to write on this subject, however, he was cast back into those disturbing and circuitous thoughts that had confounded him in Hertfordshire. But, being influenced by the evidence of Elizabeth's character and honour in the very act of refusing him, he was now completely satisfied that she could be trusted with this secret; in any event, defending himself against her accusations was required by his honour, notwithstanding the risk.

At this point Darcy hesitated; having come to the point, he recognised that Elizabeth's championing of Wickham under such circumstances as last evening's could only have come from a high regard for the man. While it pained him to imagine Elizabeth could have feelings for him, no matter to what degree, he had to feel that the mere fact of any such favour made it all the more important that she should know the truth. Inasmuch as he could have no idea what Wickham had told her, from what part of their association he had drawn his lies, the only avenue open to him was to tell her every thing. The tale was long, but every detail was etched clearly in his mind.

> With respect to that other, more weighty accusation, of having injured Mr. Wickham, I can only refute it by laying before you the whole of his connection with my family. Of what he has *particularly* accused me, I am ignorant; but of the truth of what I shall relate, I can summon more than one witness of undoubted veracity...

Having now given her full details of his association with the man, it still occurred to him that Elizabeth would have no means of judging between the history he presented and the one Wickham had offered her, whatever it might be, not to mention but what she would almost certainly prefer to believe Wickham over him. This delay in responding to her accusations on his behalf might easily be seen an equivocation to gain time in order to concoct a fable; he recalled the notable preference Elizabeth had demonstrated for Colonel Fitzwilliam, however, and was persuaded that she would believe *him*, where she might not chose to believe Darcy. He finished his letter thus:

> This, Madam, is a faithful narrative of every event in which we have been concerned together; and if you do not absolutely reject it as false, you will, I hope, acquit me henceforth of cruelty towards Mr. Wickham. I know not in what manner, under what form of falsehood, he has imposed on you; but his success is not, perhaps, to be won-

dered at. Ignorant as you previously were of every thing concerning either, detection could not be in your power, and suspicion certainly not in your inclination. You may possibly wonder why all this was not told you last night. But I was not then master enough of myself to know what could or ought to be revealed. For the truth of every thing here related, I can appeal more particularly to the testimony of Colonel Fitzwilliam, who from our near relationship and constant intimacy, and still more as one of the executors of my father's will, has been unavoidably acquainted with every particular of these transactions. If your abhorrence of *me* should make *my* assertions valueless, you cannot be prevented by the same cause from confiding in my cousin; and that there may be the possibility of consulting him, I shall endeavour to find some opportunity of putting this letter in your hands in the course of the morning. I will only add, God bless you.

Fitzwilliam Darcy."

As he finished, having expressed himself as completely and rationally as he could, he knew that with his final words he was giving over every thing that mattered to him; he felt all his love and hope fall away into that vast, dark chasm that divided him from Elizabeth. For just a moment, his loss welled up inside him, forsaken and barren, but his eye chanced to light on Wickham's name in his letter; his anger rose up in an instant, sweeping his quavering weakness away.

The sun was lighting the sky from beneath the horizon by the time he had finished; reference to his watch gave it as close on five o'clock. Darcy sat back down to wait for the household to stir; enervated and stupid, his mental energies banked low, his mind would catch snippets of the scene last night, but would pass on directly without consideration or emotion. Perkins appeared eventually; rousing himself from his lethargy, he asked his man to bring him coffee, and a change of clothes; Perkins looked about the room at the guttered candles, and the bits of quill strewn atop the desk, and left directly without speaking. When Perkins had gone, Darcy went to the window and leaned against the frame, staring out across the lane to the Parsonage for a long while; he felt himself to be balanced on a knife's edge between the anger that shielded him still, and a bleak desolation that threatened to unseat his very reason. How long he might have stood there, locked in stasis between two powerful forces, he did not know: Perkins's silent appearance with his coffee and clothes brought him back to himself. Even the mundane and trivial irritation of Perkins's arrival tipped the scales: his anger flared and centred him. His honour remained to him, if nothing else—and that all woven into the contents of the letter at hand; all that remained was to convey it to Elizabeth. He drank and dressed without attending, then gave his letter a final cursory review. Signing and dating it, and determining to give it to her at the earliest possible moment, he set out for the grove.

On reaching it, however, he was loath to return to those spots where he had so recently found such enjoyment in Elizabeth's company; therefore, as it was really too early to expect her to be out, he staid in those portions of the grove closest to the Parsonage. He wandered back and forth amongst the trees, not letting himself think of his coming meeting with Elizabeth; his emotions were too raw, and his injuries too deep: if he thought too long on what it would be like to face her, he feared either his resolve would fail or his anger would again break free. But the exhaustion of a sleepless night helped him maintain control; and, putting one foot in front of the other, again and again, trying to see only the path before him, listening only to the breeze and the birds—anything rather than attending to the deep anguish that roiled beneath the surface—he waited out the morning.

After a considerable length of time spent pacing amongst the trees, passing from one side of the Lodge to the other, as he once more turned back down the lane, he spied a lady walking away from the Lodge further along. Quickly following, he saw it was in fact Elizabeth; she had just reached one of the gates in the paling, and was looking in. He called out to her, and, seeing her stop, made his way directly to the gate.

He could not bring himself to meet her eyes, knowing he would surely see no welcome there—not now, not ever—and he could not bear to see again that look of censure and disgust she had fixed on him the evening before. He therefore kept his gaze away from hers, and holding himself in, that nothing of what he felt might show, with the careful manners that had been worked into him since infancy, he told her: "I have been walking in the grove some time in the hope of meeting you. Will you do me the honour of reading that letter?" He bowed as she took it from his hand, and, still without looking at her, turned and made his way back towards Rosings.

He sought out Colonel Fitzwilliam on entering the house, meaning to inform him of the office he had assigned him with respect to Elizabeth. On seeing him approach, however, his cousin cried out: "Darcy, there you are! I was going to trot over to the Parsonage, to take leave. Care to join me?"

After a brief hesitation, Darcy nodded without speaking; he must pay his compliments to Mrs. Collins and her husband at some time before he and his cousin left the next day, and, as he was already up and about, he might as well make the return trip now and be done. Besides, there was the possibility that Elizabeth might not yet have returned, and he would be spared the necessity of attempting to converse with her; if it were otherwise, he could let his cousin take the burden of conversation from him.

"Fitzwilliam," said he to the Colonel as they walked along, "there is something I want you to do for me."

"Of course, Darcy. What is it?"

"There is a possibility that Miss Bennet will ask you about Georgiana and Wickham. If she does so, I want you to tell her what you know."

That Colonel Fitzwilliam was exceedingly surprised at this request was clearly marked by his expression, and he asked, "What on Earth could have brought this about? Why should Miss Bennet have any need to know about Georgiana and Wickham?"

"It is a matter involving my honour, Fitzwilliam; Wickham fed her a lie about me that has damaged my character in her eyes. I have given her an account of the man, complete and accurate, to counter this lie; she may wish to verify it with you: that is all."

"'That is all'?" demanded the Colonel. "*All*? You have told Miss Bennet things I have withheld from my own parents!"

"I have, yes."

"Dirks, what has got into you? To have revealed your sister's...error in judgement...I could have sworn you would never share that with any living..." the Colonel's voice trailed off, and he stared at his cousin. "Miss Bennet is the lady," he stated.

Darcy looked at him, but said nothing. Colonel Fitzwilliam pressed him: "Dear Lord — Dirks — is Miss Bennet the one you want to marry?"

"She was," Darcy acknowledged in an emotionless voice, "but that matter is closed, Edmund, and I would ask that you not mention it again; nor would I have Georgiana told of Miss Bennet's presence here amongst us: it might distress her."

"In Heaven's name, Dirks, what..." the Colonel stopped on seeing his cousin's face. "Very well; if that is what you want."

"Thank you, Edders. Truly — thank you."

The Colonel's face was troubled, and he was quiet the remainder of the short walk to the Parsonage. As they drew near the house, Darcy told his cousin, "Fitzwilliam, I shall not stay long, but if Miss Bennet should happen not to be in, might you wait for her a bit? I would have this matter settled before we leave, if possible." His cousin frowned and looked pensively at his friend, but only nodded. Darcy placed a grateful hand on his shoulder.

It so happened that Elizabeth was *not* yet returned, to Darcy's great relief, and he staid only minutes before departing. On regaining his rooms, he sent Perkins down to Lady Catherine with the message that he was indisposed, and would come down when he felt more himself. He settled into a chair, staring directly ahead; in time his weariness worked on him, and he nodded. He did not stay long at rest, though, and he passed the remaining morning hours dozing fitfully: falling into a dark and exhausted sleep, only to awaken shortly thereafter, from a discomfort which was as much mental as it was physical.

He went down to dinner, just to get out of his rooms: neither he nor the Colonel had much to say; their aunt, attributing this to their disappointment at leaving Rosings, kindly took upon herself all discussion required at table that evening. Darcy, of course, was disinclined to even attempt conversation, and Colonel Fitzwilliam seemed very preoccupied, and looked often in Darcy's direction. This state of affairs lasted through breakfast the next morning; Darcy, having slept as little on his last night at Rosings as he had on his first, had little energy for anything save the barest minimum demanded by courtesy. The Colonel, ever the gentleman, roused himself at the end to say his thanks and pay his respects properly before they set out. Darcy said what he could, but all he could wish for was to be in the coach and on his way home.

The two spoke little on the trip, as the Colonel did not wish to intrude on his friend's temper, saying only "You know I shall not press you, Dirks; only do let me know, when you can, what this has all been about." Darcy nodded, but still found nothing to say. They parted sombrely at Knightsbridge, and Darcy went on alone. When he arrived back in Grosvenor Square a short ride later, he forced himself to revive sufficiently to greet his sister, then, pleading fatigue from his trip, he went up to his rooms.

Taking off his travelling clothes, he went to wash the dust off his face at the washstand; splashing the water on his face, he pressed his hands against his eyes and stood there for some time, vacantly listening to the drops of water fall from him into the basin. His strength and resolve seemed to fall with them, each one leaving him weaker and more vulnerable; for the first time since he had left the Parsonage on that evening nearly two days before, he stopped fighting against the injuries he had received at Elizabeth's hands: his utter exhaustion, coupled with an unprecedented and extreme weakness of spirit, rendered him unable any longer to resist; as his spirits ebbed, an expanding pain in his chest caused him to slowly pull in on himself; his breath came in shallow draughts, and he sank down until only his elbows held him, head nearly level with the basin. His tortured emotions crushed him utterly: he could find no release, no way to escape his suffering. He recognised that something essential within him had died, the loss of which he did not know how to survive; he had been cut off, in some manner, from his life—when he tried to think of next steps or new directions, he could sense no future ahead of him at all: he had no prospects of happiness, foresaw neither strength nor purpose; it was as if his very soul had been dissevered from him. He staid there, transfixed by the deep, oppressive pain of heartbreak, and the sharp agony of shame, for a very long while: how long, he did not know. A chance noise of some one passing by his door brought him upright at last, lest any one should enter and see him in this state. He wrapped his wounds and pain back up as best he could inside him, binding them in with that pride which would allow no one to see him laid thus low; but anger no longer befriended him, and he was without protection from his injuries: pride alone kept him from his knees. Suffering unceasingly from the wounds that do not heal, for the first time in his life, Darcy of Pemberley had no slightest idea of what to do, where to turn, or how he might go on.

Correspondence

EDITOR'S NOTE
N.B.: It is not necessary to follow the correspondence in its entirety to understand or appreciate the history contained in the body of the work; when important to the movement of the story, the letters, either in part or in whole, have been included in the text. As the written word was so important a means of communication during the time before the advent of electronic communication, though, the letters, even those with no part to play in the story, are included separately to give the reader a chance to follow the story from a different, and perhaps even deeper, perspective, and at a pace more consistent with that experienced by the story's characters.

The correspondence between Mr. Darcy and his sister is given in chronological order by correspondent. The various threads interweave in time, making it all but impossible to follow each thread individually with a proper chronology; it is necessary therefore to separate them in this way. References are given to the appropriate replies, where applicable, to facilitate following the chain of correspondence correctly.

Letters from Miss Georgiana Darcy

*****

Bath
Thursday, January 9, —

Dearest Fitzwilliam,

We are arrived in Bath; the roads were poor, especially through Wiltshire, but Aunt Eleanor and I are none the worse for wear. We have only just finished settling in, and we are in the drawing-room with every one—a very lively scene, I declare! I am nicely out of the way here in the corner at the secretaire, where I can see and hear every thing as I write.

Goodness, but our young cousins are a noisy group! —although of course they are very young. I have just had one (Fitzwilliam, I can *not* think of his name—is that not horrible? It will come to me, though) try to pull me out of the chair where I sit, to come play, and he has undone my sash in the process. But there is one very dear little one, little Thomas, so sweet and quiet as he sits by the fire at his mother's feet! I have got him to smile, and I have promised myself to get speech of him before the evening is gone. He is shy, not yet five, with the fairest hair and biggest eyes of any child that ever was seen.

My aunt is very much in her element, and to listen to her talk with her sisters you would think them still in earliest youth: so eager to hear and to tell all the news from each side! —they can none of them speak fast enough. I have just counted up the number of people in the room, and there are a round dozen: sisters, sons, daughters, nieces and nephews; how different from our life at Pemberley! Their Christmas holidays must be a sight to behold. I am sure to have a pleasant stay here amongst them.

Little Thomas has just waved a tiny wave at me, and I shall end this to see if I might further my acquaintance with the gentleman.

Write soon, Fitzwilliam, and tell me how you do.

Your loving sister,

Georgiana Darcy

*For reply, see Darcy, January 15.

*****

Bath

Friday, January 17, —

Dear Fitzwilliam,

Bath seems, if such be possible, even gayer and more bustling than London. We have been to the pump rooms nearly every day, this evening we are to go to a concert in the Octagon Room, and Wednesday there was a chorale in the Upper Rooms. It has rained twice, yesterday for the whole day, keeping every one cooped up, and the young ones suffered for it: so boring to be within the whole day long! Some of the boys did, in fact, escape from their governess to the outer world, only to return in a wonderful state of disarray and dirtiness.

Oh, there is altogether such a coming and going, such staying and leaving, such a fine commotion amongst all our friends; it is beyond describing! Shall I confess to you that I find it wearying at times, and am only too happy to be here at the secretaire where I might step aside from the crush for a half-hour of repose? Little Thomas has come to stand by me as I write; we have become fast friends — in large part, I believe, because I am the quietest of his relations. He is of delicate sensibility, and likes having his feelings catered to; not at all like his boisterous elder brothers. He stands to my left and holds my hand when he can, asking all manner of questions. He is fascinated by words on a page: I think he conceives pen and ink to be some sort of magic; he is very curious as to how I might be speaking with my brother thus silently: I believe he finds the idea very appealing. He is altogether a most charming little boy.

I have received yours of the 15th, and I think I agree with you, Fitzwilliam, that a little time from the pressing concerns and commotion of Town would do you good. I would happily seek an invitation for you to come to Bath, but for the fact that I fear the children would be almost as vexatious to you as are the fashionable set in London; they, some of them, are made more free by association, and their fond and indulgent parents see in this only good. Therefore I shall resist the inclination to ask you here, for your own sake.

Your description of the finding in Egypt fires my imagination with visions of the Pharaohs, and the knowledge and wisdom that might still be trapped in the writings of the ancients. It is, perhaps, unfortunate that it is taken by the French, but did you not tell me once that science transcends national boundaries? Surely so rare a find will not be hoarded up and secreted away from the world in this modern age, when even heads of state are philosophers of renown? I trust that this will be the case.

I must ascend now to dress; we are off to the theatre to-night, although I do not know what we are to see; I always forget to ask these things. I shall let you know when next I write. Till then, be well, dearest Brother; and I hope you may find some amiable destination to lure you from Town. Your caring and affectionate sister,
Georgiana Darcy

*For reply, see Darcy, January 26.
*****

Bath
Tuesday, January 28, —
Dear Brother,

We have had a delightful visit, but I begin to be anxious to be home. My aunt, too, has said that she has had a sufficiency of relations, and has begun to think of returning to London.

In your letter of the 26th, you mention that you contemplate a visit to Oxford; I hope you find the looked-for guidance from Mr. Pender. I wish I might see your university one day: your descriptions and stories about it always make me long to make the visit myself.

I have tried, Brother, to take your admonitions to heart and forbid the familiarities I spoke of in the younger set here—I cannot but confess, however, that I have largely failed: not that I disagree, of course, but they mean no harm, and see in me, I think, one who is not so distant from them in age that they need hold me in awe; nor would I have them do so, in truth—I have no wish to be awful and forbidding in character, or even simply by virtue of my age. I find myself caught betwixt and between: neither suited to join in their frivolity, nor in the more stately and meaningful discourse of my aunt and her relations. In either case, silence seems my best response, and the course I find easiest to follow.

I have tried the library here several times, but, as Bath is meant for diversion, the library's contents have never been much thought of. It does offer a convenient shelter, however, as I believe I am the only inmate of the house who goes into it.

I hope and expect to see you soon, Brother, and as Aunt Eleanor has not spoken of a stop in Hampshire, I trust we will be back in London by the second week in February, at the latest. Until then, please take care of yourself; I remain:
Your loving and homeward turning sister,
Georgiana Darcy

*****

*Grosvenor Square
Thursday, April 10, —

Dearest Fitzwilliam,

I have received your letter from Tuesday, and yes, you are entirely too cruel, indeed! It is one thing for you to say such things to me, but I pray you again, promise not to speak them aloud to any one; it terrifies me to imagine the result of such disobliging expressions getting abroad. I wonder you can even think them, Brother; what my father would say I do not know! And I certainly shall not ask the Rector to pray for any one capable of such meanness. There!

Now! I am pleased that the Colonel will have more pleasures open to him than in years past, but what of you, Fitzwilliam? Will you truly have nothing to do there but labour on Lady Catherine's books? I know that is why you go, but, if I mistake not, was that not your complaint last year, the lack of diversion? I remember you saying that Aunt Catherine's library was "pedestrian, at best"; is there nothing at all to divert you for an entire fortnight? That would be such a shame.

I always feel such sympathy for my cousin—imagine living with Lady Catherine, and always being so ill; poor thing, how she must long to breathe free and be strong! Whenever I have, in prior years, thought myself trodden down or ill used by the world, I have often used Cousin Anne as a reminder of those things for which I should be thankful.

I have been enjoying the use of *our* library while you are absent; Mrs. Annesley has offered to bring me any number of books, including novels, from a lending library she frequents. Would this be proper, Fitzwilliam? I admit to a certain curiosity, but one hears such dreadful things about novels and the low impressions they create, I am very hesitant. I shall wait for your guidance in this matter.

Correspondence

That, dear Brother, is all from here, I am afraid. I hope you continue well, and that you will be free to return home soon.

Your affectionate sister,
Georgiana Darcy

*For reply, see Darcy, April 14.

*****

Grosvenor Square
Wednesday, April 16, —

Dearest Fitzwilliam,

Your letter of the 14th, was, I confess, too deep for my poor brain; the one part I did understand and find amusing, though, was your adieu, wherein you said there was little more to be said for you: after four pages of dense philosophical debate, it is no wonder that there should be little more to be said! But you are *too* bad to Mr. Collins, and he a clergyman—for shame, Fitzwilliam! I vow you only say these things to make me blush, and why you would bother, when you are too far away to see your success, I cannot imagine.

From what I could make of your letter, it is a question of marriage: when it is acceptable and when not, and with whom, is not it? Is this something you have under consideration, Fitzwilliam? In writing that last I had thought I was teazing, but on reflection, I now ask it in earnest: is this something you have under consideration, Fitzwilliam? I do hope you would not let me be surprised by a decision such of moment. No, I know you would not. It is well; I breathe again.

Mrs. Annesley has suggested I mention to you a Mrs. Francis Burney, an author of one of the novels she had in mind for me to read. Do you know her works, and whether they might be altogether wholesome? Oh, and let me not forget to mention that Aunt Eleanor has instructed me to tell you that there will be another dinner *and* a ball, on your return from Kent; while you may be certain I would never take such liberty, I did think it would amuse you to hear.

Your devoted sister,

Georgiana Darcy

*For reply, see Darcy, April 20.

*For reply, see Darcy, April 20.

*****

Letters from Mr. Fitzwilliam Darcy

*****

Dear Georgiana,

Well, we have had our ball. It began well enough, though it was not until the third set that I could secure Miss Bennet's hand. As you predicted, I was very well pleased to stand up with her. But I regret to say that the evening was not to end as well as it began.

To begin with, I had a worry I did not share with you in my last—something I wish I did not have to report: I have again seen the man who betrayed you. He has but recently joined the regiment stationed here in Meryton, and, owing to Mr. Bingley's ignorance of the fact, he was included in the invitation issued to the officers of that corps. I confess that this had an influence on my decision to stay, as I hoped to give Miss Elizabeth Bennet some measure of warning about the man. While he thankfully did not attend the ball, I fear he has in some way already garnered Miss Elizabeth Bennet's good opinion; this had a rather dampening effect on the time I spent with her.

This was not the only circumstance which interfered with my hopes for the evening, however, nor even the most pressing: my attentions were drawn away from Miss Elizabeth Bennet perforce, as it appears Mr. Bingley has formed a strong attachment to Miss Jane Bennet, the elder sister. The lady, while a fine young woman, unfortunately does not return his affection equally; given her family's connections and general deportment, this unequal attachment is of grave concern. I believe him to be sufficiently enamoured of Miss Bennet that he will offer for her, and it is my intention to remove to London to-morrow that I may give him to understand what he is about. You may therefore address future correspondence to Grosvenor Square.

I still mean to be at Pemberley on the eleventh December to escort you back to Town; hopefully by then this will all have blown over. Please forgive my brevity, Dearest, but there are many details to attend to, if, as I hope, I am to depart early to-morrow morning. May God bless,
Your loving brother,
Fitzwilliam Darcy

*****

*Grosvenor Square
Wednesday, January 15, —

Dearest Georgiana,

Thank you for your letter informing me of your safe arrival; I am sorry to hear the roads were incommodious. The house has been very quiet since your departure, or it seems so to me; quite a change from the scene before the holidays: I believe I shall remember your dinner…pardon me, my aunt's dinner…for quite some time. Really, there has been so little going on here I must charge my thoughts to come up with enough to fill a page. Every one has left Grosvenor Square,

Correspondence

of course, and London's fashionable set seem more addicted to gossip than ever this Season, which you know I find irksome, so I have not been much inclined to go out amongst them. I have been filling my days with books — both perusing them and purchasing them. On my honour, I some times feel that the best and only reason for staying in Town is for having access to literature.

I have just finished reading an account of a singular discovery in the town of Rashid, Egypt, last summer: a stone which appears to be inscribed with a message in three different tongues, the last of which is recognizable as Greek, whilst the other two appear more ancient still, and are thought to be like unto the hieroglyphs found on many of Egypt's antiquities. Fascinating! The one regrettable aspect is that it was discovered and taken by Bonaparte's army. Heaven knows what the French may do with such a scientific treasure in their egalitarian zeal: the sanctity of scientific knowledge does not always hold its proper place in the esteem of *les citoyens*.

As for our relations in Bath, given the mortuary silence of Grosvenor Square, I might almost envy you a bit of liveliness. Where was the mother, or the governess, of the one who un-sashed you, may I ask? I do not like to see such license given to children; it does not do to train them up to such disobliging and disrespectful habits. I beg you will not suffer such again without giving proper notice to those responsible for their charges; I will not have you subjected to indignity, even by a relation. I protest, it appears to me that our once-great nation is on an ever-increasing race towards anarchy, what with the decadence of the capital's first circles and our profoundly lax approach to rearing our children. One is tempted to retreat, firmly and forever, to the security and propriety of the North, and never leave Pemberley again.

Ah…well, perhaps that is excessive. I find my tolerance of impropriety has ebbed to an all-time low; I think a holiday from Town would be well: I shall think on this further. Meanwhile, enjoy Bath, and be assured that I remain,
Your silent, but loving brother,
Fitzwilliam Darcy

*For reply, see Georgiana, January 17.

*****

*Grosvenor Square
Sunday, January 26, —

Dearest Georgiana,

I have settled on an "amiable destination" to "lure" me from Town: I have decided to make an excursion to Oxford, to visit my old professor, Mr. Pender. It will not be for long; I merely wish to consult with him on an affair that is most efficiently dealt with in person, and it gives me the excuse I needed to leave London. I shall leave this Wednesday, and return, I expect, on Saturday; certainly within the week, regardless. This will likely be my last, therefore, until your return.

Again, dearest, let me ask that you not accept impertinences from our cousins. Even though I am sure you do so out of an abundance of regard and forbearance, it is not a good thing, either for you or for them. As mistress of Pemberley (I know…but you are, in fact) you must try to hold yourself above such treatment. It is, of course, a fine line to walk, especially amongst friends, but it is one I would have you learn to navigate. A word to the parents by your aunt would surely be sufficient.

And so, you have made a friend in young Cousin Thomas, have you? Perhaps I should ask if it was your conquest, or his—it sounds as if he has quite stolen your heart. Just remember not to pack him up with your other belongings when you return: by your account, I am sure he would be sorely missed for the uniqueness of his quiet nature and sweet disposition.

There is little else to share from London; I look forward to seeing you in a fortnight's time, or thereabouts. Until then, I am,
Your loving brother,
Fitzwilliam Darcy

*For reply, see Georgiana, January 28.
*****

*Rosings
Tuesday, April 8, —

Dearest Georgiana,

Well, the Colonel and I are arrived at Rosings: please have the rector say a prayer for wayward travellers, that we may wend our way safely home from these strange and barren shores.

In truth, this year promises better than last; Lady Catherine' new parson, Mr. Collins, is newly married, and his wife has her sister and a friend staying with her, so at least there is a more diverse company here than in prior years. Do you recollect the old parson, Mr. Teesdale, and how he used to fawn on Her Ladyship? By comparison with Mr. Collins, he seems in retrospect a paragon of manly pride; Collins is as wonderful an example of meekness as I have ever seen; he is exactly the man for Her Ladyship, however, and she is prodigiously pleased with him. He follows after her like a puppy, and, if asked, I am sure he would be as happy to lick her boots as any puppy ever seen (is that too *very* cruel, do you think?).

Colonel Fitzwilliam has great plans for Lady Catherine's horseflesh, as they have seen not one iota of exercise since last we were here, so he has hopes of staying away from my aunt's notice very continually. And I believe he hopes to make himself agreeable to the two ladies visiting Mrs. Collins; he has already made himself known to them, so it may be that his time here will be more congenial than he had anticipated.

For myself, I foresee an extended stay in the Rosings library, as a first glance at Lady Catherine's books shows them to be in a state of considerable disarray. Prudent is not a word one would apply to Her Ladyship; fortunately, given her retired style of living, even her profligacy is unable to exceed the estate's income.

I fear that is all I know for now; but, as this will not be a long visit, perhaps you will forgive me a sparse and sporadic correspondence. Truly, Dearest, I will write again as soon as I have anything to say,

Correspondence

Your far distant (we might almost be in the New World, so strange as are some of the customs here), but loving brother,
Fitzwilliam Darcy

*For reply, see Georgiana, April 10.

*****

*Rosings
Monday, April 14, —

Dear Georgiana,

You have my most sincere contrition over my ill-usage of Mr. Collins; could you but know him, though, I cannot but think you would be less disposed to think me in error. I jest, of course, but indeed, he is one of the more dependable diversions here in Kent, and has yet to disappoint me by uttering anything resembling sense in my presence. I shall not try your credulity by even attempting to describe his sermon-making. As to his over-hearing me, I assure you that it would be he, not I, who would be apologising should that occur; the man is incapable of feeling an affront, or he should never have become such a favourite with my aunt—and now I am being bad, again; let me pass on.

I have been reflecting this morning on a philosophical question, Dearest, and I wish to write my thoughts more for my own clarity, than your edification; I hope you will forgive me for thus claiming your time as my own. The question I have in mind this morning is: how often the regulation of society must interfere with the regulation of one's domestic arrangements—in particular, where and how one might dispose of one's hand in marriage.

You may recognise in this a reference to Mr. Bingley, as regards his inclination for Miss Jane Bennet, of Hertfordshire. Actually, I had occasion to discuss somewhat of this with Colonel Fitzwilliam on our journey hither, and I felt he had arrived at a good working structure to set out from: the various elements that dictate what is proper, in thinking how to direct one's heart in the most suitable direction, would be: the issues of Society, the issues of Family, and the issues of Breeding. As the Colonel put it, Society speaks to the issues of standing and station; Family speaks to questions of familial allegiance, such as Whig v. Tory, or perhaps Irish v. English; and Breeding speaks to the more personal matters of taste, education, and pursuits.

In my estimation, it is the issues of Society wherein lies most of the conflict, in determining how properly to direct the heart. Where the heart might choose without regard to any of the above, it is only where it chooses contrary to the dictates of Society that lasting trouble ensues, I believe. Families will eventually be reconciled, as all parties have an interest in doing so, and of course, those issues of breeding existing between the main parties will soon be softened and soothed over in favour of their attachment; or, as it more often seems, their sense of decorum. But it is Society that maintains a cold and unforgiving eye on unsuitable unions, as it has no interests to motivate conciliation.

But what, I wonder, is the benefit of such obtrusion? How do Society's strictures on marriage benefit its members? That is my difficulty: as all things must have a reason, I know that there is some driving benefit, some hidden good that derives from Society's proscriptions on unions of various sorts, but when I look carefully, none I have been able to think of seems to hold up under scrutiny. I cannot seem to find my way through to it, yet I have turned my mind to it on more than one occasion. Well, Dearest, I do not suppose I shall resolve this any time soon; but I thank you for the opportunity to express my thoughts; putting them down on paper always seems to make them clearer.

Now, as to Rosings: Lady Catherine and Cousin Anne have changed little, I believe, since you were last in company with both. My cousin is, perhaps, even less inclined to speech than before, but as her mother rarely allows any one an opening, it does not seem to be a matter of concern to either. As you say, she is indeed a fine example of what you and I might congratulate ourselves on having, which she lacks; although I must say that, having, over the years, attempted to breach the walls of her silence on many occasions, I am not entirely convinced that she is the one to be pitied. Regardless, as the new parson is completely willing to say whatever he thinks might most please Lady Catherine, at any time and on any topic, there is always *some* conversation going forward, even if no one of sense takes any share in it.

The Colonel is well, and sends his regards; he continues to find ways to leave me to my own devices here at Rosings, while he is out most of the time, either riding or visiting at the Parsonage. Really, I cannot blame him, and, as he is only here to oblige me, I do not begrudge him his absence.

We are together in the evenings, when the want of his discourse would be most felt, so it is well enough.

I appreciate—and to a degree I share—your concern over the reading of novels, but like all things created by the hand and mind of Man, there is good and there is bad; I shall be happy to guide you for a bit when I get home, until you feel better able to discern the difference for yourself, before any damage may be done, to either your understanding or your character.

There is little more to be said for us at present, so I will end this. Be well, and may God bless,

Your affectionate brother,

Fitzwilliam Darcy

*For reply, see Georgiana, April 16.

*****

Rosings
Sunday, April 20, —

Dear Georgiana,

I write to inform you that I shall be extending my stay here in Kent yet a while longer, I had originally hoped, as you know, to be home to-morrow, or possibly Tuesday; but I find I have still some things to attend to. I regret, therefore, that I shall not be back with you until Saturday.

We continue well, here, so you must not entertain any alarm on that account, but there are certain unresolved affairs that I wish to see finished before I leave; you may trust, as you might imagine, that I would not delay my return simply in order to enjoy my aunt's company for an additional week.

The authoress you mention is unknown to me personally, but I have heard of her. The bookseller has made a passing recommendation on her works. We shall investigate together when I return. And, that I may return the sooner, I shall now leave off to see to some of the affairs which await me here. Be well,

Your devoted brother,

Fitzwilliam Darcy

*****

Rosings
Tuesday, April 22, —

Dearest Georgiana,

I am thinking this evening about how society might best bring about its manifest goals of order, justice, and harmony for the people that constitute it. Is it through the collective goodwill and understanding of the citizenry that these goals are approached, or by the dictates of society itself? In law this might be expressed as the difference between *in se* and *prohibitum*; i.e., is the good sought as a good in itself, as being apparent to all, or is the benefit to be gained generated through the proscriptions and general guidance of the man-made rules of society?

I am inclined towards the latter; my reasons are in large measure the result of a consideration of the nature of heredity, and the difference between of God's Laws for man, and God's Plan for man; I shall use my cousin George as an example of this later. God's Law prescribes righteous conduct *in prohibitum*; that is, it is placed over our innate sense of right and wrong, to provide guidance and structure to our fallible natures. Yet God's Plan, which is the higher and must take precedence, must certainly provide for free will; it must as well make allowance for the effects of heredity, and how it must influence behaviour. It must be part of God's Plan that we are gifted with a sense of right and wrong, and yet we can still follow the inclination of our free will.

Heredity, as part of God's Plan, ought to tend towards righteous behaviour; but, like free will can countermand God's Law in our tragic species, so can heredity, as part of God's Plan, be overcome by habit and inclination. Here we take up our example, Lord St. Stephens: his family background is of the highest, yet he follows the dictates of his desires to the detriment of himself and his family, trundling along after Mr. Fox like a little duckling follows its leader, and being led into low company and irreligious pursuits.

This being so, that good *in se* can be put aside by habit and inclination, might not too, the tendencies of heredity be also set aside in a beneficial way? I met a young man not long ago, whose background was of the lowest, yet he himself was one of Oxford's brightest students, and an altogether charming young man. If God's Plan, heredity in this instance, can be defeated on one side by free will, might not it also be advanced on another? There is great symmetry in Nature, and if human intervention can bend the Plan one way, might it—must it not—also be able to bend it the other?

Correspondence

And is not the heart the organ most attuned to right and wrong? It is the heart that tells us what is right, and what is wrong in our daily lives; this then would make it the best and most appropriate means of measuring God's will. So, the rules of society, while they were intended to further good amongst mankind, operate *in prohibitum* and have been created by God's most fallible instrument, the wisdom of Man, and have been bent and twisted by centuries of interest and desire; largely the product of the mind, they must therefore be constantly ratified by the heart before we can accept them as promoting good *in se*.

Yes, Dearest, I believe this is correct; it seems rigorous and sound; I am satisfied. I shall hope to hear your thoughts on this soon, as I plan to be home this coming Saturday. God keep you safe until my return,

Your loving brother,

Fitzwilliam Darcy

*****

Rosings,
8:00 A. M., Friday, April 25, —

Miss Elizabeth Bennet,

Be not alarmed, Madam, on receiving this letter, by the apprehension of its containing any repetition of those sentiments, or renewal of those offers, which were last night so disgusting to you. I write without any intention of paining you, or humbling myself, by dwelling on wishes, which, for the happiness of both, cannot be too soon forgotten; and the effort which the formation and the perusal of this letter must occasion should have been spared, had not my character required it to be written and read. You must, therefore, pardon the freedom with which I demand your attention; your feelings, I know, will bestow it unwillingly, but I demand it of your justice.

Two offences of a very different nature, and by no means of equal magnitude, you last night laid to my charge. The first mentioned was, that, regardless of the sentiments of either, I had detached Mr. Bingley from your sister; —and the other, that I had, in defiance of various claims, in defiance of honour and humanity, ruined the immediate prosperity, and blasted the prospects of Mr. Wickham. —Wilfully and wantonly to have thrown off the companion of my youth, the acknowledged favourite of my father, a young man who had scarcely any other dependence than on our patronage, and who had been brought up to expect its exertion, would be a depravity to which the separation of two young persons, whose affection could be the growth of only a few weeks, could bear no comparison. —But from the severity of that blame which was last night so liberally bestowed, respecting each circumstance, I shall hope to be in future secured, when the following account of my actions and their motives has been read. —If, in the explanation of them which is due to myself, I am under the necessity of relating feelings which may be offensive to yours, I can only say that I am sorry. —The necessity must be obeyed—and farther apology would be absurd. —I had not been long in Hertfordshire, before I saw, in common with others, that Bingley preferred your eldest sister to any other young woman in the country. —But it was not till the evening of the dance at Netherfield that I had any

apprehension of his feeling a serious attachment.
—I had often seen him in love before. —At that
ball, while I had the honour of dancing with you, I
was first made acquainted, by Sir William Lucas's
accidental information, that Bingley's attentions to
your sister had given rise to a general expectation
of their marriage. He spoke of it as a certain event,
of which the time alone could be undecided. From
that moment I observed my friend's behaviour attentively; and I could then perceive that his
partiality for Miss Bennet was beyond what I had
ever witnessed in him. Your sister I also watched.
—Her look and manners were open, cheerful, and
engaging as ever, but without any symptom of
peculiar regard, and I remained convinced from
the evening's scrutiny, that though she received
his attentions with pleasure, she did not invite
them by any participation of sentiment. —If you
have not been mistaken here, I must have been in
an error. Your superior knowledge of your sister
must make the latter probable. —If it be so, if I
have been misled by such error, to inflict pain on
her, your resentment has not been unreasonable.
But I shall not scruple to assert that the serenity of
your sister's countenance and air was such as
might have given the most acute observer a conviction that, however amiable her temper, her
heart was not likely to be easily touched. —That I
was desirous of believing her indifferent is certain,—but I will venture to say that my
investigations and decisions are not usually influenced by my hopes or fears. —I did not believe
her to be indifferent because I wished it; —I believed it on impartial conviction, as truly as I
wished it in reason. —My objections to the marriage were not merely those which I last night

acknowledged to have required the utmost force of passion to put aside in my own case; the want of connection could not be so great an evil to my friend as to me. —But there were other causes of repugnance; —causes which, though still existing, and existing to an equal degree in both instances, I had myself endeavoured to forget, because they were not immediately before me. —These causes must be stated, though briefly. —The situation of your mother's family, though objectionable, was nothing in comparison of that total want of propriety so frequently, so almost uniformly, betrayed by herself, by your three younger sisters, and occasionally even by your father. —Pardon me. —It pains me to offend you. But amidst your concern for the defects of your nearest relations, and your displeasure at this representation of them, let it give you consolation to consider that to have conducted yourselves so as to avoid any share of the like censure is praise no less generally bestowed on you and your eldest sister, than it is honourable to the sense and disposition of both. —I will only say farther that, from what passed that evening, my opinion of all parties was confirmed, and every inducement heightened, which could have led me before to preserve my friend from what I esteemed a most unhappy connection. —He left Netherfield for London, on the day following, as you, I am certain, remember, with the design of soon returning. —

The part which I acted is now to be explained. —His sisters' uneasiness had been equally excited with my own; our coincidence of feeling was soon discovered; and, alike sensible that no time was to be lost in detaching their brother, we shortly resolved on joining him directly in London. —We accordingly went—and there I readily engaged in the office of pointing out to my friend, the certain evils of such a choice. —I described, and enforced them earnestly. —But, however this remonstrance might have staggered or delayed his determination, I do not suppose that it would ultimately have prevented the marriage, had it not been seconded by the assurance, which I hesitated not in giving, of your sister's indifference. He had before believed her to return his affection with sincere, if not with equal, regard. —But Bingley has great natural modesty, with a stronger dependence on my judgment than on his own. —To convince him, therefore, that he had deceived himself, was no very difficult point. To persuade him against returning into Hertfordshire, when that conviction had been given, was scarcely the work of a moment. —I cannot blame myself for having done thus much. There is but one part of my conduct in the whole affair, on which I do not reflect with satisfaction; it is that I condescended to adopt the measures of art so far as to conceal from him your sister's being in Town. I knew it myself, as it was known to Miss Bingley, but her brother is even yet ignorant of it. —That they might have met without ill consequence is, perhaps, probable; —but his regard did not appear to me enough extinguished for him to see her without some danger. —Perhaps this concealment, this disguise, was beneath me. —It is done, however, and it was done for the best. —On this subject I have nothing more to say, no other apology to offer. If I have wounded your sister's feelings, it was unknowingly done; and though the motives which governed me may to you very naturally appear insufficient, I have not yet learnt to condemn them.

With respect to that other, more weighty accusation, of having injured Mr. Wickham, I can only refute it by laying before you the whole of his connection with my family. Of what he has particularly accused me, I am ignorant; but of the truth of what I shall relate, I can summon more than one witness of undoubted veracity. Mr. Wickham is the son of a very respectable man, who had for many years the management of all the Pemberley estates; and whose good conduct in the discharge of his trust naturally inclined my father to be of service to him; and on George Wickham, who was his god—son, his kindness was therefore liberally bestowed. My father supported him at school, and afterwards at Cambridge; —most important assistance, as his own father, always poor from the extravagance of his wife, would have been unable to give him a gentleman's education. My father was not only fond of this young man's society, whose manners were always engaging; he had also the highest opinion of him, and hoping the church would be his profession, intended to provide for him in it. As for myself, it is many, many years since I first began to think of him in a very different manner. The vicious propensities—the want of principle, which he was careful to guard from the knowledge of his best friend, could not escape the observation of a young man of nearly the same age with himself, and who had opportunities of seeing him in unguarded moments, which Mr. Darcy could not have. Here again I shall give you pain—to what degree you only can tell. But whatever may be the sentiments which Mr. Wickham has created, a suspicion of their nature shall not prevent me from unfolding his real character. It adds even another motive. My excellent father

died about five years ago; and his attachment to
Mr. Wickham was to the last so steady, that in his
will he particularly recommended it to me to
promote his advancement in the best manner that
his profession might allow, and, if he took orders,
desired that a valuable family living might be his
as soon as it became vacant. There was also a leg-
acy of one thousand pounds. His own father did
not long survive mine, and within half a year
from these events Mr. Wickham wrote to inform
me that, having finally resolved against taking
orders, he hoped I should not think it unreasonable for him to expect some more immediate
pecuniary advantage, in lieu of the preferment by
which he could not be benefited. He had some intention, he added, of studying the law, and I must
be aware that the interest of one thousand pounds
would be a very insufficient support therein. I rather wished than believed him to be sincere; but,
at any rate, was perfectly ready to accede to his
proposal. I knew that Mr. Wickham ought not to
be a clergyman. The business was therefore soon
settled. He resigned all claim to assistance in the
church, were it possible that he could ever be in a
situation to receive it, and accepted in return three
thousand pounds. All connection between us
seemed now dissolved. I thought too ill of him to
invite him to Pemberley, or admit his society in
Town. In Town, I believe, he chiefly lived, but his
studying the law was a mere pretence, and being
now free from all restraint, his life was a life of
idleness and dissipation. For about three years I
heard little of him; but on the decease of the incumbent of the living which had been designed
for him, he applied to me again by letter for the
presentation. His circumstances, he assured me,

and I had no difficulty in believing it, were exceedingly bad. He had found the law a most unprofitable study, and was now absolutely resolved on being ordained, if I would present him to the living in question — of which he trusted there could be little doubt, as he was well assured that I had no other person to provide for, and I could not have forgotten my revered father's intentions. You will hardly blame me for refusing to comply with this entreaty, or for resisting every repetition of it. His resentment was in proportion to the distress of his circumstances — and he was doubtless as violent in his abuse of me to others, as in his reproaches to myself. After this period, every appearance of acquaintance was dropt. How he lived I know not. But last summer he was again most painfully obtruded on my notice. I must now mention a circumstance which I would wish to forget myself, and which no obligation less than the present should induce me to unfold to any human being. Having said thus much, I feel no doubt of your secrecy. My sister, who is more than ten years my junior, was left to the guardianship of my mother's nephew, Colonel Fitzwilliam, and myself. About a year ago, she was taken from school, and an establishment formed for her in London; and last summer she went with the lady who presided over it, to Ramsgate; and thither also went Mr. Wickham, undoubtedly by design; for there proved to have been a prior acquaintance between him and Mrs. Younge, in whose character we were most unhappily deceived; and by her connivance and aid he so far recommended himself to Georgiana, whose affectionate heart retained a strong impression of his kindness to her as a child, that she was persuaded to believe herself in love, and to consent to an elopement. She was then but fifteen, which must be her excuse; and after stating her imprudence, I am happy to add that I owed the knowledge of it to herself. I joined them unexpectedly a day or two before the intended elopement; and then Georgiana, unable to support the idea of grieving and offending a brother whom she almost looked up to as a father, acknowledged the whole to me. You may imagine what I felt and how I acted. Regard for my sister's credit and feelings prevented any public exposure, but I wrote to Mr. Wickham, who left the place immediately, and Mrs. Younge was of course removed from her charge. Mr. Wickham's chief object was unquestionably my sister's fortune, which is thirty thousand pounds; but I cannot help supposing that the hope of revenging himself on me was a strong inducement. His revenge would have been complete indeed.

This, madam, is a faithful narrative of every event in which we have been concerned together; and if you do not absolutely reject it as false, you will, I hope, acquit me henceforth of cruelty towards Mr. Wickham. I know not in what manner, under what form of falsehood, he has imposed on you; but his success is not, perhaps, to be wondered at. Ignorant as you previously were of every thing concerning either, detection could not be in your power, and suspicion certainly not in your inclination. You may possibly wonder why all this was not told you last night. But I was not then master enough of myself to know what could or ought to be revealed. For the truth of every thing here related, I can appeal more particularly to the testimony of Colonel Fitzwilliam, who from our near relationship and constant intimacy, and still more as one of the executors of my father's will, has been unavoidably acquainted with every particular of these transactions. If your abhorrence of me should make my assertions valueless, you cannot be prevented by the same cause from confiding in my cousin; and that there may be the possibility of consulting him, I shall endeavour to find some opportunity of putting this letter in your hands in the course of the morning. I will only add, God bless you.

Fitzwilliam Darcy.

*****

FINIS

Books by Stanley Michael Hurd:

Darcy's Tale, Volume I: Into Hertfordshire
Darcy's Tale, Volume II: Into Kent
Darcy's Tale, Volume III: The Way Home

Darcy's Tale Deluxe Edition (All three volumes in one edition)

Made in the USA
Middletown, DE
06 October 2015